The Bonfire Buddleia

The Bonfire Buddleia

Published by Hut 22 Books in the United Kingdom 2025

Tel: +44(0)7921 887519

www.hut22books.com

jo@hut22books.com

ISBN 978-1-0683088-0-2

Typesetting and Cover Design by: Charlotte Mouncey, www.bookstyle.co.uk

Printed and bound in Great Britain by Clays Ltd, Elcograf S.p.A.

The Bonfire Buddleia

Jo Bavington-Jones

For my sisters. Different but the same.

Sisters are different flowers from the same garden.

Unknown

Chapter 1
The end of the beginning

Mags

I suppose it began with the funeral. It started with an end.

I remember getting the phone call from Mum. 'Uncle Ken's died. Tell your sisters.'

No *hello*, no *how are you?* That was Mum, short and to the point. And the point was often sharp.

I was silent for a moment as I digested the news. 'Oh,' I said eventually, trying to evaluate how I felt about it. 'How did he die?'

'Heart attack,' came the response.

'Oh.' Again.

'Anyway, tell your sisters. I'll let you know about the funeral.' She hung up. Apparently we were done.

I sat with the phone in my hand, staring at nothing and letting memories of Uncle Ken scroll through my mind like slides from one of those old-fashioned projectors we'd had in the early seventies. That was the era my mind took me back to: a time of innocence.

Ken wasn't really an uncle, not a biological one. He was my eldest sister Rose's godfather in an age when your mum's and dad's friends were always called Uncle or Auntie. He'd been our neighbour when we were little and had earned the honorary title by being a good one, I suppose.

I remember him being a regular visitor to our house when we were kids. Every Saturday morning, in fact. I looked forward to his appearance, and would hover by the back door, watching for him to come through the gate between our back gardens. He would always spot me and wave. Sometimes I ran out to greet him, sometimes not, depending on weather and the proximity of wellies. I was a lazy child I think; I must've been five or six.

Uncle Ken nearly always wore a dark navy fisherman's sweater, had thick, wavy, greying hair, black-rimmed glasses and a rugged face that was always tanned. He had the look of someone who spent most of his time outdoors. I'm surprised at how well I can still picture him from nearly fifty years ago. But Uncle Ken made himself memorable. He bought my undying affection so easily. And he did it with chocolate. Yes, every Saturday morning, he brought chocolate bars for me, and my sisters, Cami and Rose. We weren't often allowed such treats and it quickly became the highlight of my week. I think I would've sold my soul to the devil for a Mars bar back then. It would probably take at least a box from Hotel Chocolat now.

Looking back, Mum looked forward to Uncle Ken's visits almost as much as me, because he often took her three daughters out for a couple of hours, giving her some peace and quiet. He'd pile us into his estate car with his German Shepherd, Saxon, and take us off on an adventure somewhere. We could often be found dangling from ropes in castle moats or deep in the woods building dens. Health and safety be damned back then. I guess they were the sorts of things our dad should've done with us, but he'd never been that sort of dad. He'd been more of a hands-off dad. I don't remember anything of the time before my parents separated. I was only two though. Cami and Rose do remember, and I think that made it harder for them. I think they felt abandoned. Anyway, Uncle Ken kind of filled the father-shaped hole in our lives for a while, and in the early years we had a lot of fun, although it is a miracle none of us suffered a broken arm or leg.

My sisters weren't quite so cheaply bought as me. They would wait for me or Mum to shout, 'Uncle Ken's here!' before they appeared to receive the chocolate offerings.

Some Saturdays – I don't really know how often – Uncle Ken took Rose out on her own.

'She's my goddaughter,' he would say by way of explanation. 'Sometimes, she shouldn't have to share me.'

I was jealous of their relationship and would sulk on those occasions. I wanted a godfather who made me feel special. My own godparents, as lovely as they were, didn't live next door. Or even in the same county. It wasn't fair. I would stomp off with my sweet treat and sulk. So, either way, Mum got her peace and quiet on Saturday mornings. I sulked, and Cami was a mouse who always had her nose buried in a book. Cami was the quiet one, the one who never complained or caused trouble. I think she was in Rose's shadow though, and she didn't blossom the way she could have. Should have. Like a flower planted in the wrong place. Cami was so pretty, but she simply didn't realise it, overshadowed by the loud, demanding beauty of her older sister. Easier just to hide away and not draw attention to herself. I remember envying my older sisters, borrowing clothes without their permission, and trying to grow up faster to catch up with them. I didn't know it wasn't a race. Maybe that's why

I'm the one who wears makeup and takes more interest in my appearance. I wanted to be as grown up as them.

I pull myself back to the present with a sigh, and dial Cami's number.

Cami

Mags just gave me the news about Uncle Ken. I can't say I feel very much at all really. He must've been well into his eighties, so not a bad innings, and not really much to be sad about. Much better to go like that than a long, drawn-out illness. That's how I'd like to go, anyway.

I can't even remember the last time I saw him… must've been his eightieth birthday, I think. Yes, that was it – there was an afternoon tea thingy at that hotel. Mags and I had done a quick tour of the room to show our faces and then bagsied a couple of chairs nearest the bar, washing down scones and sandwiches with copious amounts of gin. Rose wasn't there – she said she had a wedding to go to. Never did find out whose. Some friend from university, I think. Mum had berated her at the time: 'He's your godfather, he's known you since you were a baby… blah, blah, blah… you should be there…etc., etc.,' but Rose wouldn't budge. Didn't think anything of it at the time. God knows we'd all rather have been at a friend's wedding than in a room full of geriatrics telling us about when they were young, and tutting. A lot. With ageing seems to come a good degree of dissatisfaction. Can't wait.

Still, I suppose Uncle Ken's death is the end of an era, and he was good to us as kids, and to Mum. Mainly by giving her a break from us most Saturdays when he would arrive with chocolate bars for us. Mags used to be hopping up and down with excitement in the kitchen waiting for him. I didn't see the point; I'd get the sweets soon enough. Revels were my favourites. Except the coffee ones. We always used to try and guess the flavours before we bit into them.

Better than the sweets he brought, was Saxon. I loved that dog, and running with him was the best part of our expeditions into the wilderness. Uncle Ken used to make us promise not to tell Mum about some of the stuff we got up to, saying she'd only worry, as he lowered us into a castle moat on a rope, or led us over a river by way of a fallen tree. We did have a lot of fun, and none of us suffered more than a scraped knee. More by luck than judgment.

Some Saturdays, I'd be left at home with Mags, who'd sulk like a baby, stomping off to her room. She hated being left out. It didn't really bother me – he was Rose's godfather, after all, and she was entitled to time alone with him. I was just as content to read or do a jigsaw, to be honest. I always thought Mags was a bit of a spoilt brat when we were kids, a bit of an attention-seeker. If she ever lost at a game, which was pretty much always being the baby, she'd upturn the board in a fit of anger.

Looking back now, there was something a bit off about Uncle Ken. As I got older, I remember he gave me the creeps a little bit. Not to the extent that Jimmy Saville did every time we watched *Jim'll Fix It*, but just a hint of something that made me uncomfortable. He never gave the feelings any substance though, so I shrugged them off. I didn't like people generally, men especially. Much better off with a dog. Two husbands had fallen by the wayside as I tested the theory that you're better off with a canine companion. I wouldn't make the same mistake a third time.

I try to remember when the outings with Uncle Ken stopped. I think it was when I was about fourteen. Rose, at fifteen, had rather outgrown the Saturday morning adventures in favour of more exciting ones with her friends. And boys. Rose was so beautiful when she was young, and there was always a queue of boys waiting to go out with her. I was a bit jealous, to be honest, but I didn't have her confidence. Or her looks. I've always been the plain one.

She'd gone a bit wild though, if I'm honest. She seemed angry a lot of the time, and rowed with Mum constantly. Doors slammed often in our house as Rose stormed out. I took sanctuary in my room, happier in my own company. Maybe I should've been there more for Mags, looking back, but it was all about survival during those years, until Rose went off to university. Mags seemed fine anyway, bright and bubbly and increasingly beautiful. Another sister to envy and resent.

With a sigh, I dial Rose's number.

Rose

I haven't stopped shaking since I hung up the phone. He's dead. The old bastard's dead. Good. I hope he rots in hell for all eternity. And that's what I told Cami when she gave me the news.

'Woah! What?' Cami'd said.

'I said, good, and I hope he rots in hell,' I repeated more slowly.

'That's what I thought you said. Still don't understand though.' I could hear the confusion in my sister's voice as she waited for an explanation. She wasn't getting one. Not yet anyway. Maybe not ever.

'No, you wouldn't. No reason why you should.'

'So tell me,' Cami pushed.

'No. I can't. I can't talk now, Cami, I have to go.'

'Rose, wait…'

But I'd already hung up the phone.

I hadn't let myself think about Uncle Ken for so long. Hearing he'd died, while welcome news, was likely to release a maelstrom of emotion that I'd had bottled up for decades, and I really didn't know if I was strong enough to survive it. Caring for my husband, David, since his stroke took every ounce of strength I had. And often more. Any feeble reserves I might once have had, had long since dried up and I ran on fumes most days. I coped by shutting off from the past as much as possible, and not acknowledging how utterly fucked up I was. If I stop to look back, I fear I will fall and never be able to get back up. So, maybe I just blot the phone call from my memory bank, and carry on as if it never happened. Maybe I'm just delaying the inevitable shitstorm, but I don't know what else I can do.

Mags

'Hey, Cams, what's up?' I'm surprised to be speaking to my sister again so soon.

'Hey, Mags. I just got off the phone with Rose and you'll never believe what she said when I gave her the news.'

'So tell me,' I prompt.

'She said, and these were her exact words: *Good, and I hope he rots in hell!*'

13

'What? Really? Why on earth would she say that? Are you sure?'

'Er… yeah… not the sort of thing I'd make up, is it?' Cami sounds a little aggrieved.

'But why…?'

Cami interrupts. 'I don't bloody know!'

'That's really weird though, isn't it? He was her godfather.'

'Yeah, I know. I don't understand it either.'

'Well, didn't you ask her?'

'Didn't really get the chance – she hung up on me.'

'Do you think I should phone her?'

'Um… honestly? I think you should leave it. For now, at least. We'll have to speak to her again with funeral arrangements soon anyway. Perhaps sanity will have prevailed again by then.'

'Yeah, I guess – God knows she's not been in a good headspace since David's stroke. I feel guilty for not doing more to help.'

'I know. Me too. It's difficult though, we have our own lives to lead.'

'Still, maybe we should try and find some time to get up to visit soon.'

'Sounds like a plan. Right, I s'pose Mum'll ring you with news about the funeral?'

'Yep. Sadly, I seem to be the chosen one for the conveying of bad news.'

'That's because you're the nice one, Mags, and least likely to kick up a stink.'

'Hmm, I don't know, maybe my number's just easier to remember or something?'

'Well, rather you than me. Sorry, Mags, but the less I have to do with the old bat, the better. My tolerance threshold seems to be decreasing with age, and I really won't put up with her shit anymore.'

'I don't blame you. I s'pose, being the youngest, I haven't quite reached that point yet. I do have to bite my tongue though, and count to about a million every time I have to deal with her.'

'A million wouldn't be enough for me now. She was a crap mother and I'm done with making excuses for her.'

'I hear you,' I respond with a sigh. 'Right, well, let me know if you speak to Rose again. Take care.'

'You too, Mags. Bye for now.'

Like Cami, I'm puzzled by Rose's response to the news of her godfather's passing but, with an internal audit coming up at work, other thoughts soon push the puzzlement to one side.

Chapter 2
Shades of grey

Mags

It's not many days before Mum phones me again with details of the funeral.

'You can pick me up and take me home afterwards,' she instructs.

I bite back the urge to say no, not unless you ask me nicely. Somehow, she still has the ability to make me feel like a small, sulky child, but it would be nice if for once she didn't just assume; tell me what I'm doing rather than asking if that's okay with me. Because sometimes it's very much NOT okay with me, but I am the obedient child, the one who simply smiles in the face of, well, pretty much everything. I've always done my crying in private. Easier for everyone else that way. Mum once accused me of being drunk because I was so exaggeratedly happy. On that particular occasion I happened to be stone-cold sober.

I sigh and agree to her terms, as usual.

'Tell your sisters,' she ends before hanging up.

'Tell them yourself, you old bitch,' I mutter, too late for her to hear, of course, but it makes me feel a little better. I wish, for about the millionth time, that I could stand up to her.

My mother is definitely my number one trigger. I press my fingers to my temples to push the overwhelming urge to reach for something to take the edge off how I'm feeling, back into my head. I've fought hard for my sobriety and I refuse to let her be my undoing. I never want to give her that satisfaction; of her accusation being accurate.

I go to the fridge and grab a bottle of Coke, unscrewing the top with a slightly shaky hand and taking a few swigs. Drinking straight from the bottle – one of the perks of living alone. I wonder idly if I'll ever be able to adapt to living with someone again. As there's currently not a man in my life, this is not an immediate concern. What is, however, is informing my sisters of the funeral arrangements. Putting the lid back on the Coke, I grab the phone and dial Cami's number.

'Hey, sis, what's up?' Cami's voice comes down the line.

'The Mother just rang with Uncle Ken's funeral arrangements.'

'Oh, okay, let me grab a pen.'

I wait for her voice to break the silence once more, trying to ignore the pounding in my brain as it demands something to quiet it. Sometimes I wished Coca Cola still contained cocaine.

'Right, fire away,' she says.

I reel off the date, time and place. 'Can you let Rose know?' It's an unnecessary request, of course, because this is how we work.

'Yep. Will do. Hope she reacts better than the last time we spoke. Most odd,' Cami says.

'Yeah, I am worried about her,' I agree.

'I was worried before this news about Ken. I think she's really struggling.'

'We must take some time off to go and stay with her for a

while. What do you think? Maybe after the funeral?'

'Definitely. I'll have a look at the annual-leave calendar at work and let you know some dates.'

'Okey dokey. I take it you will be at the funeral? I've been told I'm taking Mum. Lucky me.'

'Sorry you got the short straw again,' Cami consoles.

'She is my cross to bear. If only she wasn't so cross all the time,' I sigh.

'Mm,' Cami agrees. 'Rose had the right idea moving away.'

'Didn't she just?! Although I bet she wishes she wasn't so far from you and me now, since David's stroke.'

'You're probably right, although she's always making excuses for not coming to visit.'

'Yeah, I know. I mean, I know our childhood wasn't amazing, but…' I let the sentence hang and can hear Cami's breathing in the silence that ensues.

'Right, I'm gonna phone Rose before I forget. Take care and speak soon.'

'Yes, good luck, bye, Cams, take care.' I hang up the phone and become aware once more of the pounding in my brain. I'm still working on making new neural pathways; ones that bypass those that always led to a fix.

Cami

As I hang up the phone to my younger sister, I wonder if I imagined the slight wobble to her voice, and I can't quite shake the feeling that she was really on edge. But contact with our mother has a way of winding us all up. *I'm* annoyed and I didn't even have to speak to her. Sometimes though, I do wonder if

Mags is just putting on a brave face for the world, and that there's a darkness in her to match my own.

I run my fingers over the thin fabric of my trousers, feeling the slightly raised areas of skin on the tops of my thighs; parallel lines of scar tissue. I blink and shake away the memory that's trying to push its way to the fore, hitting Rose's contact and listening to the call connect.

'Hi, Cami.' I can hear the exhaustion in my sister's voice.

'Hi, Rose, how are things?' I already know the answer.

'Oh, you know, same shit different day.'

'I know. I'm sorry.' Worthless words.

'How about you? Any new men on the horizon?'

Me and men. It's a bit of a running joke. I have a tendency to attract weirdos when I'm out walking the dog. But Rose knows there's only room for one man in my life, and he has four legs and a tail.

'Just the usual odd bods,' I inform her.

'Mm,' Rose replies, her thoughts clearly elsewhere. The Maldives probably.

'Um… anyway, the reason I'm phoning is I've got details of the funeral. Uncle Ken's funeral. If you…' I don't get the chance to finish my sentence as Rose interjects.

'Don't bother, Cami. I'm not going.'

'But…' I begin.

'Don't. Just don't.' I can hear the strain in her voice, just from those few words, so I don't.

'Okay.' I don't understand, but I realise I can't push her on the subject. Not now anyway. 'Okay, so Mags and I were wondering if we could maybe come up and annoy you for a few days sometime soon? If you'd like?'

Rose doesn't reply right away and when she does I can hear that she's close to tears. 'I would like that. I'd like that very much,' the words tremble down the line.

'Great. We'll sort it. Will you be alright 'til then?' I'm seriously worried about Rose now as she's clearly close to breaking down.

Rose sniffs. 'I'll be okay.'

'Maybe don't answer the phone if Mum rings,' I suggest. Although I know our mother rarely phones her eldest daughter, Rose's refusal to go the funeral will no doubt get the old bitch's hackles up. I know from my own experience that dealing with Mum when you're feeling fragile can only make matters worse.

'Good advice. She's the last thing I need at the moment,' Rose sighs. 'Changing the subject... how's Mags? She fallen in love this week?'

I chuckle. Our youngest sister has a bit of a reputation for falling in love at the drop of a hat. And out again just as fast as you can pick the hat back up.

'As far as I know there's no one on the scene and hasn't been for a while. I know she's on a couple of dating sites, but she says by the time she's discounted all the ones holding fish, in the gym, in the bathroom or off Crimewatch, there's not a lot left.'

'Maybe it'll do her good to be on her own for a while?' Rose suggests.

'Yeah, maybe. I know she thinks she needs a man in her life, but...'

'But she needs to learn to love herself first,' Rose finishes my sentence for me.

I sigh. 'Yep. But Mags has always got her sense of self-worth from men, and there's never been a shortage of them to oblige.'

'Perhaps she's growing up at last?' Rose suggests.

'Perhaps. Anyway, I think work's keeping her busy – I know she's auditing this month.'

'I'm sure it won't be long before some new man sweeps her off her feet. For five minutes.'

'You're probably right. Let's just enjoy the peace until then.'

'Yes, indeed. She should enjoy being single for a while. I'd happily change places with her.'

Rose doesn't need to say any more. I know how desperately unhappy she is and that she feels as trapped by David's stroke as he is. She'd talked of leaving many times before, her plans now halted like the blood supply to David's brain. To leave now would make her look callous, cold, cruel. A heartless wife deserting her handicapped husband.

'Right, Mrs, I'll speak to you soon and we'll sort out a date to come and stay. WhatsApp me any days that won't work for you.'

'Okey dokey, will do. I'm really looking forward to seeing you. And Mags. I can't remember the last time we spent any real time together, all three of us,' Rose says.

'Hopefully she won't be mooning over some new man by then,' Cami laughs.

'If she is, I'll be jealous to be honest. Even the plumber's starting to look attractive.'

'Oh, God, Fat Tony?! You are in a bad way!'

'Never a truer word spoken,' Rose sighs.

'Well, we'll do our best to put a smile on your face. Mags' dating stories are always a giggle. And if that fails there's always gin.'

'Hurrah for gin. And chocolate. And gin chocolates.'

'Ha! Take care, Rose. Just hang in there until we can come and rescue you.'

'Thanks, Cami. You too. Lots of love.'

Rose

I realise I'm smiling as I hang up the phone. I'm genuinely looking forward to spending time with my two younger sisters. The real reason for the call is pushed to one side in favour of their impending visit.

There was a time when I resented Cami and Mags, when I almost hated them. It wasn't their fault, but I'd sometimes wished I was an only child. And while the thought of being alone with Mother was a hideous one, it would have been easier in some ways. If I hadn't had to protect my sisters, maybe my life would have been very different. Maybe I could've said something, spoken up. Would Mum even have believed me though? I honestly don't think she would have. Because she wouldn't have known what to do with that knowledge. Maybe she did know, but she didn't want to face up to it? She should have seen. She was my mum; she was meant to protect me. I could've run away if it wasn't for my younger sisters. I could've escaped. Anywhere would have been better. But I couldn't abandon them to the same fate. And so I stayed. And I said nothing. And I resented them.

Shit. I don't want to open this Pandora's box. I stuff the thoughts that are trying to escape back in and close the lid firmly. I hear David calling for me, and for once I'm glad of it.

Chapter 3
Shades of black

Mags

The day of the funeral arrives and I brace myself for a few hours with Mum. I could've done with something to take the edge off, but I'd meditated as I did every morning now, and written my list of gratitudes. They're a part of my daily routine, and I always send them to a close friend – that gives me an added incentive and accountability. I've never shared them with my sisters. There's so much I've never shared with my sisters. Maybe I never will, for fear of being found wanting, of being judged. I like being liked by them, and I'm in no hurry to return to the bad old days when they didn't want me around. We were in the same boat, for once in our lives, and I was not going to be the one to rock it.

I'm grateful Cami will be at the funeral as moral support. There's definitely an element of safety in numbers around Mum. Sharing the load, reducing the burden by fifty percent. Although there's no guarantee she won't focus all her bitter disappointment on just one of us. You never knew who she'd pick on; you just had to expect the worst, and be prepared to draw blood from your own tongue.

I douse my wrists in a blend of essential oils designed to

combat stress, inhaling deeply, before pulling on a dark woollen coat, flicking my long brown hair over the collar. I wonder about a hat. I'm not really much of a hat wearer, but I rummage around in the hall cupboard and retrieve the black felt number I call my Agatha Christie hat. It's freezing out, with a light blanket of snow on the ground, and there's always a lot of standing around at the crematorium. Checking my appearance in the mirror, I conclude the hat looks pretty good, and add a slick of nude lipstick to the mouth that will soon be smiling grimly. Black leather boots and gloves complete the ensemble, and I'm ready to do battle.

Sadly, I live only about fifteen minutes' drive from the woman I call my mother. I wish on a daily basis that I lived at least in another county. Continent would be better still. I envied Rose the distance she'd put between herself and Mum as soon as she possibly could. I turn up the radio during the drive, listening to Capital as usual. Two pop and rap songs are bookends to a Christmas one. Far too soon, I'm pulling up outside *her* house, the same house I'd grown up in. Taking a deep breath, I walk up to the front door which I know will be unlocked, letting myself in.

'Only me,' I call out, so as not to worry her.

'Well, who else would it be?' comes a voice from the kitchen.

I pull a childish, sneering face and mutter under my breath. 'Oh, I dunno, a deranged killer... a hitman hired by your daughters...?'

I walk up the hall to the kitchen.

'Hi, Mum. You look nice.'

She doesn't acknowledge the compliment, but looks up from her seat at the kitchen table, which is still covered by the same oilcloth of my childhood; a now faded confection of her favourite blowsy blooms. How I hated that tablecloth; the backdrop for so many arguments between Mum and Rose. Mum insisted on calling her by her proper name, Peony, which further inflamed matters.

'What on earth have you got on your head?' she demands.

My little bubble of confidence is burst, my armour pierced, just like that, and I can feel tears pricking at the corners of my eyes and the pounding starting in my brain.

'It's cold out.' I squeeze the words out, when what I really want to do is fling the hat from my head, run upstairs and throw myself onto my childhood bed. To sob quietly into my pillow and wonder why my mother hates me.

She makes a sort of huffy noise, and shakes her head, as if to say the weather is no excuse to look ridiculous. I wonder again why she feels the need to be so critical, so hurtful. Even if she thinks the hat looks awful, why does she feel the need to tell me? Why not just keep her trap shut? No, she opens her trap and I fall in once more, spiralling to the ground and landing with a painful thump. And yet she was always telling us as kids, 'If you can't say something nice, don't say anything at all'. Do as I say, not as I do. That's Mum.

I stand silently and watch as she applies a far too bright lipstick to her thin lips. She has a mean mouth. Figuratively and literally. I can't remember the last time she smiled at me. There must have been a time when she wasn't so embittered, but if there was I can't remember it. She felt the universe had dealt her a bad hand and accepted no responsibility for the way her life had turned out. Why couldn't she see that she had three beautiful daughters, and why wasn't that enough?

Finally, she's satisfied with her appearance, having donned a hideous black woollen hat which I would never have criticised aloud, and we leave the house. I hold open the car door for her and help her on with her seatbelt. She doesn't say thank you, and I no longer expect it. As I walk round to the driver's side, I take a deep, steadying breath before getting in and starting the engine. I quickly turn off the radio before she has a chance to moan about 'the racket'. Always trying to please her, invariably failing.

My fingers are clenched around the steering wheel as I drive the twenty or so minutes to the church. I'm conscious of the tension in my jaw and neck too, and can feel a headache starting. It was these tension headaches that had started me on a slippery slope so many years earlier. Now the strongest thing I can take for them is paracetamol or ibuprofen. I roll my neck in an effort to release the taut muscles and shrug my shoulders up and down a couple of times.

Naturally Mum, who's been silent up until now, sitting rigidly upright in her seat, both hands clutched around her handbag, notices.

'What on earth are you doing? Stupid girl. Just drive will you?' she says, turning towards me, and tutting.

I can feel her eyes boring into me as if I'm some alien creature she cannot comprehend. I don't need to look at her to know her mean mouth will be pursed in distaste and her grey, slightly watery, eyes awash with disapproval. Don't mistake the watering for emotion. It's purely an age thing. My mother turned off the tears tap many years ago. Along with anything soft or maternal. Not that there was much of that to start with as far as I could remember.

Silence resumes and I try to relax my jaw and hands to no avail. It will be a while before I can take anything for the headache, which only makes me feel more uptight and anxious.

Finally, we pull into the car park next to the church. I turn off the engine and look around for Cami's car, which I spot in the far corner under the snow-laden boughs of a yew tree leaning over from the graveyard. The car park is filling up rapidly. Ken was obviously a popular man.

'Is that Camellia's car over there?' Mum says, pointing her gloved finger. She always uses our full Christian names.

'Yes, that's Cami's,' I confirm, silently adding *thank God*.

'What about Peony? Which one's her car? I suppose she's late as usual. Thoughtless and inconsiderate as ever,' Mum practically spits out the words.

The pounding in my head increases. We haven't told Mum that Rose isn't coming, deciding it would be safer to tell her in a more public setting where she's less likely to cause a scene. I really don't want to tell her on my own.

'Um… Rose's car isn't here. Come on, let's get out and join Cami.'

'Maybe they came in one car,' Mum says. 'Make a change for your sister to do something sensible.'

Christ, just shut up, you hateful old witch! I think to myself, before reaching into the back seat for my handbag. I catch sight of myself in the mirror as I turn back, and pull the hat from my head, throwing it into the back, and running my fingers through my hair in an attempt to tidy it. No doubt, the state of my hair will be just as reprehensible as my hat, but I no longer have the confidence to wear it.

I'm trembling as I go round to open Mum's door for her,

but it has less to do with the freezing temperatures, and more to do with my emotional state. I offer my arm to help her out of the car, but she pushes it away.

'I'm quite capable of getting out of the car, you know. I'm not dead yet.'

I turn away and mutter *sadly* under my breath, spotting Cami getting out of her car, and waving. The cavalry.

Cami walks gingerly across the frozen car park and pulls me into a hug.

'Breathe, Mags,' she whispers in my ear before releasing me. 'Hi, Mum,' she says. 'You look nice.' She catches my eye and raises her eyebrows as if to say why do we bother being nice to her?

Mum huffs. 'Camellia. At least you're on time. Unlike your sister. Where is Peony? Late again, I suppose.'

Cami looks at me with resignation. We both know the moment of truth is rapidly approaching. We can't keep her in the dark much longer.

'Let's get into the church, Mum. Hopefully they've got the heaters on,' Cami distracts.

Realising the ground is slippery, Mum begrudgingly lets Cami and me take an arm each and lead her slowly to the church, stopping now and then to greet fellow mourners also making their way out of the frigid air.

Once inside, we shake hands with the vicar, with Mum's face briefly transformed by a smile. By the time we reach a pew, her normal sneer is back.

Cami and I exchange glances. I nod the briefest of nods.

'So, Mum... er... sadly Rose can't make it after all. David's really not well enough to be left with just the carers,' Cami says.

This was the line we'd agreed on, designed to reduce fallout as much as possible. I hold my breath and watch as Cami's words are digested. Surely she wouldn't, couldn't, react badly in front of all these people, especially the vicar. We're counting on the fact that she still cares about appearances.

The silence grows uncomfortable, so I fill it, as is so often my way. 'She really wanted to be here,' I lie.

Cami raises her eyebrows at me, as if to say don't overdo it.

'Well, I suppose it can't be helped, but I must say I'm disappointed. After everything Ken did for her, for all of you.'

I start to breathe again. This is a huge concession coming from Mum, especially where Rose is concerned.

'One of you can give her your order of service,' she instructs. 'And take photographs. That's the next best thing to being here, I'm sure.'

While neither Cami nor I have any intention of carrying out either of those instructions, we nod. It's just easier.

Soon the rows of pews are all full and, when I turn to look, there are quite a few people standing at the back also. Uncle Ken was clearly well-loved. I wonder idly how many of them had been bribed with chocolate.

I've avoided looking up the nave towards the altar, where the coffin rests in front of the choir but, as the vicar begins the service, my eyes are drawn inexorably to the dark wood casket containing Uncle Ken's body. I shudder involuntarily, and tears threaten, not because I'm overly sad at Uncle Ken's death, but because my emotions are never far from the surface. I'd probably have cried at Hitler's funeral. It just makes you think about your own mortality and how fleeting life is. The person who's died isn't suffering anymore; it's those that are left behind who are screwed.

I haven't really heard the vicar's introduction, lost in my own dark thoughts, but I suddenly become aware that the people around me are opening their hymn books. I grab the one in front of me and hurriedly turn to the first number shown on the board. 'Lord of all Hopefulness' I see with a groan. Four dreary verses.

Lord of all hopefulness,
Lord of all joy,
Whose trust, ever child-like,
No cares could destroy,
Be there at our waking,
And give us, we pray,
Your bliss in our hearts, Lord,
At the break of the day.

I can make out Cami's soft, quiet voice and Mum's thin, reedy one. This would be when Rose would come into her own. She always had a beautiful voice, and sang in the church choir in her village. I do my best to fill Rose's singing shoes, but I'm a poor substitute. I think about the lyrics that we're singing and wonder if it is actually the Lord missing from my life, rather than a mortal man. The twelve-step programme had called on me to accept God into my life, but I'd never managed that. I substituted something I called a Higher Power instead. It did the same job, I'd thought at the time. But maybe I needed a thirteenth step? Maybe God was the answer? The hymn comes to an end, and I push the thoughts aside as the vicar begins the eulogy.

As I listen to the vicar speak of Ken's life, I look around the church, trying to pick out people I know. There, in the front pew is a woman I guess is his sister. I vaguely remember Mum telling me she'd been widowed a few years back, and assume the people around her are her children, their spouses and offspring. All boys. Ken's great-nephews. Ken had never married or had children of his own. Maybe that was why he'd taken such a keen interest in my sisters and me.

I can pick out a few more familiar faces in the congregation, mostly Mum's generation, from the village. I recognise one elderly couple in particular, and seeing them brings a lump to my throat. Funerals must be especially poignant to them as their only child, Anna-May, had disappeared when she was fifteen and a body had never been found. Although I didn't have children of my own, I'm not sure I would have been able to keep going in the face of such heartbreak. How awful to never know what happened to your child and, worse, to imagine what horrors she might have been subjected to. I shudder and force my attention back to the vicar.

After the vicar has delivered the potted history of a life which seemed to have been spent helping others, he calls on Peter, one of Ken's great-nephews (so I was right) to deliver the bible reading. Peter looks to be about twenty-one, tall and good-looking, and he reads the one about 'my father's house has many rooms' in a very composed manner for one so young. Like I said, even if I'd been at Hitler's funeral, I would've blubbed.

After that comes a succession of friends and neighbours who speak of Ken's great generosity, his selflessness and largeness of heart. I've never been to a funeral where more people have volunteered to get up and speak. And, to be honest, most of what's said ties in with my own memories of him. He was a good and kind man, who would clearly be missed.

We sing a rousing 'Jerusalem' when the stream of Ken fans finally dries up, before the vicar leads us in prayers. I pray for the strength to get through the rest of the day, and for it to be rather warmer at the crematorium, the irony of which is not lost on me.

The coffin is carried out to a rousing rendition of Elgar's 'Nimrod: Lux Aeterna' which finally tips me over the edge and has me reaching for the tissue in my coat pocket. Thank God for waterproof mascara. I'm relieved that the first part of the funeral is over, but know that the worst is yet to come.

As we follow the procession out of the church, Cami sees the state I'm in.

'Why don't we go to the crematorium in my car?' she suggests, squeezing my arm.

'Yes, please,' I nod gratefully, wiping away more tears and blowing my nose as quietly as possible.

Mum looks at me in disgust. 'Pull yourself together, Magnolia! For goodness' sake!'

I resist the urge to ask what does she know about goodness? But I say nothing. Just take her arm and lead her across the car park. The thought did flash into my mind that part of me wished this was her funeral. Would I shed tears for her? I wondered. Maybe more for myself, and my sisters. And definitely not as many as for the Führer.

The crematorium is only another ten miles away, and the roads are quiet and gritted. A bit like my teeth, as Mum has decided now we're in the confines of the car and away from people whose opinions count for something, she can say what she really thinks.

'And did you see what that sister of his had on? Not even

wearing black. At her own brother's funeral. Floozy. Always thought she was a cut above the rest of us, she did. Well, I should think Ken's turning in his grave,' she rants.

I catch Cami's eye in the rear-view mirror and we raise our eyebrows. Neither of us bothers to point out that Ken isn't even in his grave. Or that he is, in fact, being cremated. We'd learned as children to pick our battles. This one definitely isn't worth the exertion. Or the backlash. So, we just let her rant on.

I tune out whatever vitriol is spewing from Mum's lips and let my thoughts drift, much like the snow along the sides of the road. I wonder, not for the first time, why Rose was so vehement about not attending today. Cami'd said she didn't even want to know when it was, but apparently Rose had asked for the date and time in a subsequent text exchange with her. It was all most odd, but Rose had a lot on her plate and maybe it was just all too much to bear. Maybe we'd find out when we went to stay in a few days' time.

Before too long we're pulling into the crematorium car park along with the rest of the convoy from the church. We huddle around in groups, stamping our feet and rubbing our hands together in an attempt to keep warm. The crematorium is set among rolling hills and, while the snow-covered land is breath-takingly beautiful, it's also exposed to the elements. I become transfixed by Mum's breath condensing in the cold air as she continues her tirade in lowered tones. She stops occasionally to smile and wave at some she knows. *Two-faced cow*, I think to myself, pulling a face at Cami and miming throttling Mum when she's not looking. In turn, Cami mimes a Psycho-style stabbing action, and we try not to laugh. Even at this most sombre occasion, we are reduced by our mother to silly girls.

Finally, we follow the pallbearers into the building and take our seats once more. There is a brief address before the curtains close and the coffin disappears from view. This is the bit I find really tough, and which is topped only by a traditional burial and the moment a coffin is lowered into the ground. I guess it's the finality of it, but it gets me every time. Cami, seated next to me as a shield from our mother, reaches over and squeezes my hand, in a gesture that means the absolute world to me. I know that we will get through this day together. We are stronger together.

Rose

'Alexa, set an alarm for gin at eleven a.m.' It's the day of the funeral and, while I didn't want to be there, I hoped acknowledging it might give me a little bit of closure. Maybe the ball of pain and anger trapped inside me for decades, like a cancerous mass, will start to dissipate. I can hope.

Chapter 4
In the wake of the wake

Mags

Finally, the ordeal's over and I drop Mum off at home. I can tell she's tired as she's more crotchety than ever. I get her settled in her recliner with a cup of tea and the TV remote before taking my leave.

'Bye, Mum, see you soon. Look after yourself.'

Her reply is a hand raised in acknowledgment, which is more than I sometimes get.

I close the front door with a sigh of relief, locking it behind me as I know Mum will probably fall asleep in her chair and, for some unfathomable reason, I still want her to be safe. Go figure.

Instead of heading home, I detour to Cami's as arranged. I turn the radio on again and the closing bars of 'Last Christmas' fill the car. I don't really want to think about last Christmas to be honest. Suffice to say I was not in a good place. And for once it didn't involve my family, who I'd told I was going away for the festive season. They didn't need to know it was to rehab. The twelve months since have meant a lot of hard work and dedication to stick to the programme, and I still just take one day at a time. Days like today are more of a struggle. I suppose

I will always be an addict… but now I am a recovering one.

Cami opens the door as I walk up the path to her tiny cottage. She's changed out of her funeral garb and is back in jeans and a jumper. Her Jack Russell, Jacks, bounces over to greet me.

'Hey, you, come on in,' she smiles warmly at me.

'Thanks. Ooh, it's nice and warm in here,' I say, shrugging off my coat and hanging it on the hooks by the front door. I reach down to unzip my boots and remove those too, before following Cami into the lounge.

She's lit a fire in addition to the central heating and the small sitting room is cosy and welcoming.

'What can I get you?' she asks. 'Tea, coffee… something stronger?'

I resist the urge to say yes to something stronger. 'I'm still a bit awash with tea after the wake to be honest. Unless you've got a peppermint one?'

'Yep. Peppermint tea it is. Make yourself comfy,' Cami says before heading to the kitchen.

Jacks has joined me on the sofa, and I stroke his ears absent-mindedly as I look around the room. Cami's taste is what you'd call cottagey, and there are a multitude of rugs, blankets and cushions, in shades of burgundy and dusky pink, to add to the cosy feel. A bookshelf to one side of the fireplace is crammed with novels by the likes of Jane Austen and the Brontë sisters. In spite of what Cami will tell you, she definitely has a romantic streak. A small Christmas tree twinkles in the corner. As I focus my gaze back on the flickering fire, I find myself staring into the flames and then drifting, my eyelids growing heavy. I'm fighting sleep when Cami returns with two steaming mugs.

'You look knackered,' she says, putting a tea on the table next to me.

'Feel it, to be honest,' I reply, rubbing my fingers across my eyes.

'Well, it was a double whammy today – Mum *and* a funeral. That's enough to suck the life out of anyone.'

'Ain't that the truth. Really glad you were there – not sure I would've got through it otherwise.' I smile my gratitude.

'Yeah, you would. You're stronger than you think.'

'Not sure I am where Mum's concerned,' I groan. 'She just has a knack for making me feel small and stupid.'

'It's not just you, trust me,' Cami says, pulling a face.

I reach for my mug and we sit quietly for a few minutes. Finally, I break the silence, but not because I need to, for once.

'Did you see Mr. and Mrs Lawrence at the church today?' I ask Cami. The Lawrences were the couple whose daughter disappeared.

'Was that them sitting near the front on the other side from us?'

'Yeah. I was thinking how bloody awful funerals must be for them, you know, after losing Anna-May. I mean, I know funerals are shite for everyone, but it must bring back all the pain.'

'Yeah, it must. They had that memorial service for her, didn't they? Years and years ago.'

'Yeah, one year after she went missing. But with no body, they can't really mourn properly, or have a grave or anything. Must be awful.'

Cami just nods and sips her tea. 'Still, it was a good turnout for Uncle Ken. He was obviously well-liked.'

'Mm. Loads of people there to pay their respects. Was that his sister in the front pew?'

'Yes, Margery. I s'pose she'll inherit the house as Ken never married.'

'I assume so. Presumably she'll sell it – I can't imagine her wanting to live in it with that big garden to take care of.'

'Unless one of her sons wanted it?' Cami shrugs.

'Mm. Maybe,' I say, before silence descends once more.

It's Cami who breaks it this time. 'You know all those photos at the wake?'

I nod.

'I got dragged round to look at them with Mum when you were queueing up for teas, and she made me take pics to show Rose,' Cami raises her eyebrows.

'I meant to go and look at them but somehow didn't get round to it. There always seemed to be a crowd of people around them.'

Cami picks up her mobile phone from the coffee table, opens the photos and passes it to me. 'There are quite a few of us as girls, taken on our Saturday outings or in the garden at ours or Ken's.'

I begin scrolling through the photos, pausing at the ones of me and my sisters. They're mostly from the 1970s and have that slightly orangey, washed-out appearance old photos have.

'Oh God, look at our hair! And the trousers!' I groan.

'Oh yes. And the tank tops,' Cami laughs.

'So much orange and brown! Ugh! Some things should never come back into fashion. And I'm looking at them.'

'Yep. The seventies were not a good time for fashion,' Cami agrees.

'Or much else to be honest. Ooh, look at this one of Rose with Uncle Ken – jeez she looks like she wants to kill someone!'

I pass the phone to Cami.

'She must be about fourteen there, I think. She was pretty angry a lot of the time by then. Teens did not suit Rose.'

'No, they definitely didn't. Thank God you weren't like that, Cam. It would have been unbearable to have two sisters who were always spoiling for a fight.'

'I always thought it better to keep a low profile, stay under Mum's radar,' Cami admits.

'Probably wise. I think I stupidly kept on trying to get Mum's attention away from Rose, and to make them both happy. Never worked. Just hurt myself doing it.' I'm not sure if I've ever spoken so openly to my sister about the bad old days.

There's another pause before Cami speaks.

'I'm really sorry I wasn't a better sister to you, Mags.'

I realise there are tears trickling down my cheeks, not for the first time today. I am so touched by Cami's apology that I don't know what to say. 'Don't be daft. I was probably so good at putting on a happy face that you thought I was okay,' I smile sadly at her, wiping the tears away.

'Well, you did always seem stupidly happy considering how shit things were at home most of the time,' Cami concedes.

I nod. 'Yep. That's me – happy face. Smiley Mags, nothing ever gets her down.'

'I'm sorry, Mags. I think deep down I knew you weren't happy, but it was easier just to bury my nose in a book than face up to it.'

I shake my head. 'Please don't feel bad. We were both just surviving the best we could.'

'Yeah, I know, but we could've been there for each other – it might've made things easier.'

'We were just kids,' I shrug. 'Anyway, we can be here for each other now and I for one am very happy about it.'

'Me too, Mags. Better late than never.'

I return my attention to the photos. 'Some of these must be from Mum's photo albums,' I say as I find another one of the three of us taken with Ken and his dog in our back garden.

'Yeah, I think Margery contacted her asking if she had any. I suppose she asked everyone who knew him well.'

I examine the faces of the three young girls in the picture. Mine is smiley, happy, innocent; Cami's expression gives nothing away, but I notice she has her hand on Saxon's neck; Rose looks stony-faced. As I study the photo even more closely, I see clenched fists at her sides, and Uncle Ken's hand resting on her shoulder. I feel an inexplicable shudder.

'What was Rose's problem?' I ask Cami. 'What was she so bloody aggro about all the time?'

Cami shrugs. 'Dunno. I assumed it was all just growing up stuff, hormones.'

'Yeah, I guess.' I continue scrolling, but lose interest when there are no more photos of us, passing Cami back her mobile.

We chat for a while about arrangements for our impending trip to Rose's before saying our goodbyes and sharing another hug. This new closeness with my middle sister is bringing me so much joy. I really hope I can cultivate the same warmth of feeling with my eldest one, for heaven knows Rose is not without thorns.

Chapter 5
Shades of brown

Mags

'I just winked at the vicar.'

'I take it you're joking?' Rose says, without looking up from the maths paper she's marking. I don't miss her eyebrows lifting though, or the red pen pausing over the sheet.

'Nope. Definitely not joking,' I assure her, grabbing an apple from the fruit bowl and plonking myself on the chair opposite her at the scrubbed-pine kitchen table. 'He was looking at sherry. Bit of a cliché, I thought. Would've been much better if he'd been looking at – I dunno – cans of extra strong lager to swig on a park bench. I asked him if they stock Absinthe.'

Rose looks up at me over her glasses, an expression of bemused resignation on her face. 'Why on earth would you wink at Reverend Flory, Mags?'

'He thought I was you,' I inform her, pulling a sorry-not-sorry face.

'Oh, for God's sake. I have to face him at choir practice tonight, you div.'

'Hey, it's not my fault the whole village seems to think we're one and the same person,' I defend myself with a shrug.

At that moment, Cami walks in with Jacks, back from their

afternoon constitutional. I raise a hand in greeting, my mouth now full of apple.

'Hello. Nice walk?' Rose asks. 'Wink at anybody?'

'Yes, thanks. What? Why?' Cami says, unwinding her scarf from around her neck.

'Mags winked at the vicar in the Co-op.'

Cami shifts her gaze to me. 'Why did you wink at the vicar in the Co-op?'

'He thought I was Rose.' I shrug face and shoulders as if to say this should be explanation enough.

Cami cocks her head to one side for a moment before deciding this is perfectly acceptable. 'I actually got waved at by quite a few people who clearly thought I was you while I was out with Jacks.'

'Did you bother to disillusion them?' Rose asks.

'Nope. Doesn't seem any point. They'll still make the same mistake next time we're out.'

'Exactly,' I agree, waving my now half-eaten apple in the air. 'I blew a kiss to the builders working on that barn conversion down the road yesterday too.'

Rose sighs the sigh of the long-suffering older sister. 'I wish you'd both remember that I still have to live in the village after you two have buggered off again.'

Cami comes and joins us at the table, Jacks taking up his place by her feet. Rose returns to her marking and a comfortable silence overtakes us. Even my apple crunching seems a little loud, so I place the still-too-large core on the mat in front of me, and sit back in my chair. For once, I'm happy to be silent, not giving in to my normal urge to fill a silence with exaggeratedly happy talk. I'm grateful that the silence between us is comfortable. That hasn't always been the case.

I look over at Rose, her head bent over the GCSE test paper. Now fifty-seven, there are many more greys threaded through her dark-brown hair. From time to time, she drags her fingers distractedly though the shoulder-length tresses. I just know that there are a hundred other things racing through her brain, even as she grades the paper. Rose is actually her middle name. She was christened Peony Rose but, after enduring years of being called Pee-on-me or just plain Pee, she'd adopted her middle name. Our mother, with her usual lack of foresight had named us all after flowers.

I switch my gaze to Cami – Camellia Lily, and yes she suffered with Cami Knickers throughout her childhood. She's taken out her mobile phone and is absorbed by something – probably a funny animal video knowing her. I can't see any greys lurking in her slightly shorter, layered, chestnut-brown hair. The one good thing our father gave us: good hair genes. Her blue eyes crinkle as she chuckles at the images on the screen. Cami's just a year younger than Rose.

At fifty-three, I'm the baby. Mags. Magnolia Marguerite. Can you believe that? Thanks, Mum. Practically child abuse. I'd dabbled with Maggie and Rita, but settled on Mags. It wasn't until secondary school that the nickname Paint started. And for a while Dulux. I run my fingers through my own long, straight brown hair: the colour and the percentage of greys somewhere between my two sisters'. Different but the same.

That's us. Three sisters. The Flower Fairies as our mother referred to us. Different but the same. The same but different. I'm tall where they're not. They wear glasses, I opt for contact lenses in my green eyes. I sometimes wear makeup, they never do. We don't dress alike either, although the unwelcome arrival of middle-aged spread may be changing that sooner rather than later as elasticated waistbands become appealing.

So, when you see us together, we're actually far from clones, but there is some strong familial likeness that makes us indistinguishable when seen separately. When we go out as a two- or threesome, you can hear pennies, and see jaws, dropping as realisation dawns. And it never stops amusing us.

We sit like that for a while, until Cami finishes with her phone, and gets up to put the kettle on. A few minutes later, she places mugs of tea in front of us. Our tea, like our hair, comes in varying shades of brown. And only I take sugar. The same but different.

'Done!' Rose says with relief, closing the booklet and putting it to one side. She takes off her glasses and rubs her tired eyes. She always looks tired these days, and there are more lines around her brown eyes, which somehow look sad even when she's smiling. There's still a shadow of the rare beauty of her youth, but so much pain has punctured her life.

'How many students are you tutoring now?' I ask her.

'Just three. Keeps my hand in, and takes me away from everything for a few hours a week.' She sounds wistful.

'Miss being at school?'

Rose nods. 'Never thought I'd say it, but yes. I miss teaching a class full of rowdy oiks who have bugger all respect for teachers, a subject that half of them have no aptitude for.'

I just nod. There's nothing I can say that will make it better. Rose's life changed forever when her husband had a massive stroke two years earlier. But that wasn't the half of it. Not even a fraction. Cami and I didn't know it at the time, but Rose's life had been shattered decades earlier.

Cami and I'd arrived at Rose's a couple of days earlier, and hadn't done a great deal to be honest. Just started getting used to being comfortable together really. And taken some of the burden of caring for David off her shoulders, allowing her to escape for a long soak in the bath or a few hours in her craft room. Apart from walking the dog, and a trip to a garden centre for winter pansies, we'd barely left the house. I think she just needed a break from the drudgery; a buffer between her and her now dependent husband.

Neither Cami nor I have mentioned the funeral, and Rose hasn't asked about it. Whilst curious about her point blank refusal to attend, we don't want to jeopardise this new-found harmony.

'Are we ever going to talk to Rose about the Uncle Ken thing?' I ask Cami one evening, after David's gone to bed and Rose is reading in the bath.

Cami grimaces. 'I dunno. I don't want to upset her and spoil our visit.'

'No, I know. I do kind of want to get to the bottom of it though.'

'I think not this visit. Another time, maybe. When life's not so shite.'

It's my turn to grimace. 'Is there ever going to be a non-shite time again?'

'Christ, what a depressing thought.'

'Mm. Not the best,' I agree.

We sit quietly for a while, the television burbling unwatched in the background, and Jacks snoring gently next to his mistress.

Rose appears after a time, wrapped in a fluffy towelling robe, her cheeks pink from the bath. She looks much more relaxed than when we arrived.

'That was so lovely. Such a treat to be able to relax and not worry about David for a while. Thank you, you two. I feel almost human again,' she says, smiling gratefully at us.

'You're very welcome, although I don't feel we've done much to help,' I say.

'Oh, you have! Trust me! Just being here and taking the pressure off is huge. I desperately needed a break.'

'Glad it's helped. We'll have to try and get up here more often in future,' Cami says, smiling.

I nod my agreement. 'Absolutely. It's a nice change of scene for us too.' I realise in that moment I will do whatever it takes to build and maintain this sisterhood of ours.

Chapter 6
Genie in the bottle

Mags

Later that night, as I lie in bed, listening to the unfamiliar creaks of my sister's house, I think back to the day of my brother-in-law's stroke two years ago. I remember getting the call.

'David's had a stroke. Sounds like a bad one. He's in Addenbrooke's. Can you let Mum know? I'll call Dad.' Cami, disseminating the awful news down the family pipeline. The route's different if it doesn't originate with Mum.

'Shit. Yes, of course. How's Rose?'

'That's all I know at the moment, Mags. Speak later,' Cami'd said and hung up.

I dialled our mum's number, wishing I hadn't been given the task. I relayed the news, such as it was, to Mum, and promised to keep her in the loop. 'Try not to worry – he's in the best place,' I added lamely before saying goodbye.

I texted Rose a brief 'Thinking of you. Sending love and strength. xx' message and then poured myself a very generous Jack Daniels and Coke. It was at a time when I still relied on my crutches of booze and worse. Sitting in my kitchen, nursing the drink, I barely noticed the evening drawing in and the temperature dropping. Coming to with a shiver, I got stiffly up to put the heating and lights on and close the curtains. After refilling my glass, I curled up on the sofa, flicking through the channels on the TV to try and find something to distract me. All I could do though was think how life can change in an instant. A click of the fingers and a person's world can be turned upside down.

Not for the first time, I wished I wasn't on my own. I'd turned my own life upside down when I'd left my husband three years previously. I never for one second regretted leaving, but I will admit to being lonely. I'd just assumed I'd have met someone else, but it hadn't happened, in spite of numerous memberships of dating sites which had yielded nothing but amusing anecdotes to tell my sisters. We none of us had a great track record at marriage. Cami and I both had two failed attempts under our belts. Cami swore blind she couldn't live with anyone ever again, and devoted herself to a succession of Jack Russell Terriers. I, on the other hand, still hoped for a third time lucky. While Rose was still on husband number one, it had not been a match made in heaven.

We'd learned the rules of the marriage game from parents who'd chalked up seven marriages between them. We were mere amateurs in comparison to the mother and father who'd perfected the art of how not to do it. Perhaps if we'd had a better example, we wouldn't have messed up so spectacularly. But failure is the norm in our family. Failure and disappointment.

David had been in hospital for several weeks, having suffered a fairly catastrophic left-sided stroke, and then been in rehabilitation for months. Rose was exhausted and, in between hospital visits, had to have the house adapted to accommodate a wheelchair. Rooms were repurposed, a wet room constructed, doorways widened, and ramps installed. Life as she knew it was over.

Two years on and, although David could just about get in and out of his wheelchair with the use of a stick, he still had no use of his left arm and required constant care. I'm not sure I could have coped the way Rose has. I suppose she had no choice though. Life happens whether we want it to or not, and we just have to get by the best we can: to survive. That in itself is an achievement.

When I look back now, with the benefit of that mixed blessing called hindsight, I think what happened to David and effectively to my sister, was part of the catalyst I needed to address my own illness.

I suppose I have what people call an addictive personality. My mother would just say I was weak. Maybe she's right, I don't know. All I know is I crave things that give me relief, albeit false and temporary, from the harsh realities of life. Things that stop the pain for a while; stop the little gremlins in my brain from tormenting me. I didn't just feed them after midnight, I fed them constantly for they were always ravenous.

I don't remember exactly when I took that first drink. I must've been about eleven or twelve, I think. There was never much alcohol at home: Mum was pretty much teetotal. There was the occasional bottle of wine, and one of Harvey's Bristol Cream at Christmas. But that was where having a slightly off-the-rails older sister came in handy. When Rose was out doing whatever she did with her cool friends, I would sneak into her bedroom and pretend to be her. I'd try on her clothes, which were far too big obviously, and use her make-up and hairbrush. I was always careful to put everything back the way I found it, even removing my hairs from her brush. For one so young, I think I was already adept at deception. I could think outside the box and inside the bottle.

Once when I was snooping in her room, I found a bottle of clear liquid shoved down behind the pink velvet headboard of her single bed. I remember unscrewing the lid and taking a sniff. I wasn't prepared for the burn down my throat when I put the bottle to my lips and took a big swig. My eyes watered and I coughed, but I liked the way the liquid felt when it hit my stomach. It felt warm. And somehow comforting. I was too worried Rose would know if I drank any more. She would see that the level in the bottle was lower.

I think it was that same day I found a five-year diary – one of those ones with the little brass padlocks. At eleven, or twelve or however old I was, I wasn't actually that interested in what was written on the pages inside. I just shoved it back in its hiding place. But that little bottle of clear liquid magic had made a lasting impression on me, and given me a thirst for more.

As I put everything back in order in Rose's bedroom, I worried that Mum or one of my sisters would know I'd drunk the vodka. I breathed into my hand, but couldn't smell anything really. I cleaned my teeth just in case anyway. The warm feeling in the pit of my stomach faded all too soon, but the memory of it stayed. A seed was planted in my brain that day, and I would spend the next forty or so years trying to keep it alive, not caring that I was slowly killing myself in the process.

With no access to much alcohol, I had to content myself with the occasional swig from the bottle behind Rose's bed. I would limit myself to times when things were really bad at home; when the screaming matches between my eldest sister and my mother were the fiercest; when things got thrown and smashed, and doors slammed. 'If you walk out that door, young lady, don't you bother coming back,' Mum would scream. And Rose would scream back even louder. That's when I learned the word 'fuck'. Rose spat it at Mum, before 'off', or 'you'.

It helped to know the bottle was there. I remember once when I reached down behind the bed and the space was empty. I didn't like the feeling that washed over me then. It was a kind of panic in my chest. I needed that warmth in my tummy, that comfort. I needed to know the bottle was there when the pain got too much. What I really needed, of course, was my mother to show me some attention, to tell me I was loved, wanted, cared for. In the absence of that, I looked for something else to fill the gaping, aching, pain in my chest. If my mother wouldn't put her arms around me and tell me everything was going to be all right, I had to find something, or subsequently someone, who would, even if they only meant it for an hour, a night, a month, a marriage. My life had just been a succession of Band-Aids. Of crutches.

But David's stroke made me realise I had to take control of my life, my health, my addictions. I had to try and depend on me; to love me; to be alone with me. I'm not stupid. Well, maybe I am. But I know it's not healthy to get your sense of worth from other people; it has to come from within. But I had no idea how to find it within me. I never wanted to dig that deep into my damaged psyche to look for it anyway. Easier then to find a man, men, who were only too willing to tell me I was wonderful, beautiful, desirable. And, although I didn't really believe them, it was still nice to hear; a little food for my starving little heart. A little bit of warmth in my tummy. And when there wasn't a man, there was vodka.

I know my sisters probably think I'm a fool where men are concerned, and that I fall in and out of love too easily. I suppose it's all or nothing with me; it's extreme highs and lows, and not much in between. When there was a new man in my life, before the honeymoon period was over, I didn't need my other crutches. So I never called myself an addict. I could quit anytime I wanted. I was in control. Who was I kidding? I just substituted one substance for another. Alcohol. Sex. Love. Sex. And worse.

At last my eyelids are becoming heavy, and I close my eyes on the tears that are welling there, letting sleep finally claim me, grateful I don't have to think anymore just now about how utterly and completely I have screwed up my life.

Cami and I are leaving the next morning, heading back to our own lives once more. Rose definitely seems more relaxed though, and we've promised to make our visits a more regular occurrence. I really believe we will all benefit from time together. I always wished we'd been united by our childhoods, rather than forced apart. This time feels different, feels more permanent. I'm hoping it will be healing for all three of us.

'Thank you both so much for coming,' Rose says as we load our bags into Cami's car. 'It's been so lovely.'

'It has, hasn't it?' I agree, smiling at her.

'Yep, really lovely,' Cami says, pulling us into a group hug. I don't think we've ever hugged together like that before, and tears threaten once more. I blink them away. I don't want to be the cry-baby sister anymore.

We say our goodbyes to David, hug Rose one last time and

load Jacks into the back seat. He immediately starts barking, ignoring my instruction to shut up. Rose catches my eye and I stick my fingers in my ears as we grimace at one another. Cami and her beloved Jack Russells. They can do no wrong. It helps that she's a little bit deaf, mind you.

'Shut up, Jacks!' I say again, to no avail.

'Drive carefully,' Rose says. 'Let me know when you get home, and see you again soon.'

'Will do,' Cami says.

'Definitely,' I say, and then we're pulling off the drive. I turn and wave at Rose until she disappears from view. Thankfully, Jacks settles down and I can hear myself think once more.

Rose

I wave until Cami's car disappears from view and stand on the drive for a minute or two more, wrapping my arms around myself until the December chill finally sends me back indoors. The house feels a little empty after the fullness of my sisters' presences, but I don't feel sad, comforted by the knowledge that they will be returning soon. I make a little promise to myself that I will endeavour to do better until they return; I will encourage David to do his physio and try to be more positive for him. For me. Can I say for us? Maybe not, maybe never. But I will try and make the best of this god-awful situation.

I'm grateful my sisters didn't mention the funeral, or ask about my refusal to attend. A little part of me wanted to try and explain. One evening after David had gone to bed, and we were sitting in the lounge, I tried to find the words. In my head at least. But I didn't know where, or how, to start. And I was so enjoying the peace that had overtaken us. I didn't want to shatter it. I didn't want to risk this new-found harmony with my younger sisters, who I resented for so many years, irrationally, I know. Nothing that happened to me was their fault.

Maybe next time they came I could prise open the box of the past, just lift the lid a little and see how I feel. I would like them to understand why I was such a nightmare back then; to know it wasn't my fault. Or theirs. We were just three children who were let down by the adults who were supposed to protect us, keep us safe.

David calling from the downstairs loo snaps me back to the present.

'Coming!' I call out.

Chapter 7
Charlie and other men

Mags

It's a couple of days since we got back from Rose's and I'm back at work in the quality assurance department of a small pharmaceutical company. I fell into the job and it's most definitely not my vocation. It pays the bills though, and for the not inexpensive counsellor I now see once a week. I'm doing internal audits at the moment which are by far my least favourite part of the job. And trust me, they have stiff competition. The stress of the job has made the wheels on the wagon decidedly wobbly in recent weeks, and I have to work harder than ever to stay on track.

It helps to have the added incentive of continuing to rebuild the relationships with my sisters though, and I don't want to do anything to jeopardise that. Every time I feel the panic rising in my chest, I bring Rose and Cami to mind now, and draw strength from them. Gone are the days when I would sneak off for a fix in the loo, or a swig from the silver hip flask I kept in my handbag. Like all addicts, I was adept at deception, an accomplished liar. And I was always able to function, so I told myself I didn't have a problem. Well, actually that part was true: I had several. And more than to anyone else, I was lying to myself. Admitting I had a problem was the first baby step of my recovery.

I'd been shopping for Christmas on my days off, and had splurged on a mini break for me, Rose and Cami in the new year. It was a bit of an indulgence, four days in a cabin complete with open fire and hot tub, but I thought it would be the perfect way to strengthen the growing bonds between us. In order to make it work, I'd had to involve Rose's eldest daughter, who'd agreed to look after David. She was sworn to secrecy, of course, and Rose and Cami would get details of the break when they opened their presents of white towelling robes and slippers, the kind you get at spa hotels. Just got to get through the C word itself before that; my first sober one since I was a child. I thanked God, or at least my Higher Power, that I didn't have to spend it with Mum who'd decided to go and stay with her sister in Devon. Hallefrigginglujah. If anything could tip me over the edge at Christmas, it would be Mum. I wonder idly if Auntie Ann can be persuaded to keep her indefinitely.

Cami has invited me for lunch on Christmas Day and I'm quite content to spend the rest of the break quietly at home, and avoiding the people and situations which would have made me want to use. I'm enjoying the feeling of being clean and sober too much to fall back now. I know I'll always be an addict, but I truly believe I am a recovering one. That doesn't mean I can ever stop 'doing the work', but with every day that passes, every week, every month, sobriety becomes more and more the norm. When I think about what I've been through to get to this point in my life, I realise I'm feeling new and unfamiliar emotions. I am feeling pride, and maybe, dare

I say, starting to love myself just a little. It's a revelation. I never thought I was worthy of anyone's love before, least of all my own.

*

Finally, the audits are over and so is a quiet and restful Christmas. Cami and I Skyped Rose for present opening.

'Look in the robe pocket,' I instruct both sisters when they've unwrapped their gifts from me.

I watch and wait as they dig around and proceed to read the cards I'd hidden for them, with details of the cabin break.

Cami grins at me and plants a kiss on my cheek. 'Yippee! A cabin in the woods! Can I bring Jacks?'

'No!' Rose and I yell in unison, laughing.

'Sorry, sis, it's a girls only trip,' I inform her, hoping she receives the news graciously. She's probably never been away from her little dog for this long.

'Fair enough,' Cami says. 'He'd probably pee in the hot tub or something anyway.'

Rose and I pull matching expressions of disgust and Cami laughs.

'I think I can just about cope for four days without him, but I'm not sure what I'm going to do with him. I can't put him in kennels.'

'Mm,' Rose agrees, her face dropping. 'I can't put David in kennels either. I can't just disappear for four days, Mags.'

'Yes, you can. You both can. Because I've sorted it all – Bella's coming to the rescue to look after David, and my lovely neighbour is happy to have Jacks. You've met her, Cami – Audrey. She used to have that Jack Russell called Sparky. So neither of you has any excuse not to come.'

Rose looks like she's about to cry, but she holds herself together. 'Oh my God, thank you, Mags. I absolutely can't wait.'

'Yes, thank you,' Cami says. 'It'll be great.' Cami's looking at the photo of the hot tub as she speaks, and a slightly pensive look briefly crosses her face. I guess she's not as cool about leaving Jacks as she wants us to believe.

'I really hope you can both relax and properly enjoy it,' I smile from Cami to Rose's on-screen face.

'What do we need to bring?' Rose asks, ever practical.

'Well, I thought I'd do a supermarket shop for most of what we might need. But feel free to bring whatever you fancy too,' I tell them.

'Charlie Hunnam?' Rose suggests.

Cami and I laugh. 'Only if you share,' I tell her.

'How about you get the basics and we'll get the booze and the treats,' Cami says.

'Perfect. Um… I'm on a bit of a detox at the moment, so I'll be sticking to juices and sparkling water.' It's a little white lie, but I'm not ready to tell them I'm on the wagon.

'New Year resolutions starting early, eh?' Cami says.

'Yeah, something like that,' I nod.

'Well, I definitely plan on having bubbles in the bubbles,' Rose says. 'Four blissful days, with nothing to do except relax. God, what a treat. Best present ever. Thank you, Mags. It really is so generous of you.'

Cami nods her agreement. 'It really is.'

'Well, I don't have anyone else I can spoil, so why not you two?' I say, gratified by their response.

We wind up the call soon after, and I say a silent little prayer that the time away will bring the three of us closer still.

*

I return to work for a few days between Christmas and New Year. I don't even bother staying up to see the new year in. The associations with alcohol are still too great on occasions such as that. I'm more in tune with my body now, and I listen when it tells me to rest. Previous years would have seen me dancing 'til dawn and then passing out, sometimes in my bed, sometimes not, and sleeping off the excesses. Other times, I wouldn't sleep for three days in a row, with my old friend Charlie for company. And I don't mean Hunnam. I'm not proud of my past behaviour, but I am trying to do better, be better, and not beat myself up about the stuff I can't change or control.

*

The place I've booked for us to stay is not a million miles away from Rose's – I figured she'd rest easier knowing she wasn't too far away from David and her daughter in an emergency. So, the night before, Cami and I drive up to Rose's, figuring we can then get an early start and not waste a minute of our precious mini-break. I'd paid a little extra for early check-in and late check-out too.

On the drive up, in my car this time, with no small dog accompanying us and shedding wiry brown hairs everywhere, Cami and I return to the topic of Uncle Ken and the funeral.

'So, are we going to broach the subject while we're away?' I ask, not taking my eyes off the road. It's sleeting a little and visibility isn't great.

'Um… maybe. I think we'll just have to play it by ear a bit, to be honest. She's so fragile still.'

'Yeah, you're probably right. Maybe just see if it happens naturally. Have you still got those photos on your phone?'

'Yep. Just in case,' Cami confirms.

'It would be nice to understand her reaction,' I say, thinking out loud.

'Yeah, I know. Maybe he's just a reminder of an unhappy time – she and Mum did row pretty spectacularly back then.'

'God, didn't they just? I think that's when I learned all the swear words,' I chuckle.

'Oh my God! The things she used to say to Mum! I wouldn't have dared.'

'No, me neither. Although I do think about doing it fairly often,' I muse.

'Well, yeah, me too, but I wouldn't actually do it. I don't think I would anyway.'

'She does push me to my limit, but still I find myself doing and saying the right thing, and keeping the peace.'

'Mm, like you did all those years ago. You were always the little peacemaker. I just hid in my room.'

'I tried. Not sure it actually did any good. I just wanted everyone to get on. Still do, I s'pose. Maybe shouting and screaming myself would have had more of an impact?'

Cami laughs. 'It would certainly have shocked Mum and Rose. Might have shut them up for five minutes.'

I sigh. 'God, I really hated home back then.'

'I know. Me too. I'm not sure if it was better or worse when Mum had a man in tow?'

'Ugh. She sure could pick 'em. Remember that awful Welsh

guy? What was his name?'

'Emlyn? Rose used to call him Emlyn Huge, remember?'

'Yes! I'd forgotten that. Rose really hated him. She said he deliberately left the bathroom door unlocked when he was in there, hoping she'd walk in on him.'

'Judging by the nickname, maybe she did. Although he was really fat too.'

'Yeah, yuck. What on earth did Mum ever see in him?'

'Christ knows. Maybe he was good in bed?'

'I'm surprised he could even find it under that belly!'

'Did you realise at the time that he was married?' Cami asks.

'I don't think I did, to be honest. I s'pose I was too young to really think about that sort of stuff.'

'Yeah, I think his wife knew about Mum too.'

'She was probably relieved to have him taken off her hands.'

'Talking of hands, what about Terry with the enormous ones?'

'Ew, yeah, the really hairy hands. Looked like a couple of tarantulas on the end of his arms.' We're laughing now, but at the time it had been very unfunny. Terry scared me with his dark moods and brooding looks.

'He really gave me the creeps,' Cami says as if she's reading my mind. 'He once pulled me onto his lap and I could feel that he was turned on through his trousers.' She shudders at the memory. 'When I tried to get off him, he pulled me back down. Mum just laughed. Bitch.'

'God, it's no wonder all our relationships with men have been so screwed up,' I groan.

'I know, right,' Cami agrees.

We're both silent for a while, lost in thoughts of men and

failed attempts at relationships. Neither of us has mentioned our stepfather, consciously or otherwise I don't know.

A thought suddenly occurs to me. 'Do you think Mum and Uncle Ken were ever a thing?'

'I have wondered that in the past, but I came to the conclusion they weren't. No evidence to support it, but I never got that impression.'

'You don't think he was gay, do you?' I ask. 'I mean, he never married. And I don't remember him ever having a girlfriend or anyone living with him. Do you?'

'Nope. But I don't think he was gay. Could be wrong, of course. I was wrong about my first husband. He turned out to be gay.'

'Holy flaming shit balls, Cami! Robert was gay? How have I never known that?' I turn briefly away from the road to look at my sister.

'I know. Stupid me. I didn't see it either. Just thought he had really good taste in home décor for a man,' Cami laughs.

I cock my head to one side, picturing the home my sister had shared with her first husband. 'He really did. I just assumed the impeccable taste was yours.'

'Well, I did pick up a few tips from him. Unbeknownst to me though, he was picking up more than tips. I actually found him in bed with a man he met in a gay bar he used to frequent on 'work' trips to London.'

'Bloody hell.' I'm quiet again as I digest the titbit my sister just revealed. I still can't believe I didn't know. When Robert and Cami had divorced, he'd moved away and we'd lost touch. It hadn't felt right to keep in touch with my sister's ex, even though Robert and I had always got on really well. I knew why now, we had more in common than I'd realised. 'Is that why you never had children? With Robert, I mean.'

'No, that's not the reason, Mags. I never wanted children. Ever.'

We'd never discussed the fact that neither of us had children. Rose was the only one of us to produce offspring.

'I just assumed it never happened for you. Didn't like to mention it.'

'I made sure it never happened. I had my tubes tied when I was twenty-one, straight after university,' Cami says calmly.

I can't believe my ears. The car has turned into a confessional. How can we be sisters and know so little about one another? But Cami had always been private, secretive.

'Oh my God! Really? Bloody hell.' I'm gobsmacked and can't keep the shock and surprise from my voice.

'I just always knew, Mags. Why would anyone want to bring children into this shitty world?'

'But you could have done it so much better than our mum did! You could have given a child all the love we never had.' I knew I should probably shut up.

Cami doesn't say anything.

'Have you ever regretted your decision?' I push.

'No. Never. It's the reason me and Steve broke up though. He hit forty and decided he couldn't live without a child of his own. Cue the younger model with her tubes intact.' Cami sounds so matter of fact.

I did know that Cami's second husband had married a younger woman and gone on to have twins. By IVF ironically. I felt bad that I hadn't taken more interest in my middle sister's life. I'd been too busy looking for my next fix, and it had made me selfish.

'I wish you'd told me. I wish I'd asked. I'm sorry, Cami,' I tell her quietly.

The sleet on the motorway has worsened and I focus my attention back on the road. It also helps take my mind off my own childless state which, unlike Cami's, was not through choice.

Cami reaches over and turns on the radio and the strains of Daft Punk's 'One More Time' fill the car. It's the perfect mood-lifting song and we both sing along at the tops of our voices. I reckon even Jacks would have told us to shut up as he couldn't hear himself bark. By the time we pull onto Rose's drive, we're both feeling good again, all thoughts of the past forgotten. For now, at least. If this weekend goes as I hope it will, my sisters and I will be revisiting the past and hopefully exorcising some ghosts. It's time.

Chapter 8
Packing and unpacking

Mags

Our niece, Bella, greets us at the door.

'Yay! Favourite aunties!' she says, launching herself at us for a hug.

Cami and I laugh.

'Er... only aunties!' I point out.

Bella just pooh-poohs this with a wave of her hand. 'Come in, come in, it's freezing out here. How was your drive? Awful weather,' she babbles.

I'd forgotten what a chatterbox she is, and it makes me smile. Bella is the older of Rose's two daughters and is a clinical psychologist. It had occurred to me when I was planning the trip, that I should maybe invite her too. She could probably help us navigate the complex corridors of our psyches no end. But I didn't think Rose would've liked that. She'd always tried to protect her girls from the tough stuff and the worst of our family history.

When Bella pauses for breath, I tell her that the drive wasn't too bad in spite of the sleet. 'It's lovely to see you, niecelet. Thank you for stepping in to look after your dad.'

'Yes,' Cami echoes. 'It's much appreciated.'

'You're so welcome. I think it's great the three of you are going away together. I know it will do Mum a world of good,' Bella says, smiling broadly. 'I'm a bit jealous to be honest – the cabin looks so cute. And that hot tub!'

'Maybe we can make it a foursome next time? Well, fivesome actually, because your mum's bringing Charlie Hunnam,' I tell her. If there is a next time. If we're still speaking after this one.

Bella busies herself making tea while Cami and I take our overnight bags to our rooms and then go in search of Rose. We find her in her bedroom, dithering over what to pack.

'Layers, PJs, swimsuit, book, sponge bag,' I tell her.

'Phone charger, glasses, medication,' Cami contributes.

'So far I just have Champagne, Kettle Chips and a very large box of chocolates,' Rose says sheepishly.

'Excellent priorities,' I nod approvingly.

'What flavour Kettle Chips?' Cami enquires.

Rose promptly bursts into tears. Cami and I exchange 'what the heck' faces.

'Shit! It's okay if you only got lightly salted,' Cami says, going to Rose and putting an arm round her trembling shoulders.

Rose smiles and laughs through her tears. 'I'm sorry, this is stupid. I'm just so happy.'

'Er… yeah, looks like it,' I say, pulling a mad face at her.

She laughs again. 'They're tears of relief, I think. I feel like a pressure cooker when the valve thingy finally gets opened. There's been a bit of a build-up.'

I ferret in my pocket for a tissue and pass it to my big sister. 'Here you go, snotty.' I think about the several boxes of tissues in one of the shopping bags in the boot of my car. I've got a feeling we'll be needing them.

'Thanks, Mags. Sorry to be such a dick. I'm so looking forward to this, I can't tell you.'

'You just did, Rose. Right, I'm going to see if that daughter of yours can make a decent cup of tea,' I say, heading out of the bedroom. Cami stays to help Rose pack.

Back in the kitchen, I thank Bella once more for stepping in. 'I really appreciate this, B. You are an angel.'

'I'm glad I could help, honestly. And I've been feeling guilty about not doing more to help Mum and Dad. This will give me the perfect opportunity to assess Dad's emotional wellbeing and maybe put some techniques in place to help him and Mum.'

'You mustn't feel guilty, B, it's such a pointless emotion. You're a wonderful daughter – if I'd had one I'd have wanted her to be just like you – but you have your own life to get on with. Mum wouldn't want you to feel bad. God knows, none of us would want you to feel about us the way we do about Granny most of the time.' As the words leave my mouth, I hope I haven't said too much. I don't know what Rose has said about our mother.

'Aw! Thanks! How is Granny?' Bella asks. 'Mum hardly ever mentions her. We kind of learnt as kids not to mention her – it made Mum a bit prickly.'

'She's fighting fit apart from a little bit of arthritis.' I pause for a moment, wondering if I should say any more. 'Granny wasn't the easiest woman to live with, to be honest. She and your mum used to argue quite a bit.'

Bella nods. 'Yes, that's the impression I got. There's always been tension on the few occasions I've seen them together. Mum always finds excuses for not visiting too. And now, with Dad…' Bella tails off, looking sadly in the direction of the study where her father sits in his wheelchair at the computer.

'I don't think peace will ever break out between Mum and Granny, but I'm hoping this trip will bring your mum and your favourite aunties closer.'

Bella smiles. 'I hope so. Right, tea. How do you take it?'

'The colour of my hair and one, please.'

Later that evening, with David in bed and the gentle hum of the massager going, the four of us congregate in the lounge. Rose has opened the Kettle Chips – sweet chilli and sour cream thankfully – on the understanding that I have more in the car. She, Cami and Bella are drinking wine, which I have refused in favour of a tonic with lime. I can pretend it has gin in.

'So, all packed now?' I ask Rose.

She nods. 'Yep, thanks to Cami.'

'Always easier to pack for someone else,' Cami says.

'You'd have made a great mum,' Rose says. I hold my breath, bearing in mind the earlier car confession.

Cami just smiles serenely and says, 'Dog mum.'

I exhale. I wonder if Rose knows Cami's decision not to have children was very much a conscious one. There have been many periods during our lives when the two of them have been as thick as thieves, with me very much on the outside. I was probably preoccupied with men and my other vices anyway. I take a mouthful of my drink and think gin thoughts.

Bella, unaware of the tension surrounding the subject of children, has decided to push the point, professional curiosity possibly getting the better of her.

'So, why didn't you have children, Auntie Cams?'

'I never wanted them. I don't think I'm the maternal type. It's no biggie,' she says matter-of-factly.

'No regrets?' Bella asks.

Cami shakes her head. 'Nope. I knew from a very young age and have never wavered from that position.'

But Bella's not done, and she turns her attention to me.

'How about you, Auntie M?'

I can feel my cheeks go pink as the glare of the spotlight hits me. This isn't something I talk about. Except to my counsellor after about a million sessions. 'Um... I just wasn't that lucky, I s'pose,' I say, shrugging.

I can feel three pairs of eyes on me. They're not going to settle for that, I can tell. More than ever I wish there was more than tonic water in my glass. I can feel my heart rate quickening, and a band tightening around my head. The gremlins are waking.

Before I can chicken out, I take a deep breath and begin.

'Okay, you want the truth? I guess I owe you that much. Before I carry on though, will you all promise me something?'

Three heads nod.

'Of course,' my sisters say in unison.

'Promise you won't think badly of me?' My heart is beating out of my chest. Why am I doing this? But I know why I'm doing it... because I have to, for the sake of my recovery and because I don't want all these secrets between us. And if I want the unadulterated truth from my sisters, I have to offer the same. Cami's already made herself vulnerable. Now it's my turn.

When they've promised not to judge me, I take another deep and steadying breath and close my eyes, letting my thoughts drift back in time.

'Well, I suppose the first thing you need to know is that I'm an addict.'

If any of them is shocked, they don't show it, and I continue:

'I'm actually in recovery, and I've been clean and sober for a year. I spent several weeks last winter in rehab. I'm still taking one day at a time and I see a counsellor every week to try and unpack the emotional crap I've kept buried under drink and drugs my whole life. And men, too, I suppose. I've been addicted to them as well. To anything that took me out of myself for a while.' I pause, unable to look up at the faces in the room; afraid of seeing judgment there.

But I've started now and the worst is out, so I might as well continue. Maybe it will be cathartic.

'You might want to open another bottle of wine,' I say, finally looking up from my lap where my hands are clenched around my glass. 'It's not pretty.'

'It's okay, Mags, keep going. No one's going to judge you,' Cami says.

'I'm not sure how far back I should go. It could take a while.'

'That's okay, we've got all night,' Rose says.

'Don't say I didn't warn you,' I say with a grimace. 'I suppose it all started in your bedroom, Rose.' I dare to look at her, and see confusion on her face. I explain about my secret visits to her bedroom, and the bottle of vodka behind the headboard, praying silently that it's ancient history enough for her not to mind. She doesn't speak, so I carry on.

'That first taste of what alcohol could do to my mood, and to the emotional pain, left me wanting more. There was hardly ever any alcohol in the house unless Mum had one of her god-awful boyfriends staying, but whenever there was, I would sneak whatever I could. And when Mum married Alan it was pretty easy.' (Our stepfather had been an alcoholic, a functioning one, but one nonetheless. He had died of cirrhosis of the liver some years previously. He should've served as a stark warning to me.)

'I don't know if you remember the headaches I used to get in my teens? Real stonking tension headaches. Mum got me some codeine tablets once. I spent the next ten years of my life taking about eight a day. I used to go to different pharmacies to buy them because you're only meant to take them for three days, and I was ashamed. I wasn't taking them for headaches anymore. I was addicted to them.

'By the time I left school to go to uni, I was drinking every day, and taking the codeine tablets. Christ knows how I ever graduated. I spent most of the time pissed or stoned. Yep, that's when I started smoking dope too. I just told myself everyone was doing it, that it was normal, harmless.' I shrug. 'And maybe it is for some people. But not for me. I was just always chasing a better high, anything that stopped me having to feel, to deal with real life.'

Still no one speaks.

'This is very much a potted history you're getting here. Pun intended,' I say with a sad smile. 'After I graduated and started work, I began to hang out with a crowd who regularly used cocaine. And I'm not talking scuzzy junkies – these were young professionals with power suits and jobs to match. So I started doing it too, and it made me feel invincible. It also made me reckless and stupid. I'm horrified now when I look back. There is nothing glamorous about snorting cocaine off a toilet seat.'

I hadn't realised it, but silent tears are streaming down my face unchecked. I reach into my pocket, only to find it empty because I gave my tissue to Rose. Cami passes me the box from the side table and I wipe my cheeks.

'Well, I've started, so I guess I'd better finish. To cut a very long and tawdry story short, I slept around and wasn't safe doing it. I didn't care what I did, or who I did it with. It was all about the next high and I would do anything to get it. When I was twenty-three, I found out I had pelvic inflammatory disease. And years later, when I tried to have a baby, I found out the infection had made me infertile and there was nothing they could do for me. I kind of figured it was my punishment, that I didn't deserve to be a mother. No one to blame but myself,' I finish with a shrug.

The room remains silent. I hold my breath. I'm too afraid to look at anyone. Too afraid I will see disgust and rejection, as I'd seen on my mother's face so often.

Then suddenly, two pairs of arms are wrapped around me, and two faces close to mine. I can feel the wet cheeks of my sisters, their tears mingling with my own. And I feel safe. And accepted. And loved.

Chapter 9
The cabin

Mags

We talk into the early hours, finally heading to bed at about ten to three. It's just as well we don't have a long drive, or anything to do other than relax, as it's three zombies who meet in the kitchen at about eight o'clock. I'm grateful to at least have no hangover. Rose and Cami both look decidedly fragile. I'm still getting used to feeling clearheaded when I wake, and not relying on one substance or another to get me through the day.

I take a turn at making the tea, as my sisters sit at the table holding their heads.

'Shouldn't have opened that third bottle,' Cami groans.

'Or had that gin liqueur,' Rose grimaces.

Before I can joke about what a couple of lushes they are, ironically of course, the back door opens and Bella walks in.

'Morning, alkies!' she says, grinning broadly. 'And recovering alkie,' she adds, winking at me. 'Thought you might appreciate these,' she says, holding up two McDonalds bags.

'Oh God, you are an angel,' Cami tells her.

'It's been said before,' Bella says, putting the bags on the table between hungover sisters. 'Sausage and Egg McMuffins, food of the hangover gods.'

'And hash browns?' Rose asks.

'Of course! What do you take me for, Mother? Some sort of heathen?' Bella laughs.

Even without a hangover, I happily tuck into the food, abandoning tea-making as Bella makes a pot of coffee and hands out paracetamol. It's a novelty to be the one not taking drugs. By the time we've finished, Rose and Cami are starting to feel and look a bit more human.

After breakfast, we all head off for showers and by nine-thirty, the car's packed and we're on our way.

'Have a wonderful time,' Bella tells us. 'And don't worry about anything here. I've got it.'

The atmosphere in the car is happy and relaxed. I'm still a little bit gobsmacked at how easy it was to tell my sisters some of my sordid past, and how non-judgmental they both were. It's hard to describe how I feel now... sort of cleansed somehow. I'd included what happened in my morning gratitudes, and writing it down made it feel even more special. I wondered why it had taken me so long to confide in them. I suppose I wasn't ready before. And maybe they weren't either.

In a little under an hour, we turn off down a wooded track. Rose and Cami had both nodded off a few miles back, but I was content enough listening to the radio and thinking about the next few days.

About a mile further on, I hang a left and am soon pulling up outside our log cabin.

'Hey, wake up sleepyheads, we're here,' I say.

'Oh! It's lovely!' Rose cries as soon as she opens her eyes. The wooden building is set back in a small clearing, surrounded by pine forest.

I smile. We're off to a good start.

Cami yawns and stretches in the back seat. 'Jacks would love it here,' she says.

'No!' Rose and I yell together.

'If you tell us he's stowed away in your bag, I will not be a happy bunny,' I tell her.

'He eats bunnies,' Cami laughs. 'Happy or otherwise.'

'Come on, let's take a look inside before we unload the car,' I say.

The key is in a little safe by the front door, and I check my booking form for the code. Once inside, we're delighted to find that the fire has already been lit in the big stone hearth in the main living room, and the cabin is toasty warm and welcoming. There are fresh flowers on the table in a small but well-equipped kitchen, and a welcome basket containing a selection of goodies.

'Mm, these scones look amazing!' Rose says, examining the contents of the basket. 'Strawberry jam. And a note saying clotted cream is in the fridge. Yum!'

'It really is perfect, Mags, good job,' Cami smiles at me. 'Let's check out the bedrooms.'

I'd booked a cabin with three bedrooms as I wasn't sure how my sisters would feel about sharing, and I figured we might need our own space to escape to from time to time. We hadn't spent this much time together since we were children. Two of the bedrooms open on to a wooden deck which holds a table and chairs and the hot tub. I unlock one of the doors and we all go out to check out the view into the forest.

'Idyllic!' Rose declares.

'Hopefully we'll see some deer while we're here. Apparently there are Red, Roe, Fallow and Muntjac,' I inform my sisters, counting them off on my fingers. I'd done my research. 'Ooh, stick your hand in here,' I say a few moments later, having lifted the Jacuzzi lid a little way.

Rose follows suit. 'Let's unpack quickly so we can get in,' she declares.

Cami is still standing by the railings at the edge of the deck, staring into the forest. She doesn't seem as enthused by the prospect of a soak in the hot tub as me and Rose.

'Cami? You coming? We're going to unload the car.'

My middle sister turns and smiles, but there's a shadow of something else leaving her face as she does so.

It doesn't take long to empty the car and unpack the shopping and our personal effects.

'Er... have you brought enough tissues?' Cami enquires as she unloads four boxes from one of the Tesco's bags.

I look at her and shrug. 'You know what a cry-baby I am,' I joke. 'There's just a box for each bedroom and one for the lounge really,' I offer by way of actual explanation.

Cami nods, as if to say fair enough.

With everything unpacked, and the hot tub calling, Rose and I head to our rooms to put our swimsuits on. Cami hangs back. 'Not sure I fancy it just yet. Maybe later tonight? Under the stars?' she says.

Rose and I accept this explanation, and before long we've changed and are wearing our matching robes and slippers and heading to the deck. We take a side of the heavy lid each and pull back to reveal the steamy, bubbling tub.

'Oh my God, bliss,' I say as I climb in and sink into the

hot water.

Rose quickly follows suit, making a sound more usually heard in the bedroom, I think.

We both close our eyes and for a couple of minutes just relax totally.

'Bugger, forgot the bubbly!' Rose says, breaking the idyll.

'Maybe we should save that for when Cami's in too?' I suggest.

'Oh, yes, you're right. Soft drinks for now then. I'll go. What do you want?'

Just as Rose is about to clamber out, Cami appears as if by magic.

'You're just like Mr. Ben,' I grin. 'Sure you won't join us? It's bloody lovely.'

'Could only be improved by the presence of Mr. Hunnam,' Rose adds.

'No, thanks. I'm going to go for a walk and explore a little bit. Just wanted to see if you need a drink or anything before I go?'

'You're a mind reader,' I tell her. 'Can I have a sparkling water please? With a slice of lime if you can be bothered. Ta.'

'Mm, same for me please. Thought we'd have the Champers later when we're all together,' Rose informs our sister.

Cami smiles that gentle smile of hers and disappears back inside, returning a few minutes later with our drinks. 'Right, won't be long,' she says, leaving via the deck and disappearing down a rough path into the trees.

'Don't get lost!' I call after her.

She acknowledges with a backward wave of her hand, and Rose and I return to the business at hand: complete relaxation.

We don't speak for a while, just letting the massage jets do their work.

It's Rose who finally breaks the silence. 'Cami doesn't know what she's missing. I might just spend the entire four days in here.'

'It is utter bliss, isn't it? Cami's probably just missing her hound and her routine of walking him.'

'Yeah, she'll probably come back with a deer on a lead.'

'Ha! Yeah, Munt-Jacks!' I giggle.

'Or a strange man she's picked up,' Rose adds.

'If anyone can pick up a random man in the middle of a forest, it's Cami.'

We laugh before silence descends once more.

It's me that breaks it this time. Something has just occurred to me that I've never really considered before. 'Do you think Cami simply doesn't like the water?'

Rose opens her eyes. 'What? Why?'

'Think about it...' I say, '... all those holidays at Granny's when we used to go to the beach. Or to the swimming pool. Cami never wanted to come. And when she did, she never went swimming.'

Rose pauses to consider what I've said. 'You know, you're right. She'd never wear a swimming costume, even when Mum nagged her. She'd always wear those long shorts she lived in during the summer.'

'Yeah, and she'd never do more than paddle, would she?'

'I never really thought about it at the time. Probably just put it down to her shyness.'

'Mm, she was always pretty self-conscious, wasn't she?'

'She hated being the centre of attention, always. I suppose

that's never changed.'

We both close our eyes again, lulled by the warmth, and I let my mind drift where it will. I think Rose may actually have fallen asleep at some point. That's how Cami finds us some time later.

'You still in that thing?' she says as she steps up on to the deck.

'Yep. We're staying in here for the duration,' Rose tells her.

'We decided you can wait on us,' I add.

'Yeah, hope you don't mind?' Rose says.

Cami just laughs. 'Cheeky gits. I'm going to start a jigsaw,' she says, heading indoors.

'Some things never change,' I say with a smile.

Chapter 10
Come on in, the water's lovely

Mags

We spend the rest of the morning lolling around the cabin, just chatting and doing the jigsaw, which is of a Swiss mountain scene with far too much snow and sky for my liking. Cami's already completed the edges by the time Rose and I are dry and dressed. I make a pot of coffee and we decide we can't wait until afternoon tea to eat the scones.

'Jam or cream first?' I ask them, feeling a little bad that I don't already know the answer.

'Er, jam of course!' Rose says.

'Yeah, jam. What are you? Some kind of monster?' Cami says, mock shuddering.

I laugh. 'Hey, I concur! Just didn't want to assume.'

'To assume makes an ass of u and me!' my sisters chorus.

'Oh my God, how many times did Mum say that to us?' I groan.

'But she did at least teach us the correct way to eat scones,' Cami says.

'Did she, though? I can't remember having scones as kids. I s'pose we must have,' I cast my mind back.

'We definitely did. Not homemade ones though,' Cami

informs me.

'Hm, okay, well that's no surprise. Mum wasn't much of a cook, was she?' I say.

Both sisters shake their heads.

'Wasn't much of a mum either,' I say quietly. I busy myself with preparing the scones the correct, Cornish, way and push thoughts of Mum away. Her presence is most definitely not welcome in the cabin.

We gloss over lunch, full of delicious scones as we are, and head out for a walk in the early afternoon. We let Cami lead the way, as she's already explored the area behind the cabin. The temperature has dropped and we're wrapped up in hats and gloves, our noses turning rapidly red. No one seems to mind the cold though as it's crisp and dry, the sky a bright white.

After we've been walking for about half an hour, Cami suddenly stops in her tracks and gestures for us to do the same. She turns, with a finger to her lips, and then points up ahead. There, only about twenty or so feet away is a Muntjac deer, grazing quietly just off the path. Well, of course, that's my and Rose's cue to look at each other and say 'Munt-Jacks' rather too loudly for the deer's liking and it pauses with its head up, looks in our direction and then scampers off.

Cami gives us a filthy look. 'You dicks!'

Rose and I try to look repentant. 'Sorry!' we chorus before giggling again.

We continue walking and I think, not for the first time today, how much I'm loving being with my two big sisters. In spite of the cold, I'm filled with a warm glow. And it has nothing to do with vodka.

Before it starts to get too near dusk, we head back to the cabin. Cami makes tea and we sit in front of the fire to thaw out. We're all soon yawning, the late night catching up with us. Rose's head is nodding as she dozes in her chair, and Cami takes herself off to bed for a lie down. I fight sleep as I know a nap now will prevent me from sleeping at bedtime. My routine is still a critical part of my recovery and a regular sleep pattern helps keep me on track.

As the evening draws in and my sisters continue to snooze, I get up and close all the curtains to keep the warmth in, tossing another couple of logs on the fire we've kept going all day. At about five-thirty, I put a moussaka in the oven and settle down to read while I wait for Rose and Cami to wake. I don't hear Cami when she pads back into the lounge, until she plonks herself down on the sofa.

'Hello. You really are like some kind of ninja, Cami. I think you missed your vocation. You should've been a spy or an assassin or something. A private detective, maybe,' I say, holding up the Strike novel I'm reading.

Rose stirs in the chair opposite, opens her eyes and stretches. 'Oh, hello, you two. How long have I been out for?'

'Ages. It's tomorrow. You missed dinner,' I say.

'And breakfast,' Cami says.

'And Charlie Hunnam,' I tell her.

'But don't worry, Mags entertained him,' Cami informs her.

'Dirty job…' I say, feigning exhaustion with the back of my hand to my forehead.

Rose, however, has only managed to process the dinner part of the conversation. 'What is for dinner?'

'Moussaka. Hope that's okay?'

'Yum, yes, lovely.'

I look at my watch. 'Be ready in about twenty minutes.'

'Okay. I might just freshen up then,' Rose says, heaving herself out of the chair with a groan.

'Oh, God, old people noises,' Cami says. 'Are we old?'

'Very nearly,' I tell her sadly. Uncle Ken's recent funeral flashes into my mind and I wonder if we'll get the chance to talk to Rose about it tonight.

Cami turns her attention to the jigsaw and I turn mine to dinner, loading plates with pre-prepared salad and laying the table. There's a bottle of Shiraz breathing and three wine glasses ready and waiting. Mine will have cranberry juice in. It helps to not feel quite so odd one out if I have the same glass and a similar colour drink as everyone else. Stupid I suppose. I've found a candle and am dithering about whether to light it and put it on the table or not. *Would it be a bit weird? Stop overthinking it, Mags*, I tell myself. *If you want to light it, bloody well light it!* So I light it, weird or not, and move the flowers to place the candle in the centre of the table.

Over dinner the conversation is light and the laughter happy. We are becoming entirely relaxed in each other's company. It's long overdue.

'This is so lovely.' I look from Rose to Cami and smile. 'I'm so grateful to have you both in my life.' They both reach out and take a hand each and I feel a constriction in my chest. I wait for the tightening in my head to follow suit: the two have always been inextricably linked. But it doesn't come. This feeling is different. This is what love must feel like. 'And... I want to say thank you for not judging me when I told you about my awful, sordid past. I'm not proud, but I can't change what happened, what I did. All I can do is try and be a better person from now on.'

'You don't need to thank us, Mags. We're family – I know that isn't always easy – but we're none of us perfect and we accept you, warts and all,' Cami says, smiling at me.

'What she said,' Rose adds. 'God knows I've made enough mistakes to last several lifetimes, and I know I haven't always been the best sister, but I do love you, both of you. Very much.'

'Thank you,' I smile. 'And, by the way, I just want it to be known I don't have warts. Anymore!' I stick my tongue out at them.

'Good to know,' Rose says. 'There's no way you're getting Cami in the Jacuzzi if you do!'

I look to Cami. Her head is down as she focuses hard on the food on her plate. She attempts an unconvincing laugh. 'Absolutely not!'

After dinner is consumed by us and the dishes by the washer, we take our seats in the lounge again.

'Music? TV?' I ask.

'Um… not TV,' Cami requests.

'Music's fine by me,' Rose adds. 'Nothing too loud.'

'Jeez, stop being an old person!' I joke. 'In fact, your mission for the next few days is to master the art of getting in and out of that chair without making those old-person noises.'

Rose grimaces. 'I guess I'll be sitting on the sofa then.'

I laugh and get up, with exaggerated groaning, and find a suitably soothing playlist on my iPhone. 'What do you think, give it an hour for dinner to go down and then back in the hot tub?'

'Sounds good,' Rose says.

'Cami?'

'Um, yeah, okay.'

Rose and I last about forty minutes before the lure of the hot tub becomes too much and we go off to get changed. Cami promises to join us shortly, saying the moussaka's still sitting a bit heavy.

'Do you want to bring the bubbly when you come?' Rose says.

'And a sparkling water for me please,' I add.

Cami nods, 'Yep, okay.'

Rose and I are discussing the artistic merits of *Sons of Anarchy* when Cami finally appears wearing her new robe and slippers, the belt tightened fast around her waist. She passes us our drinks and places her own glass carefully on the edge of the Jacuzzi.

'Come on in, the water's lovely,' Rose coaxes.

'I will. In a minute,' Cami says, taking a deep breath. 'But before I do… there's something I need to tell you. Or rather show you.' She casts her eyes to the floor, clearly struggling with something.

'What is it, Cami, what's wrong?' Rose asks.

Cami doesn't speak. She simply undoes her robe, letting it slip to the floor, and steps into the light. Rose and I look at her and then at each other, matching expressions of confusion on our faces.

'What?' Rose asks. 'Nice cozzie, by the way.'

Still Cami doesn't speak. Instead she slips her feet out of the towelling slippers and climbs into the hot tub. She doesn't sink into the water though, but remains standing. And that's when I see the scars across the tops of both her thighs. My hand flies to my mouth and I stifle a sob.

'Oh, my God, oh, Cami!'

Rose is a little slower to catch on, but finally understands my reaction. 'Oh, my poor darling girl,' she says quietly.

Cami's face is virtually expressionless as she tries to hold her emotions in. She begins to talk, running her fingers across the roughly parallel, faded pink lines on her legs. 'It's okay,' she says, shaking her head. 'It was all a long time ago. Another life. Ancient history,' she shrugs before settling herself carefully down on the seat. She picks up her glass and raises it in a toast: 'To us. We three sisters. And to being honest.'

I'm trying not to cry, but lift my glass along with Rose, and we clink them in the centre of the steaming tub.

'I'm really sorry,' I begin, 'I think my nose just dripped in the water.'

And suddenly we're all laughing.

Chapter 11
The truth, the whole truth and nothing but?

Mags

The laughter doesn't last long as Cami begins to speak of the past.

'It started in the last year of primary school. I don't know if the boys in your class did it, but there was a phase when they would cut themselves with compasses...'

'Pairs of compasses, you mean?' Rose interjects.

I glare at her. 'Rose! Don't be such a maths teacher. Carry on, Cami.'

'Well, yes, *pairs* of compasses. Anyway, sometimes they'd just do it to show how hard they were; other times they'd use biro ink to make sort of DIY tattoos.'

'I do vaguely remember something like that,' I encourage.

'At first I thought they were stupid. Then one day, and I don't know why, I decided to try it myself. I was in my room at home, as usual, and the atmosphere had been worse than ever for a few days – it was when Mum was seeing Terry the tarantula...'

I know I probably shouldn't interrupt, but I can't help myself. 'He had a bit of a soft spot for you, didn't he?' I say.

'Sadly, yes. And more of a hard spot,' Cami shudders.

Rose remains silent.

'He was always trying to cuddle me, or get me to sit on his lap. Disgusting pig. And Mum never did or said anything to stop him.' She shakes away the thoughts. 'Anyway, that particular night, I cut my arm with my compass and… it's hard to explain… it hurt like mad, but it somehow also felt good, like a kind of release.

'I didn't do it again for a while afterwards, but one night after a particularly bad row at home, I cut my leg. It honestly brought tears to my eyes, but at the same time it gave me a weird sort of relief from all the emotion I kept bottled up. After that, every time things got too much for me, I would cut myself again. I stopped using the compass and started using a razor I found in the bathroom. I kept it in its own special little tin hidden in my pencil case.'

My attention is suddenly taken away from Cami as I hear a strangled sob coming from Rose as she clambers inelegantly from the Jacuzzi and dashes inside.

Cami and I exchange surprised looks. 'Rose?' I call out, but she's gone.

'Do we go after her?' Cami asks.

'I s'pose so.'

We both climb out and don our robes once more, heading into the cabin to find our eldest sister. She's not in the lounge and a glance in her bedroom doesn't reveal her.

'Bathroom?' I say.

We try the bathroom door and find it's locked. Sobbing is coming from the other side.

'Rose? Open the door,' I say.

Nothing.

'Rose, let us in. Whatever's wrong, we can talk about it,' Cami urges.

The sobbing subsides a little and we wait.

'Rose?' I say again.

Finally, we hear the lock being pulled back and the door opens to reveal a very dishevelled and tear-stained Rose. She's wiping her nose with several sheets of loo roll. Should have brought five boxes of tissues.

We guide her through to the lounge, all squeezing onto the sofa, oblivious to the fact that we're soaking wet.

'What is it? What's wrong?' I ask.

'It's all my fault... all of it... your drinking, Mags, and Cami's self-harming. It's all my fault!'

'What? Don't be daft. You didn't pour the vodka down my throat.'

'Or put the compass in my hand.'

Rose just shakes her head and starts crying again. 'But I might as well have done. If I hadn't been such a little bitch, rowing with Mum all the time...' she sobs. 'It's my fault, it's all my fault.' She just keeps repeating the same words over and over again and won't be quieted. 'I should've been a better sister to you both. I'm sorry, I'm so so sorry, it's all my fault.' Her whole body is shaking as Cami and I hold her tight, absorbing the awful wracking guilt our sister seems determined is hers.

'Shh, Rose, listen,' Cami says quietly. 'You're not to blame for any of this, for my or Mags' problems.'

'Cami's right. If anyone's to blame, it's Mum,' I confirm.

But Rose won't be comforted and she just keeps sobbing.

Eventually the sobs subside, and Rose begins to quiet, all cried out. The room has grown a little chilly as the fire's gone out. I give Rose a squeeze before getting up to relight it. Then I go to the kitchen and set about making hot chocolate for us all. I figure the sugary warmth will do us good.

'Here you go,' I say, handing them a steaming mug each and taking up my seat once more.

'I'm sor…' Rose starts to say, but Cami and I stop her.

'No! Do not say sorry one more time,' Cami says.

'We were all just kids, trying to survive as best we could. We weren't your responsibility, Rose. It wasn't your job to look out for us,' I tell her.

She shakes her head. 'But I helped create that awful atmosphere at home.'

'You can't blame yourself, really.'

She doesn't seem convinced, but stops pushing the point, and we sit quietly, drinking our hot chocolates.

I can't help wondering what else the weekend is going to bring up. I glance at Cami, only too aware that we didn't have a chance to really talk about the scars on her legs. Picturing them now brings a lump to my throat.

The room quickly warms and we finish our drinks in silence, simply drawing comfort from the flickering fire and the closeness of our towelling-clad bodies. Eventually though I realise how uncomfortable my damp robe and swimsuit have become.

'I'm going to change into my pyjamas,' I inform my sisters, gently extricating myself from the squash on the sofa.

'Good idea,' Cami says, reaching her mug onto the coffee table before turning to Rose and giving her shoulders a final squeeze.

Cami and I stand and reach out a hand each to Rose.

'Come on you,' I say. 'Let's get out of these damp things.'

I'm first back to the lounge and I drape a blanket over the sofa to protect us from the now slightly soggy cushions, before stoking the fire and fetching glasses of the Shiraz for my sisters. I stop to consciously acknowledge the fact that it's actually not that hard to do; that I'm not tempted to glug back a glass myself. 'Go, you,' I tell myself quietly. 'You've so got this.' I feel a smile stretch my cheek muscles and recognise this new feeling as pride, self-respect.

Before long, Cami and Rose reappear and we take up our seats once more. We forgive Rose the groans as she sinks back into the armchair.

'Sorry for losing it earlier,' Rose says.

'Apology unnecessary, but accepted,' I tell her.

'Yep, and no more need to say sorry,' Cami agrees.

'Thank you, both, but I do need to say sorry...' She puts her hands up to stop us as Cami and I start to interject. 'No, please, let me finish. One more sorry, then I promise I'll shut up.'

Cami and I nod our agreement.

'I need to say sorry to you, Cami. You were being so brave and I totally stole... I dunno... not the limelight, but you know what I mean. You should have had all our attention. I know how hard it must have been to show us your scars, and I had no right to interrupt. I'm so sorry.'

I look round at Cami, and her gaze is in her lap. She says nothing for a few moments and when she looks up I can see a single tear rolling down her cheek. I want to reach over and wipe it away, but she beats me to it. Cami rarely cries. She hates the attention it brings.

'Thank you, Rose, I appreciate that. Even though there was no need!' she adds, smiling at our big sister.

Rose smiles. 'There really was.'

'Well, anyway, now you know. Now you know why I never wanted to go swimming or in the sea. It just felt like the right time to tell you, especially after you were so brave, Mags. It's a relief to be honest.'

'Thank you for confiding in us. I'm so glad you did, and I'm so sorry you went through all that pain on your own,' I say.

'It's okay, Mags, really it is. The scars healed a long time ago.'

'The physical ones, I guess,' Rose adds. 'I think we all still bear a ton of emotional ones.'

'Well, maybe we can heal some of those together?' I say. 'It feels like the right time.'

Cami nods her agreement. 'It does.'

Rose remains silent.

I return my attention to Cami's earlier confession. 'When did you stop cutting yourself? If it's okay to ask?'

'Yes, of course. When I left home, I suppose. I found I didn't need to anymore.' Cami sounds pretty matter-of-fact about it, but it still makes my heart hurt to think of her alone in her bedroom, slicing her thigh open with a razor blade all those years ago. But even if I had known, what could I have done? Mum probably wouldn't have given a shit, and Cami would've hated me for drawing attention to it.

It's as if Cami's reading my mind. 'Mags, please don't feel bad. There's nothing you could've done. Either of you,' she adds, looking over at Rose who's still saying nothing. I know she's wrestling with her conscience and feelings of guilt.

Silence overtakes us again until Rose finally speaks. 'Do you mind if I go to bed?' she asks. 'I feel absolutely exhausted.'

'Of course not,' Cami and I say together.

Rose heaves herself up with more groaning than ever, clearly shattered by the day's events. Cami and I get up and hug her, before wishing her goodnight.

'Sleep tight,' we call after her.

With Rose gone, Cami and I talk in lowered voices.

'What Rose said about it being her fault...' I begin. 'It's kind of true. For me anyway. I'd never tell her that though.'

'For me too. It was the rows she had with Mum that created that awful atmosphere. It was like living in a pressure cooker.'

'Yeah, I felt so anxious all the time. You never knew when one of them was going to blow. Talk about treading on egg shells.'

'I wasn't quite telling the truth when I said I stopped self-harming when I left home. It was actually when Rose left home,' Cami admits.

I just nod. I know that we will never tell Rose this. It's an unspoken agreement.

'It was better after she left, wasn't it? I mean, Mum was still a bit shit, but it wasn't as tense.'

'Yep, it was loads better. Would've been even better if Mum hadn't had such lousy taste in men.'

'Amen to that,' I groan.

'I suppose she was lonely when it was just us girls,' Cami muses.

'Yeah, I guess. As kids you don't think about your parents in those terms though, do you? It can't have been easy for her after Dad left.'

'No. But she still had us, and would it have been so hard to show us a bit of love?'

'I know. I don't think I ever felt loved. Wanted. I suppose

that's why I turned to booze and drugs – to numb the pain for a while. And why I had such crap relationships with men – I became an expert at kidding myself they all loved me.'

'I think most of them probably did love you, Mags. You've spent your whole life trying to please other people: to be loveable.'

'Oh, I don't know, Cams, what a mess, what a bloody mess. All of us. Our whole lives.'

'Until now, baby sister, until now. This is where we start to put ourselves back together. Just like a jigsaw.'

Chapter 12
Abandon hope, all ye who enter here

Rose

There's no sign of my younger sisters when I come out of my bedroom the next morning, their bedroom doors still closed. I busy myself with lighting the fire. I slept fitfully and am feeling tired and heavy. Weary. I feel weary.

My dreams disturbed me often. My mind insisted on going to places, memories, I've denied it all these years and it was a battle of wills which I'm not sure I won. I've been so expert at keeping the lid on the box, but this time with my sisters is threatening my equilibrium. I feel vulnerable. I feel fractured, and that the box might burst open at any moment. I can't let that happen. I could not survive it. I'm just not strong enough.

With the fire now crackling in the hearth, I head into the kitchen to make a cup of tea. Cami's laptop is on the work surface, and I run my finger over the touchpad. To my surprise the screen springs to life. The next thing I see makes my heart stop and my breath catch in my throat.

Cami

'Rose? Rose? You okay?' She's standing in the kitchen in front of my laptop, frozen like a statue, frozen and staring. I can see as I round the work surface that her fists are clenched. Glancing at the screen, I see one of the photographs I took at the funeral: a photo of a photo. It's the one taken of the three of us with Ken in his garden. I'd uploaded them from my phone last night when Mags and I were on our trip down memory lane. Or dog-shit-alley as we called it. Looking at Rose now, she's like a mirror image of her teenaged self in the picture. Same clenched fists and jaw, same stony expression.

I put my hand gently on her shoulder. 'What's the matter?'

She just carries on staring. It's almost as though she's in a trance. I shake her, trying to break whatever spell she's under. Suddenly she blinks, and looks at me. Her expression scares me, transporting me back in time to another kitchen. Angry Rose, spoiling for a fight, and never backing down. Sending me scurrying to my room and my razor. I had hoped that Rose no longer existed, but here she is, standing right beside me.

At that moment, just when I don't know what to do or say next, Mags appears.

Mags

I don't know what the hell's going on, but I just walked into the kitchen to find Rose and Cami frozen in some weird tableau. Rose has a face like thunder and Cami looks like a frightened child. She looks over at me as I approach and her expression switches to one of relief. I can feel my face is wearing a frown as I try and read the situation.

'Hey, what's going on?' I ask. I take in the photo on the laptop screen.

'Um… I'm honestly not sure,' Cami says, letting her arm drop from Rose's shoulder.

'Rose?' I say.

She blinks and looks at me, almost like she's coming out of a trance. *What the heck is going on in her mind?* I wonder.

Rose shakes her head as if to return to the present moment. 'Nothing. Nothing's going on.' She closes the laptop and turns to the kettle. There's a mug with a teabag next to it already. She fetches two more and makes us all tea. Cami and I exchange confused looks and shrugs behind her back, silently acknowledging the fact that we need to find out what the hell is going on with Rose once and for all.

We drink our tea in the kitchen, no one speaking. The atmosphere is more than a little tense, and I'm trying to keep my breathing steady as the old familiar tightness has started in my chest. It's a relief when Rose announces she's going to have a shower.

'You know we can't ignore this, right?' I say to Cami after Rose is out of earshot.

'Whatever *this* is. I just don't get it.'

'Me neither. What is it about Uncle Ken that triggers her like this?'

'God knows.'

'I mean, he was always so good to us,' I can hear the puzzlement in my own voice.

'Do you think maybe she resented him? Thought he was trying to take Dad's place or something?' Cami suggests.

I just shrug my shoulders. 'God knows. I don't remember what it was like when Mum and Dad were together.'

'You didn't miss much, to be honest. He was hardly ever home and, when he was, Mum was just a moany old bitch to him. It's hardly surprising he left. And even when he was home, he didn't do anything with us. Never read us stories, bathed us, played with us. The only thing that changed when he left was that it freed Mum up to have a succession of disastrous relationships.'

'Yeah, she sure could pick 'em, couldn't she?' I sigh.

'I think Rose did miss Dad though. Or rather she missed the Dad she wanted him to be. I think she wanted his love and approval more than Mum's,' Cami says thoughtfully.

'Hmm, still doesn't really explain her reaction to Uncle Ken though, does it?'

'So, what do we do? Ask her outright what her problem is?' Cami doesn't look thrilled at the prospect and pulls a face.

'Oh, God. I think we have to, Cami. Don't we?' I pull a matching face.

Cami nods. 'Yep. Bloody hell. Light the blue touch paper and stand well back springs to mind.'

Having decided on a plan of action, Cami and I head to our bedrooms to quickly get dressed.

Rose

I stand in the shower for ages, letting the hot water flow over my head and body, desperately trying to wash away the feelings of pain and revulsion, the self-loathing. I close my eyes and focus on diverting my thoughts, back to the normally well-regulated paths, and skirting around the dark little patch of my brain where the unwanted memories live.

I know how confused my sisters are by my behaviour, but I can't let that be my problem. They just need to accept it and stop bugging me about it.

By the time I'm showered and dressed I'm composed once more and ready to face the day. My composure lasts just long enough to make it to the lounge where I find my sisters waiting for me, with that photo on the laptop display in front of them.

I glare at them and start to turn back to my room.

'Rose. Please. Come back.' I hear Mags' voice pleading with me, and I pause. Why can't they just leave it? I turn to face them once more.

'Close the laptop and I'll think about it,' I say.

Cami closes the laptop without saying a word, just waiting expectantly beside Mags. I can feel two sets of eyes burning into me, trying to read me, to get inside my head. Trust me, I think to myself, you don't want to go in there. Even I don't want to. There should be a sign on my forehead saying, 'Abandon hope all ye who enter here'.

With a sigh, I walk over and throw myself huffily down in my chair. At least the huffing masks the usual old-person noises. I'm fully aware how defensive my manner is as I sit with my arms crossed like a barrier in front of me. Good luck breaking that down, oh sisters of mine, I think mutinously.

Cami and Mags exchange looks. I almost feel sorry for them. I know exactly what's going through their minds, but I've spent too long building my defences to have them knocked down. I've pulled up the drawbridge and they're not getting in. I have a little bet with myself on who's going to speak first; who's drawn the short straw. My money's on Cami as the oldest, but then I see Mags take a deep breath and I know I just lost that bet.

'It's your turn, Rose,' Mags says. 'I've bared my soul and so has Cami. Now you.'

Ooh, no messing, I think, almost with admiration. *Straight in there, Mags. Nicely done.* I say nothing. I wonder if they're going to go all good cop, bad cop on me.

Cami speaks next. 'Come on, Rose. What is it about that photo, about Uncle Ken, that makes you react like this?'

I raise my eyebrows, but say nothing.

'Don't you think you owe us the truth? After everything we've told you?' Mags persists.

They just stare at me, waiting for me to speak. They'll have a long wait.

'For fuck's sake, Rose, what can be so awful that you can't tell us?'

Mags, you need to stop talking, I think. I can feel the tension spreading through my body.

Cami and Mags exchange another look and I see Mags nod slightly. Cami opens her laptop again. I start to get up.

'No.' Mags' voice is calm. 'Sit down.' I've never heard such authority in her voice. She's always been the accommodating people pleaser. I'm sufficiently shocked that I sit down again. 'We're not budging from here until you tell us what the hell is going on, Rose. Why you wouldn't come to Uncle Ken's funeral? Why you can't even look at his photo without looking like you want to commit murder?'

I retreat behind set jaw and folded arms once more. It's Cami's turn next.

'Come on, Rose, whatever it is, you can tell us. I feel so much better for sharing my secret with you both; like a weight's been lifted I didn't even know I was carrying.'

There it is, the good cop. Thumbscrews next? I can feel anger building in me, but still I stay resolutely mute.

'Talk to us. Please,' Mags implores. Okay, two good cops now.

'Was it something to do with Dad?' Cami asks.

I feel my face contort into a *what are you on about?* expression.

'Well?' Mags pushes.

'Well, what? No. For fuck's sake. It has nothing to do with our useless father,' I say.

'Then what does it have to do with? Just tell us.'

'Rose.'

Silence hangs over us. I know they're not going to give up though.

'Rose.'

I take a breath, uncross my arms and press my fingers to my eyes. My head feels like it's about to explode. 'Why can't you both just let it go? Please?' Maybe my own pleading will work?

Cami and Mags both shake their heads.

I suddenly come to a decision. This should shut them up once and for all. Before I can change my mind, I begin to speak. 'Okay, you want to know why I wouldn't go to Ken's funeral? Why I hope he rots in hell? Because he raped me. Not once, but many times, from the age of nine until I was thirteen. Happy now?' As I finish speaking, I get up, grab my coat from the hooks by the front door and let myself out of the cabin. I don't look back. I don't want to see my sisters' faces.

Chapter 13
Opening the box

Mags

I look round at Cami. Her face is ashen. I'm guessing mine is too. Neither of us has spoken since Rose dashed from the cabin. I don't know how much time has elapsed.

'Christ, Cami, we should have gone after her straight away,' I say, getting to my feet. I feel panicky and my heart is pounding in my ears.

Cami just looks too stunned to speak. 'I... I...'

'Yeah, I know. Come on, we have to go after her,' I tell my sister, shaking her by the arms. She gets up obediently and we shrug on our coats and head out after Rose. God knows what state she's in after the bombshell she just dropped. We don't bother with hats and gloves, and the freezing air smacks us awake.

'Which way?' I ask helplessly.

'Should we split up?'

'Yeah, maybe. Phones,' I say. 'We need our phones – then we can call if we find her.'

Cami nods, and we quickly retrieve our mobiles before setting out in opposite directions.

'Check in with you in a bit,' I call after Cami's disappearing back. 'Maybe see you back here if we haven't found her in, I dunno, half an hour?'

Cami waves an acknowledging hand and I set off down the path leading into the woods where it circles back around the cabin. I just hope Rose hasn't done anything stupid. I still haven't really had time to process what she told us, and now the priority is finding her. Everything else can wait.

I half walk, half jog into the trees. It's not the path we took yesterday and therefore unfamiliar territory. I stick to the one path as I don't want to get lost. I laugh nervously as a thought pops unbidden into my head – all three of us lost in different parts of the forest, endlessly circling as we search for one another.

After I've walked for about fifteen minutes, the trees start to thin out and I see a reflection of the weak winter sun on water. I know there's a lake around here somewhere, and I think I may have just found it. I increase my pace and as I approach the body of water, I see with relief the figure of my big sister sitting at the edge, her back hunched over and her arms hugging her legs. It literally looks like she's trying to hold herself together.

I quickly call Cami. 'Found her. She's by the lake. See you back at the cabin. Assuming I can persuade Rose.'

'Thank God! Okay. Call me if she won't come back and I'll come and find you,' Cami says, the relief in her voice obvious.

'Will do. Go and get warm. See you soon.'

I cover the remaining distance to the edge of the lake and sit down next to Rose. 'Hey.'

She doesn't move or acknowledge my presence. She's shivering and I can't tell if it's from the cold or emotion. Maybe both. I shuffle a little closer to her and put an arm around her hunched shoulders. My arm vibrates with her trembling.

'Come back to the cabin. We need to get you warm. Everything will be okay.'

After a time, she speaks. 'No. Everything won't be okay. It will never be okay.' Her voice is low, monotone. She sounds as though she's given up. She sounds hopeless. Well, I'm not having that. I've spent a lifetime trying to make people happy, and that training will not go to waste.

'No, you're right, Rose, it won't be okay. Not today, or tomorrow, or probably any time soon, but it will be okay. One day. If you let us in. Let us help you. We love you.'

'You don't understand. I've spent my whole life running from this because I always knew if it caught up with me, it would destroy me.' She sounds strangely matter of fact, as if she has accepted her fate.

'Well, I don't buy that, big sis,' I tell her, pulling her body in to mine. 'You're one of the strongest people I know. And you can, you will, survive this. Unless of course we get hypothermia and die. And that would really piss Cami off.'

Rose sighs.

'Come on. Let's go back,' I say again, getting to my feet, already feeling stiff with cold. I reach out for my sister's hands and, with another sigh, she heaves herself up.

We walk back to the cabin in silence. I take Rose's hand and she doesn't pull it away. Cami must have been watching from the window and she rushes out to meet us.

'Oh, thank goodness! Come on, get yourselves in and get warm.'

The fire is blazing and I quickly throw off my coat and sit on the hearth rug, holding my bare, chilled hands up to the flames until the heat becomes unbearable. Cami has gone all mother hen and is helping Rose out of her coat as if she's a child, ushering her over to her chair which she moves nearer the fire. I remove myself to the sofa, rubbing my rosy-cold cheeks with my hands. Soon I have my hands wrapped around a mug of hot chocolate and Cami has joined me on the sofa. I glance at her, not knowing what to do or say. She just smiles at me and pats my jeans-clad leg. She quickly pulls her hand away. 'Christ, your leg's freezing!' She reaches behind her for a blanket and begins to spread it over my legs, but I shake my head and gesture towards Rose. Presumably if my legs are this cold, hers are too. Cami gets up and goes over to Rose, spreading the blanket over her legs. Rose makes no sign, just continuing to stare into the flames. It's like she isn't really here.

Cami kneels down in front of Rose, putting her hands on her thighs and squeezing gently. 'Hey, you. Anybody home?' she enquires gently.

I see Rose slowly shift her gaze to meet Cami's. 'I can't do this,' she whispers. I feel the familiar prickling of tears and my eyes welling up.

'Yes, yes, you can, Rose. You can because you're not alone and you can use our strength. Mine and Mags'. Although, to be fair, looking at Mags now, she's going to be as much use as an inflatable dartboard.' She looks round at me and winks. She knew before looking that I'd be crying. I can't help laughing.

Rose smiles weakly, but then shakes her head. 'You don't understand.'

'So help us understand,' Cami says.

'I've spent four decades running from this, Cami. I always knew that if it ever caught up with me, I'd fall apart. I just can't... And now... David...'

'I know, I know, but guess what? Things that fall apart can be put back together again. And that's our job: me and the dartboard over there,' she says, nodding her head in my direction. I can't help giggling.

'We can fix you back together with gold, like that, what's it called? That Japanese repair thingy.... Kint...' I pause, unable to recall the word.

'Kintsugi,' Rose finishes. 'Golden joinery.'

'That's it,' I say, 'Kintsugi. We'll glue you back together with gold and you'll be stronger and more beautiful than ever!'

Rose smiles weakly. 'I don't want to be beautiful.'

She's finally talking and it feels like a very small win. A window.

There's a pause and my eyes meet Cami's as we wait to see if she continues. I'm holding my breath.

'He said I was his beautiful girl. His special girl.' The words are met by silent tears as they leave Rose's mouth. The tears stream unchecked down her face. I press my fingers to my mouth to stop the emotion screaming up my throat from escaping. Cami, the strong sister, is crying too, as she takes our big sister in her arms and holds her tightly as huge, harrowing, heart-wrenching sobs overtake Rose.

No one speaks. The only sounds in the room are the crackling of logs in the fireplace, and the howling, animalistic noises coming from Rose as the dam bursts completely and years of suppressed pain break through. I have never heard noises like it, or felt as if my heart might actually break. I can only imagine a fraction of how it must feel for Rose. Cami continues to hold her, never loosening her grip, absorbing as much of the pain as she can. Eventually the shuddering of Rose's body begins to ease, and the howling settles to a mewling, then a hiccoughing and finally to breathing.

I grab a handful of tissues and pass them to Cami, who hands some to Rose before wiping her own face. There follows an unattractive couple of minutes of nose-blowing and face-wiping. We all look absolutely dreadful.

'We are not pretty criers,' I pronounce.

'Blotchy frogs,' Cami adds.

'Definitely not beautiful.' Good, Rose is cognisant.

'Don't know what you mean. We're all as pretty as a picture,' I say.

'Yeah, by Hieronymous Bosch,' Cami says.

'Yep,' I nod. I get up and go into the kitchen area to fetch glasses of water for us all. 'How are you feeling now?' I ask Rose as she takes one. Cami heaves herself up off the floor before taking hers.

'I'm not really sure. My head's thumping and I feel like crap.' Rose pauses to consider. 'But maybe I feel a little bit relieved too.'

'That's good,' I smile. 'You needed that release.'

'It's been a long time coming,' Cami adds.

Rose nods. 'I know. But I simply couldn't face it. Easier to pretend that part of my life never happened. Or that it happened to someone else. And that girl died and was buried and forgotten about.'

Tears are threatening again. I take a sip of water and swallow them down with it. 'But that girl was you, Rose, and it's time to acknowledge her and hopefully release her.'

'Maybe you're right. But I'm so scared, Mags. I've coped with life by not acknowledging the past, and distancing myself from things that might remind me.'

'I know,' I nod. 'And now we understand your reluctance to come back to visit Mum too.'

Rose nods sadly. 'It was the only way I could survive. I am sorry though. I know it must have been hard for the two of you, not knowing why I stayed away.'

'It was. I wish you'd been able to confide in us,' Cami says quietly. I turn to look at my middle sister and her face is full of pain and regret. 'Maybe we could've helped?'

'I just didn't want to relive it, I suppose. Easier to bury it and try to pretend it didn't happen, than make it real by talking about it. It was a fire I didn't want to give oxygen to.'

'We do understand,' I say, wanting to reassure Rose that we don't blame her. 'And we can't change what's happened, but we can try to help you moving forward. It might be cathartic to talk about it now – you've done the hardest bit after all.'

'I don't know…' Rose says, her expression full of doubt. 'That's a lot of shit to unpack. And what the heck do I do with it once it's out?'

'Well, for starters, after this weekend, you need to find a counsellor. As much as Cami and I want to help, I think you'll need professional guidance too. I couldn't have got through my recovery without my counsellor.'

'Mags is right. I saw one years ago for a while, when life was all a bit much. I realised after the first session that I was still carrying a whole load of unresolved crap from childhood,' Cami says.

'You saw a counsellor?' I exclaim in astonishment. Cami is the last person you'd expect to hear that admission from. She's so private.

'Yep,' Cami nods. 'What a shocker, eh? It really helped though.'

I look over at Rose. She looks exhausted.

'Do you want to talk now? Do you feel you could?'

'I don't know. Maybe. I do want you to understand why I behaved so badly back then, and why I didn't tell anyone.'

'Jeez, can totally understand why you didn't feel you could tell Mum,' Cami says. 'But couldn't you have told somebody else – a teacher or someone?'

'I couldn't. I couldn't tell anyone,' Rose begins as sobs overtake her once more and she buries her face in her hands.

'But why, Rose? Why couldn't you?' I know I'm pushing her, but I feel this is a pivotal moment and something she desperately needs to unburden herself of.

'Because I was protecting you!' she suddenly blurts out. 'I was protecting both of you!'

Cami and I look at each other, horrified realisation starting to dawn on us.

'Rose…' I begin gently. 'Did he threaten to hurt me and Cami if you told?'

Rose just nods and my heart breaks wide open.

Chapter 14
Open the floodgates

Mags

No one speaks for a while. I don't know how long. My own thoughts are a maelstrom as I try to get my head around what Rose has told us. I'm starting to make sense of things now; why she seemed to hate me and Cami, and why she was so angry and unhappy, so rebellious. Poor, poor Rose. She must have really resented me and Cami: we were the reason she couldn't tell anyone what was happening to her. I almost feel guilty for being born, as irrational as that is.

As I try and make sense of how I'm feeling, I realise I'm angry with Mum. If she'd been a better parent, if Rose felt she might be believed and supported, maybe she could've told. Mum should have protected us, but she failed us all.

'I'm so very sorry this happened to you, Rose,' I tell her, finally finding my voice.

'I am too,' Cami adds. 'But now we know, will you let us share the burden?'

Rose looks over at us, her face reddened from crying, and nods. 'Yes. Please,' she says quietly. 'I'm not strong enough on my own.'

'You're not on your own. You're never on your own. You always have us,' Cami tells her.

'Cami's right, and together we're strong enough to cope with anything, I promise,' I smile.

'Thank you,' Rose says. 'I don't know where, or how, to begin. It's a lot. Are you sure?'

Cami and I both nod our heads. 'We're sure.'

'And it doesn't matter where or how you start, you just have to start,' I say.

Rose doesn't speak straight away. She seems to be weighing something up in her mind. She takes a deep breath and begins.

'The first time it happened, I was nine.'

As soon as she starts to speak, my mouth fills with bile. I feel sick to my stomach and she's barely begun. It's all I can do not to run from the room and throw up. I know I have to be strong for Rose's sake, but this is going to take every ounce of strength to hear.

Cami grabs my hand and I turn to look at her. She's fighting tears and is as white as a sheet. I give her hand a reassuring squeeze. We must draw strength from each other to get through this.

'It was just after my birthday, one of those Saturdays when he said he wanted me all to himself because I was his goddaughter and shouldn't have to share him.'

The thought shoots through my mind that I used to be jealous of those times, jealous and resentful, and would sulk in my room. Christ.

'I remember standing in the kitchen at home as he told Mum he'd got a surprise for me next door at his house, for my birthday. And I just went with him.' Rose's voice cracks.

'It's okay. Go on,' I coax, trying to swallow back the feelings of nausea. Part of me wants to stick my fingers in my ears and go la la la.

'I followed him up our garden and through the adjoining gate into his. He said my dress was pretty. It was the one I got for my birthday from Granny, with the orange flowers on. Saxon came bounding up to greet us – I remember not wanting him to get slobber on my new dress.' Rose pauses and takes a breath. 'Then we went into the conservatory and there was something big wrapped up in the corner. He told me to open it and it was a dolls' house.'

I remember the dolls' house. Ken had made it for Rose and it was another reason to be envious of her.

'I said thank you...' her voice trembles as she recalls the memory for the first time in decades. All three of us have silent tears streaming unchecked down our faces. 'And he said... he said I had to thank him properly. And I didn't know what he meant. So I said thank you very much, Uncle Ken, but he said no that wasn't what he meant. He said come here and I went over to him. He was sitting on that cane chair he always sat in. And he patted his leg and told me to sit.

'He said that I was his special girl, his only special, beautiful girl and that...' Rose closes her eyes, pain etched all over her face as she revisits the moment, '...that I could show him how much I liked my present. I didn't know what he meant. And then he took my hand and put it on his crotch. I tried to pull my hand away. I knew that wasn't right. But he held it there and I could feel his erection. I didn't know what it was then, of course. I just knew it was wrong...

'He told me I made him very happy, and that he'd show me how happy. I just wanted to run home. I remember I was trying not to cry. He held my hand there, squeezing it, so I could feel his hardness. And then... and then... he... he put his other hand up my dress. I tried to pull his hand away. I knew it was wrong, it was dirty, but I wasn't strong enough.'

Tears and snot are mingling on Rose's face as she struggles to get the words out. I can feel Cami's whole body shaking through our joined hands. We know we have to just let Rose keep talking, as horrific as it is to hear.

'He touched me through my pants. I know I was crying then, and he pulled his hand out and he wiped my tears away, telling me I was a big girl and not to cry. I told him I wanted to go home, and he said I could but I had to promise not to tell anyone about today, that it was our special secret, and other people wouldn't understand. And then he said no one would believe me and they'd say I was bad and evil, and that my sisters would be punished too if I told. He didn't spell it out until later what he meant by that.

'He took me home with the dolls' house then. Mum raved about it – she didn't even notice I'd been crying. Made me thank him all over again. He carried it up to my bedroom and Mum made me go up with him. He told me again that it was our special secret and I mustn't tell anyone because he'd hate for anything bad to happen to the two of you.

'I hated that dolls' house. I didn't even want to open it and look inside. But then Mum told you two about it and you both came into my room and were all excited about it.'

'I remember that,' Cami says. 'I remember because you told me I could have it if I wanted.'

Rose nods. 'But Mum said I wasn't allowed to give it to you, and that I was an ungrateful little cow.'

I keep silent. My memories of that time are hazy and incomplete, but I do remember coveting the dolls' house.

Rose takes a deep breath. 'Are you sure you want me to carry on?'

Cami and I nod. 'Yes, go on, you're doing so well,' I tell her.

'After that, I dreaded being alone with him. The times we all went out with him were bad enough, but when he said it was our special time, I just wanted to run away. I tried to make excuses to Mum, say I wasn't feeling well – had a tummy ache or something – but she just made me go and told me not to be so ungrateful.

'The second time it happened he took me into the lounge. The curtains were closed. I remember thinking it was strange because it was the middle of the day. He shut Saxon out in the conservatory and I could hear him whining. He made me touch him again, but this time not through his trousers and I felt his thing kind of springing up and getting harder under my hand. I was crying but he didn't seem to notice. He was making these noises. Then he put his hand round mine and started pulling it up and down.

'He put his free hand up my skirt again and inside my knickers. I kept saying I didn't like it and asking him to stop. He just kept saying how special I was and how beautiful. Please stop, I said, over and over, but he didn't. And I knew he shouldn't be doing those things to me. I knew it was wrong. I thought I must have done something to deserve it, that it was my fault.

'After that it just escalated. The third time, he took me upstairs. I'd never been upstairs in his house before. It was cold and old fashioned, like Granny's house, with dark furniture. He made me lie on the bed, on one of those feather quilts like Granny had, and he took his trousers all the way off, and his pants...'

Rose's face is contorted as she recounts the story to us. I literally don't know if I can bear to hear any more, but I know I have to, we have to, for her sake. I've wiped snot and tears away with the back of my hand, not even wanting to interrupt Rose to reach for the tissues.

'That was the first time he... he raped me.' Rose's voice cracks completely and Cami and I can bear it no longer as we both jump up, going to Rose and putting our arms around her as sobs wrack her body once more. We just hold on, and hold on, ignoring the discomfort of our limbs as we stand awkwardly either side of Rose. There is no pain we could possibly endure that could be greater than Rose's. By the time Rose has cried herself out again, our three heads of brown hair are tangled and entwined with tears and mucous.

Cami and I kneel down either side of Rose, never losing contact with her, stronger conjoined, transferring our strength to her and desperately trying to absorb some of her pain.

I want to say something to her, but I have no idea what, all words seeming inadequate. I imagine the same thoughts are going through Cami's head. Rose is just sniffing quietly as her breathing begins to return to normal. Finally, it's Cami who speaks.

'I'm so sorry this happened to you. But you have to know that none of it was your fault. And I'm sorry I didn't see that something was very wrong.'

Rose shakes her head. 'No, Cami, how could you have seen? You were eight years old. Please don't feel bad.'

We sit in silence once more. I feel so awful for being jealous of Rose as a child. I had a lucky escape. She protected me and Cami, and I resented her all those years.

'Can we go in the hot tub?' Rose asks suddenly. 'I'm as stiff as a board.'

'Yes, please!' I say, registering my own stiffness.

Cami smiles and nods.

A few minutes later and we're all in the hot bubbles, making suitably happy noises as the heat and the jets ease our aching bones. Even Cami looks like she's enjoying it. She didn't even wear her robe over her swimsuit now that she no longer needed to hide her scars. Rose's scars were all on the inside, of course, and would take much longer to heal, if they ever really did.

I look at Rose. She has her eyes shut. I wonder what thoughts are in her mind right at this moment. I turn to Cami to find she's also looking at Rose. She feels my gaze and turns to me, communicating silently through the steam. I just nod. I know.

After a while, I clamber out to get drinks. 'We're probably dehydrated from all that crying.'

A feeling of calm descends and we sit back in the hot water, each lost in our own thoughts. I know there is probably much more to come from Rose, but it doesn't feel right to push her now. Today's revelations have been a lot, and I think we all need to rest and recharge before we tackle anything more. I'm trying not to think ahead to the moment we have to drop Rose back home; worried she will be too fragile to cope with life. We have our work cut out for us over the next couple of days. And I could really do with a drink.

Chapter 15
Shattered hearts

Mags

We stay in the Jacuzzi for about an hour, too exhausted to move. Eventually though, Rose says she needs to go to bed.

'I'm absolutely shattered,' she says.

'Don't you want anything to eat?' I ask, conscious of the fact that we haven't eaten for some time.

'No, thank you. I just want to sleep. For about a week,' she smiles sadly.

'Of course, you must be exhausted. You did really well, Rose. I'm proud of you. I know that can't have been easy.'

'Thanks, little sis. I'm glad you know though. As hard as it was to tell you, I'm relieved. I hated you not knowing why I was so awful back then. You must've hated me.'

I shake my head. 'Of course we didn't hate you! You're our sister. We could never hate you.'

'That's sweet of you to say, but I was the main reason you two had such awful childhoods. Be honest. I was.'

I just shake my head. 'It wasn't your fault. Any of it,' I say quietly.

We say good night to Rose, and then Cami and I busy

ourselves with getting something to eat. Neither of us can face cooking, so we just have toast and jam, which we eat in front of the fire. After she's finished eating, Cami tiptoes over to Rose's bedroom, sticks her head round the door to check on her, and then pulls the door closed.

'Fast asleep,' she confirms.

'Poor thing, she must be shattered. I know I am.'

'Me too. That was hard to hear. I still can't get my head around it.'

'I know. I feel so awful that I was jealous of her relationship with him, when all the time that was happening to her,' I say, shuddering.

'And right next door. How did Mum not know? Not notice? The changes in Rose were so marked.'

I just shake my head. 'A lot of stuff makes sense now though, doesn't it?'

'God, yeah, totally. She got so aggressive, didn't she?'

'She must've hated Mum. And us in a way. We were the reason she couldn't tell anyone. That makes me feel really lousy.'

'Me too. I keep trying to rationalise it in my head. We didn't ask to be born though, Mags, and we were just kids. Shouldering the blame won't do either of us, or Rose, any good. We just have to try and help her through this.'

'I know you're right. It's hard not to feel guilty though.'

'It is, but guilt is a useless emotion.' Cami pauses. 'The other thing on my mind, Mags, is your own recovery. I'm conscious that this must be a huge strain on you. How are you doing, really?'

I manage a small laugh. 'I'd be lying if I said I haven't fancied a stiff drink or a line of coke more than once today, but I'm doing okay. Honestly. I'll always be an addict, Cami, and I'll probably always just be taking one day at a time, but I'm okay.'

'Okay, but you know I'm here for you too. I know this has to be about Rose now, but you're not alone either.'

'Thanks, Cami. Stronger together,' I smile.

The conversation naturally returns to our eldest sister as we process what she told us earlier.

'She said it stopped when she was thirteen didn't she? Earlier on. Before she ran out,' Cami says.

'Yes. Oh my God. Four years. Four years, Cami. How did she survive it?'

We're both fighting tears again, at the thought of what our big sister endured.

'I don't know. I wish she'd told someone. In spite of what he said.'

'Me too, but I understand why she didn't. She was really brave. And selfless.'

'When I think about what he did to her... it's almost more than I can bear,' Cami says.

'Same. She was just a baby. If the old bastard wasn't dead, I'd fucking kill him.'

'Maybe she should have come to the funeral? You know, to have at least some closure? Might've helped a bit.'

I shake my head. 'I don't think she could – that would've meant acknowledging what happened and dealing with the memories.'

'I s'pose. It makes me sick that he got away with it though,' Cami says through gritted teeth.

'None of it's fair. We've just got to try and get Rose through this. That's all we can do now.'

Cami nods. 'I know, but I'm so bloody angry.'

'It helps to understand why Rose was so angry back then, though, doesn't it? A bit. Make sense of it.'

'Yeah, it does. Do you remember the day she cut off all her hair? Mum was absolutely livid with her.'

'I do. "What have you done? Your beautiful hair! You stupid girl!" Or words to that effect. That was definitely a swig-of-vodka day.'

'I found the hair on the bathroom floor. Scooped it all up and tied it up with a bow. Put it in my treasures box. Don't know why really. Just couldn't bring myself to throw it away. Still got that box at home somewhere.'

'Why do you think she did it?' I ask.

'Honestly? I think she didn't want to be beautiful. If she was ugly, maybe he'd stop doing what he was doing to her. If you think about it, that was about the same time she stopped wearing dresses and would always have scruffy jeans and T-shirts on.'

'I think you might be right. Poor Rose. She was still beautiful though, wasn't she? In spite of her best efforts.' I bring to mind an image of my angry, but startlingly beautiful, older sister, and remember how I longed to be just like her.

'Yeah, she was always beautiful. I was so jealous of her,' Cami admits.

'You weren't the only one.'

'Hm. It's easy to start joining the dots now, isn't it? Now we know.'

'Yeah, it is. It's not a pretty picture though.'

'God, dot-to-dot books... remember... we always had them as kids, didn't we? Those really cheap things Mum used to buy us.'

'Yeah, and the magic painting books. Remember them? You just had to paint over the pictures with water and the colours would appear.'

'Yes! They were that awful cheap and nasty paper.'

We're both quiet for a while as we remember our childhoods.

'I wonder if things would've been better if Dad had stayed?' I muse.

'Yeah, maybe. Might have deterred Ken, having another man around.'

'Mm, I suppose we were kind of vulnerable, weren't we?'

'I bet Ken couldn't believe his luck when we moved in next door,' Cami says.

'I s'pose that's why he never married, or even seemed to have a girlfriend... he was into young girls,' I shudder.

'And our bloody parents played right into his hands making him Rose's godfather.'

'Oh God, it could have been any one of us!'

'I know. I wonder if we would've told?'

'God, I don't know, I honestly don't know what I would've done. Run away from home?'

'But then he might have carried out his threat to do it to me or Rose.'

'It really was an impossible situation for her, wasn't it?'

'Mm hm, and I for one am grateful for her sacrifice, as awful as that sounds,' Cami says.

'No, I know what you mean. I've royally screwed up my life as it is. I dread to think the mess I'd be in if I'd suffered what Rose did. I'm honestly not sure I could have kept going. With my addictive personality, I'd probably have ended up ODing.'

'Don't say that, Mags. I really hope you could've come to

me for help before things ever got that bad.'

'Thanks, Cami. Hopefully things will never be that bad. And I really think I've kicked all those old habits.'

'I hope so, little sis, I kind of like having you around.'

Cami's words bring tears to my eyes for the umpteenth time today. She has no idea how much her words mean.

'Don't be an inflatable dartboard,' she says, nudging me and grinning.

'Rude!' I say, laughing. 'But accurate!'

'So, how do we handle tomorrow?' Cami asks, getting back to the matter in hand.

'Um… eat lots of chocolate? Call Charlie Hunnam?' I shrug my shoulders.

'Good plan, I like it,' Cami says. 'Shall we just play it by ear a bit, but try and coax more out of her?'

'I s'pose so. We can't give up now, not when she's doing so well. I am worried about when we have to take her home.'

'I know. Me too. One day at a time though.'

'Hey, that's my motto!' I say.

'Well, it seems to be working for you, so…' Cami grins.

We part company soon after and head to bed, both exhausted after the day's events. Cami hugs me and my fragile heart swells a little more.

Chapter 16
The snowman

Rose

I'm the first one up again. Not surprising really as I went to bed so early. I went out like a light. My bedroom door was closed when I woke up. I suppose Mags and Cami didn't want to risk disturbing me. I know they must have been talking about me, and everything I told them.

I woke soon after six, and lay in bed trying to work out how I was feeling after sharing some of my sordid story with my sisters. They don't know the half of it. Do I feel relieved at having unburdened myself? I s'pose I do, a bit. I'm glad they know why I was such a moody cow back then; that there was a reason and I'm not just a horrible person. Mingled with the relief is a whole load of other stuff though. It's like a really tangled up set of Christmas lights – one where you don't know whether to persevere with untangling it, or just chuck it in the bin and buy new ones. But, realistically, I can't buy new memories, can I? As hard as I've tried to forget them, these memories are real, they're mine.

I definitely feel anger today, and not just for myself. I'm angry that he stole my childhood, but he also screwed with my sisters' too. Unfortunate turn of phrase, Rose. Well, thank

God I was able to prevent that from being literal. It could have been worse. For them. I don't see how it could've been any worse for me. My anger extends past him to Mum too. How I longed to be able to go to her, confide in her, say Mum, he's hurting me, and know that she would take me in her arms, tell me everything would be okay, and would stop him. Why couldn't she love me, and see that something was badly wrong?

I used to think about running away from home. And I sometimes wished Dad was still there. But would he have been any better than Mum? Probably not. He showed bugger all interest in us, even before he left. I couldn't leave though, could I? I couldn't risk Cami or Mags being targeted. So I just stayed, and did nothing. After the first few times I didn't even bother saying no, or struggling. I just lay there and let him do it to me. I think I even stopped crying eventually. I would just focus on a point on the wall or the ceiling and try really hard to detach from my body as he thrust himself in me.

And when he was finished I would just pull on my knickers and get dressed. I didn't speak. I was like a little zombie, just going through the motions. After he'd put his pants and trousers on – he never took off his upper clothes – he would often stroke my hair, and tell me how beautiful I was. It made me feel like I was going to throw up. I thought maybe if I cut my hair off he wouldn't think I was beautiful anymore. But nothing changed, even after I'd hacked my long hair off in the bathroom at home. He still kept on doing it. Mum absolutely lost it with me that day and we had one of the worst rows ever. I feel bad thinking about how it must have affected my little sisters; of Cami cutting herself, and baby Mags stealing vodka from my room. I know I can never make it up to them. I just hope they understand and don't hate me.

At about seven thirty, I padded through to the lounge to light the fire. By the time Cami and Mags got up, I was on my second mug of tea, and attempting some of the jigsaw.

'Morning, you two,' I say, smiling at the two tousled heads.

'Morning,' come two replies, through yawns and stretches.

'How are you both?'

Cami says, 'Nay so bad,' and Mags gives me a thumbs up as she yawns again. They both look like they haven't slept, and I experience yet another stab of guilt as that's probably down to me. I get up to make them tea as they flop down onto the sofa.

'Rough night?' I ask.

'Yeah, bloody Hunnam, wouldn't leave me alone. Honestly!' Mags says.

'You don't have to make light of it, Mags, I know it's my fault,' I tell her.

'Well, actually, I do have to make light of it, because that's my default setting, and it's not your fault. So there nur.'

'Very mature,' I can't help laughing.

'The dartboard's right, Rose, it's not your fault. And you need to stop saying that,' Cami says maturely.

'Okay, okay, not my fault.'

'That's better. And if you say it again there will be consequences,' Cami says sternly.

'As long as they don't involve withholding chocolate,' Rose says.

'Good God no, we're not monsters,' Cami says.

'Indeed not! That would be cruel and inhuman punishment,' Mags concurs.

I hand my sisters their tea and go to open the curtains.

'Oh! It's snowing! Look!' I exclaim.

Cami and Mags crowd round the window and ooh and ah like children at the winter scene outside. It must have been snowing for some time as there is a good covering over everything, and it's picture perfect.

'So pretty,' Mags says. 'We have to make a snowman later.'

'And snow angels,' Cami says.

'Can mine have horns?' Mags says, holding her index fingers up to her head by way of illustration.

I just smile at them. I'm trying not to think about another time we all made a snowman together. I shake the memory away. I will not let *him* spoil the snowy day for my sisters.

'We can make snowmen, women, dogs, devils... whatever you want!' I tell them. 'But after breakfast. I'm starving.'

'Me too,' Mags agrees.

'Me three,' Cami says.

After a breakfast of scrambled eggs and smoked salmon on toast, we quickly dress, donning hats, scarves and gloves and as many layers as possible. When we open the front door, we find it's snowing even more heavily, and the thick layer crunches underfoot.

'Oh! It's so beautiful,' Mags says, clapping her gloved hands together like a child.

It really is like a scene from the alps, the roof of the cabin inches thick, and the branches of the pine trees heavily laden.

'It's very bright,' Cami says, squinting.

She's right. There is no relief from the bright white glare, but it's so fresh and clean and clear. It's pure. And it's making me feel stupidly emotional. I scoop up a handful of snow and lob it at Mags, quickly following that up with another at Cami. It does the trick and breaks my train of thought. Soon we're all screaming and throwing snowballs.

'Truce!' Cami yells eventually. 'I've got a stitch!'

'Oh! Me too, I haven't laughed like that in ages,' Mags says. 'Can we build a snowman next? Pretty please, can we, can we?'

I can't help smiling at her childlike joy. But I need a few minutes to compose myself. 'You make a start while I get us all some hot drinks,' I say, turning and going into the cabin. As I close the door, I can hear Mags issuing instructions to Cami, who says, 'Who put you in charge, squirt?' I'm feeling a little overwhelmed by a whole gamut of emotions and I need to breathe.

I watch my younger sisters from the kitchen as I wait for the kettle to boil. Mags is trying to roll a snowball round to make the head. Cami is just standing watching and laughing as Mags has to keep stopping and stretching her back. We're not girls anymore.

'Hot chocolate,' I call out a few minutes later, closing the cabin door behind me.

'Thanks, sis. This is much harder work than I remember,' Mags yells out.

'We're getting old,' I point out.

'Well, getting old sucks,' Mags says, pulling a face.

'Can't argue with that,' I say.

Mags carries on building the snowman, but Cami comes over and takes her drink. 'You doing okay?' she asks.

'Um... ish,' I tell her.

'I know yesterday was a lot, Rose. But it will help, I promise. It'll get easier.'

I nod, not trusting myself to speak.

'Unlike Mags attempting to build that ruddy snowman,' Cami laughs, nudging me to look at our younger sister. 'You're meant to be making a man, not a molehill,' she calls out.

Mags straightens up, holding her back. 'It shouldn't be this hard. Come and help!'

Cami and I exchange looks and then head over to help.

'What do you call this then?' Cami nudges Mags. 'Snow-mouse?'

'Sod off! I'm doing my best. Which, admittedly, is a bit shit.'

'It's a snow shit,' Cami says, laughing, and running away as Mags aims a snowball at her.

I can't help smiling at the pair of them.

By the time we have something vaguely resembling a snowman, we're all puffed out, with rosy cheeks and frozen fingers.

'There!' Mags says, stepping back to admire our masterpiece. Her face falls and then breaks into a giggle. 'It really is shit, isn't it?'

'Yep,' Cami agrees.

'Let's get a selfie with it,' Mags insists, running off indoors to get her mobile. 'We can send it to Bella.'

As Mags snaps half a dozen photos of the three of us with the snowman, I can't stop the memory that's been trying to push itself to the fore all morning. The snowman was better then, and taller than us. It had a scarf, and mittens, a carrot nose, stones for eyes and mouth. There was even a snow-dog by its side. We hadn't built that one by ourselves though. And the whole time we were building it, all I could think about was what had happened earlier that day.

'Rose, what's wrong? Why are you crying?' I feel Cami's hand on my arm without really registering what she's saying. I look at the concern on both my sisters' faces.

'I... I... didn't realise I was. It's nothing,' I say, wiping my gloved hands across my face and shaking my head.

'It's obviously not nothing,' Mags says gently. 'Come on, let's go in and thaw out.'

'No, really, I'm fine. What about the snow angels?' I say. I don't want to be a killjoy. And I don't want to revisit the memory.

'Snow angels be damned,' Mags says. 'I'd probably be struck by lightning if I made one anyway.'

We head back indoors and hang all our outer clothes up to dry. Cami stokes the fire and puts a couple more logs on.

I can feel their eyes on me, expectant, waiting for me to tell them what the tears were about. I know they're not going to leave it, so I take a deep breath and start to talk.

'Remember the winter we made that huge snowman and dog?' I begin. I watch as they cast their minds back and twin looks of realisation dawn on their faces. I nod. 'Yes, *he* helped us, didn't he? What you probably don't remember was that it was on one of those *special* Saturdays when I went to see him on my own. When we built that snowman, all I could think was that I wanted to go indoors and have a bath, to wash him off me. I could feel him on me and my knickers were wet with him.' I know there are tears on my face this time. And they're reflected on the faces of my sisters.

'I used to have to wash my pants myself... afterwards... just in case Mum realised what was on them. I'd hide them in the back of the airing cupboard until they were dry and I could put them in the washing bin to go in the machine. I wanted to burn them, burn all my clothes, after every time. But I couldn't of course...' I hear a sob. It takes a few moments to realise it came from me. 'Oh God, I'm so sorry, I... I... when you got my clothes as hand-me-downs... I remember seeing you wearing that dress with the orange flowers, Cami, and I thought maybe he'd stop wanting me if he saw you. I'm sorry, I'm so sorry. It was literally just one thought. Just once. A split second. I never wanted him to look at you the way he did me. Never. I'm so sorry.'

I can't even look at Cami. 'It's okay, Rose, really,' she says quietly.

'No, it's not okay. None of it's okay. What he did to me, to us...' I sob. And then there are two pairs of arms around me again, literally holding me together.

It's Mags who finally speaks. 'Right, coats back on,' she orders.

Cami and I start to object and ask why, but Mags will brook no objections, so we bundle ourselves up once more and follow her outside.

She leads us over to the snowman. 'Kick it,' she says.

Cami and I look at each other.

'Just kick it,' she repeats. 'Or punch it. Or both.'

I raise a tentative fist and smack it against the compacted snow. Cami just stands there.

'No!' Mags says. 'Really punch it, as hard as you can. Punch it, smash it, scream at it if you want.' She demonstrates what she means by kicking the icy man in the region of his shins and yelling that he's a piece of shit.

Cami and I exchange looks once more, raising our eyebrows, before shrugging our shoulders and joining in.

It's all over pretty quickly then. It's just as well there are no other cabins in the vicinity, otherwise we may well have had the police turn up to caution us for disturbing the peace. The obscenities streaming from our mouths freeze in the icy air, as the poor snowman is reduced to a pile of chunks.

We're all three of us puffing again as we stand back and look at what we've done.

'Yeah, to be honest, he doesn't look that different,' Cami says, nudging Mags.

'How very dare you,' Mags responds, pretending outrage.

I do actually feel a little better after the release, and I remember Mags' desire to make snow angels.

'I reckon I can get down, but not sure about getting back up afterwards,' I tell her as we all head off to a virgin patch of snow to the side of the cabin.

'Same goes for me,' Cami says.

'And me. They'll find our three frozen corpses in ready-made angels,' Mags giggles.

We all select a patch of snow and get inelegantly down on the ground, where we proceed to form our angel shapes.

'All done?' Mags asks a short time later.

'Yep,' Cami and I say.

'Right! Up we get,' Mags instructs, and she somehow gets herself up and out of the indents without too much bother, just a couple of oofs. She stands at the foot of her angel, grinning broadly. 'Not bad at all. Up you get, both of you.'

I turn my head and look at Cami who hasn't moved either.

Cami manages to pull herself to a seated position.

I just lie there.

'I think the only way I can get up is by rolling over,' Cami says. 'And that will probably ruin my snow angel.'

'I think the only way I can get up is with a crane,' I say.

Mags laughs at us, before treading carefully over to Cami, offering her both hands and hoiking her up. Cami brushes the snow off her coat and jeans and takes a look at her angel. 'Not bad,' she concludes.

'Er… help,' I say.

Soon, two pairs of hands grab mine and pull me up and out of the snow. Admittedly, my angel looks like she's being doing Zumba or something. Mags makes us take photos again. When she shows me the photo on her phone, my smile is real.

Chapter 17
The dolls' house

Mags

We spend that afternoon just lazing around, eating, doing the jigsaw or reading. Rose and I eventually give up on the jigsaw and leave it to Cami, declaring it too hard.

'Lightweights,' Cami says, but I think she's secretly pleased not to have to share it.

We don't even attempt to talk about anything difficult or painful, just focusing on enjoying one another's company. Always at the back of my mind though is the fact that Rose is going to need a lot of ongoing support after we leave the cabin. I honestly have no idea if we should push her to reveal more or not at this point. It's actually Rose who makes the decision for us after dinner that night when we're back in the hot tub.

'He used to give me presents,' she begins.

I'd been leaning my head back with my eyes closed, but they snap open as my full attention is diverted to Rose.

'Afterwards,' she continues. 'After he'd done... what he did... he always gave me something to go in the dolls' house. A reward for being a good girl. And he'd pat his cheek with his finger and make me kiss it and say thank you.' She shudders at the memory. 'That day – the day we made the snowman – he'd given me a doll all dressed up for the winter. She had long brown hair like mine, and a white fur coat and boots.'

'I remember that doll,' I say. 'I really wanted it. I'm so sorry, Rose.'

She shakes her head. 'The first time he gave me one of those presents, I threw it in the bin at home, but Mum found it and gave me hell. After that I just used to chuck them in the dolls' house and shut the door.'

'I would play with it when you were out,' I admit sheepishly. 'I could never understand why it was always such a mess. I used to tidy it up and play happy families, and then mess it up again before you came back and realised. One day when I took out the dolls, I found you'd cut all their hair off.'

Rose smiles sadly. 'Another of my small acts of rebellion. All that dolls' house was for me was a constant reminder of what was happening to me. I could never escape it.'

'Why did he stop, Rose?' I hold my breath after asking the question, but she seems calm.

'Because my periods started. When I was thirteen. I suppose I was a woman then in some ways, and no longer of interest. Or he was afraid of getting me pregnant. I don't really know, only that it stopped then. I remember him telling me that it still had to be our secret though, and he repeated his threat to do the same to one of you if I told. For a while afterwards I wondered what he did with those urges, but I was just so grateful it had stopped...' A look of horror suddenly crosses Rose's face. 'Oh God, he didn't, did he? He didn't touch either of you?'

'No, no,' Cami and I are quick to put her mind at ease. 'Never.'

'Thank God,' Rose says.

'Do you think there were others?' I venture. 'Other girls, I mean. After you. Or even before you?'

Rose shakes her head as if she doesn't even want to entertain the idea of other girls going through what she had. 'I don't know, Mags. I really hope not.'

'Realistically, though, there probably were, weren't there? A perversion like his wouldn't just stop. He'd still need to scratch the itch, so to speak,' Cami says.

'I can't even bear to think about it,' Rose says finally, and we let the subject drop.

I can't stop thinking about the possibility that there were other girls, other victims, and wondering about the logistics. Rose had literally been the girl next door, and easy pickings as his goddaughter.

Sometime later, Rose announces that she wants to phone home and check in with Bella. She climbs out carefully, leaving me and Cami alone with our thoughts. Those thoughts soon turn to conversation.

'What do you think?' Cami asks me. 'Could he have resisted his urges?'

'Honestly? I dunno. Seems unlikely, but I don't see how he could've managed it.'

'Hm. Porn, maybe?'

I pull a face at the thought of what sort of porn. 'Yeah, maybe. What a horrible thought.'

Cami shudders in spite of the hot water. 'Ew, they might find it on his computer when they clear out the house. Oh God, his poor sister if that's the case.'

'It would be password protected, surely, if he has dodgy stuff like child porn on there?'

'Yeah, I s'pose. It still pisses me off that he got away with it, and that he had a long, happy life after what he did to Rose,' Cami says angrily.

'I know, me too. But there's nothing to gain from exposing him now, is there? It would only hurt his family, and Rose.'

Cami shakes her head. 'It's just not fair.'

'Nope. Not much we can do though I'm afraid. I still struggle to believe he wasn't the kind man we thought he was, don't you?'

'Yeah, although I did get a funny feeling about him sometimes. Nothing I could put my finger on though. I put it down to the fact that I just didn't like men generally.'

'I think I was probably influenced by the Mars bars,' I say, shamefaced.

Cami laughs. 'You were just a baby, Mags, and God knows there were very few high spots in our weeks.'

'More of the dots have joined up today, haven't they? I used to think it was so strange that the dolls' house was always such a mess. Sometimes, when I'd go into Rose's room, she'd have thrown a load of clothes over it. I'd have to try and put everything back the way it was when I'd finished playing. Once she asked me if I'd been in her room messing with her things. I remember feeling really panicky, but I just lied right out and said no. I became a very accomplished liar over the years – I think I was always destined to be an addict. I'm good at the lying and the deceit.'

'That's the old you, Mags, that's not you any more,' Cami says gently. 'We've all lied, anyway, whether by omission or otherwise. We can't change the past though, only how we respond to it.'

'Are you sure you haven't done the twelve steps?' I chuckle.

Cami laughs, 'I'm sure. I have done a fair bit of personal development though, to deal with my own issues.'

We slip into silence once more until Rose reappears and gets back in.

'You must be complete prunes by now,' she says.

'Yep. And in no hurry to de-prune. This is even better in the snow,' I say. 'As long as you keep your shoulders under the water.'

'Everything alright at home?' Cami asks.

'Yes, fine thanks. Bella is so capable. And patient.'

'It's much easier when you're not a full-time carer, Rose, don't forget that,' Cami says wisely.

'I know you're right, but it doesn't stop me feeling guilty. David would probably come on in leaps and bounds with someone else looking after him,' Rose says sadly.

'Bollocks,' is my contribution to the conversation.

'Very succinct, Mags,' Cami laughs.

I just grin. 'Well, honestly, I think you're a bloody marvel, Rose. I'd probably have been arrested for being drunk in charge of a wheelchair if I was in your position.'

'I s'pose it's like anything in life, you just have to get on with it as best you can,' Rose accedes.

'We're survivors,' Cami says. 'And you're both stronger than you realise.'

We smile at our middle sister. 'You too, Cami,' I say, thinking of the faded scars on her legs.

The conversation turns then, almost as if by an unspoken need to lighten the atmosphere.

'So, Mags, no men on the scene at the moment?' Cami

enquires, grinning at me.

'Oh God, don't get me started!' I say, raising my eyebrows. 'Did I tell you about the pantomime dame?'

'What? No! Really?'

'I kid you not. Although, when I say pantomime dame, I think he was actually half Hobbit.'

'Oh no he wasn't,' Rose interjects.

We all laugh. 'Seriously though, why do I only attract short men?' I moan. 'Anyway, I'm taking a break from online dating – it's too depressing for words. The same men are on there from five years ago. Honestly, every time I re-join it's like a high school reunion.'

'You should get a dog,' Cami suggests. 'I meet all sorts of interesting people walking Jacks.'

'Er, no, you meet all sorts of weirdos,' Rose corrects.

Cami shrugs. 'Yeah, actually you're right. Then I just have the problem of getting rid of them.'

'I'm trying to get along without a man for once,' I admit. 'I know I've been guilty of needing a man for my sense of self-worth, and I've had to learn that I must love myself before anybody else can. It's not been easy as I don't actually like myself very much.'

'Oh, Mags, you have the heart of a lion!' Cami says.

'Yeah, the cowardly one from *Wizard of Oz*,' I say.

'It was actually the tin man who wanted a heart,' Rose corrects.

'Stop being such a schoolmarm!' Cami and I say in unison.

We then break out into a spontaneous rendition of 'We're Off to See the Wizard,' and all is well in the world. For a while at least.

Chapter 18
Let it all out

Mags

'I can't believe it's our last day here,' Rose says the next morning as we're having breakfast in the kitchen.

'I know,' I say, pulling a sad face.

'It's been brilliant,' Cami says. 'Maybe we can make it a regular thing – book something else straight away so we've got something to look forward to.'

'I like that idea,' Rose says, through a mouthful of toast.

'We can go thirds on the cost of course,' Cami points out.

'It doesn't have to be anything fancy – just somewhere we can get away from it all for a little while,' Rose says.

'As long as it's got a hot tub,' I say.

'I think that qualifies as fancy, Mags,' Cami points out.

'Rats. Well, can we do fancy at least once a year then?' I ask.

'We could take it in turns to have a fancy birthday break,' Rose suggests.

'Good idea,' I agree. 'Can I have two birthdays, like the Queen?'

'You'll probably have a man in tow soon anyway and blow us out,' Cami says. I know she's joking, or at least half joking, but I feel a stab of guilt anyway. I'm aware that I've put my

139

men before everything and everyone else.

I pull an apologetic face. 'Soz. I promise not to put a man before the two of you in future. Scout's honour,' I say, holding up my fingers in the appropriate salute.

'Hoes over bros,' Rose says.

Cami and I laugh. 'You are so down wiv da kids, sis,' I giggle. 'Where on earth did you pick that up?'

Rose looks embarrassed. 'One of my students,' she says.

'Well, I promise, no more putting men before my sisters,' I say again. 'Unless Charlie Hunnam pops up on Match, then the deal's off.'

'Fair enough. Even I'd push David's wheelchair in the lake if Mr. Hunnam came over the horizon,' Rose admits.

'Right, what are we going to do with our last day?' Cami asks.

'Snowy walk maybe?' I suggest.

The other two nod.

'I'd quite like to beat something up, you know, like we did the snowman?' Rose admits, grinning.

'Okay then,' I say, trying not to let the surprise show on my face. 'Beating something up it is. Cami? Anything you fancy doing?'

'Um... apart from the jigsaw? I had a thought lying in bed last night actually. It's something that was suggested in therapy. You write a letter, you know, to someone you have unfinished business with or something, and then you burn it. It's supposed to be cathartic. I never actually did it back then.'

'That sounds like a good idea,' I say. 'What do you think, Rose?'

'How much paper have you got?' she says.

'How about this then, we go for a walk and beat the living daylights out of something this morning, and after lunch we do the letter thing? One last soak in the Jacuzzi before we pack up the car maybe,' I suggest.

'Sounds like a plan,' Cami agrees, and Rose nods.

We clear up the breakfast things and head off to get warmly dressed. It's stopped snowing, but the world outside the cabin remains a winter wonderland.

We head off in the direction of the lake where I'd found Rose, as Cami hasn't yet seen it. We find it easily and it really is a beautiful scene.

'Oh, how lovely!' Cami exclaims.

'Now can we kick the shit out of something?' Rose asks.

'You've created a monster, Mags,' Cami says, laughing.

I pull a face of mock horror. 'Next thing you know she'll be putting cream on her scones first.'

Rose is looking around for a suitable target.

'We'll have to build something out of snow,' I tell her.

'Sod that for a game of soldiers,' she replies, wandering off in the direction of a fallen tree at the side of the lake. Before Cami and I can catch up with her, she's found a stick and is whacking the tree with it while screaming obscenities.

Cami and I stand well back, watching with our hands in our pockets. 'Remind me not to get on her bad side,' I say.

'You're not kidding,' Cami says.

It isn't many minutes before Rose gives up, holding the now broken stick aloft, straightening up and grinning at us. 'That felt so good!'

'We could see, you crazy person.'

Rose walks over to us. 'I think I might get one of those

punching bags that boxers use – it could go in the garage.'

'Why not? You could put photos of people's faces on it to incentivise you,' Cami says.

'Just not ours,' I say.

Rose laughs. 'I do feel lighter, you know – than when we arrived. Thank you, both.'

'You're so welcome,' I smile.

We walk around the lake, talking about where we might go for our next therapeutic mini-break. Nothing too fancy rapidly turns into city breaks to Paris or Barcelona, or a spa break at some chic hotel.

By the time we complete our lap of the lake, we're all starving, so we head back to the cabin where I get the fire going again while Cami and Rose concoct a lunch of odds and ends and leftovers. We eat off our laps in front of the fire, and I think again how much I'm enjoying this time with my big sisters. I do feel a pang of regret that we didn't find our way back to one another years earlier though.

'Right,' I say. 'How about we sort out most of the packing and then reconvene for letter writing and burning?'

'Okey dokey,' Cami says. 'Have we actually got any paper?'

'Yep, I always have a notebook with me,' I tell her. 'I can tear some pages out.'

Rose hasn't spoken.

'Sound okay to you, Rose?' I ask.

'Um… yeah… I s'pose so. I feel a bit anxious about opening the can of worms up again. Is it a good idea when I have to go back to my real life again later on?'

'You don't have to do it if you don't want to. I just thought it might help, but there's no pressure,' Cami tells her.

'You might be right. Okay, I'll give it a go. Boxes of tissues at the ready though,' Rose says, sounding nervous.

'We can burn them too,' I say, thinking a ceremonial burning of tear-soaked tissues might also be cathartic.

'Christ, we don't want a towering inferno,' Cami jokes, thinking of the number of tissues we may potentially get through.

Rose heads into her room to start packing while Cami and I clear up the lunch things. We're standing side by side at the sink when she stops washing the plate in her hands and turns to me:

'I brought copies of some of the old photos with me,' she says. 'You know, the ones from the funeral? Of us, and *him*. In case Rose changed her mind and wanted to see them. Before I knew all this awful stuff that went on.'

I pause, tea towel and mug in hand, 'You're wondering if we should burn them with Rose, aren't you?'

'Well, yes, I am. What do you think?'

'I dunno. Might be too much for her?'

'Or it might be exactly what she needs. Watching his face go up in flames. What's not to like?' Cami shrugs.

'Play it by ear? Have them ready and see where the afternoon takes us?' I suggest.

'Okay,' Cami nods.

We finish the dishes and head off to our rooms to pack our stuff.

At about two o'clock, we reconvene in the lounge. I've brought my notebook and pen, and found another couple of biros in a drawer in the kitchen. I grab some books for us to lean on, and we're ready to go. I hand Cami and Rose a pen and a few sheets of paper. We all just sit there for a while, staring at the empty pages.

'I don't know what to write,' I say, eventually.

'Me neither,' agrees Cami.

'I suppose it doesn't matter what we write, does it? Nobody else will see it and we're going to throw the pages in the fire anyway, so…' Rose says.

'You're absolutely right. And it doesn't have to be sentences even – could just be words, or names,' Cami shrugs.

'Or even doodles, pictures,' I add, glancing at Cami and wondering if we can introduce the photos.

She shakes her head almost imperceptibly, as if to say no, not yet.

Rose puts pen to paper, and I can't help wondering what she's writing. Cami starts next, and I have to resist the urge to peer over at her paper. Finally, I start making a list of negative things about myself, stuff I need to let go of if I'm ever going to learn to love myself.

We're quiet for some time, all absorbed in the activity. Eventually, I run out of things to write, and look round at Cami, who nods her head in Rose's direction. When I turn to see what she means, I see a look on Rose's face that I'm not sure I can describe. It's an expression of pain, but also of fury. I recognise the fury from our childhood, but the pain is deeper than I can bear to delve. It literally makes my heart hurt.

I write on my paper, and nudge Cami to look: *Should we intervene?*

Yeah, maybe, she writes, holding her hand over the other stuff she's written.

Share what we've written?

Cami nods. 'How are you getting on over there?' she addresses Rose.

No answer. I'm not even sure Rose heard her.

'Rose?' I try.

Finally, she looks up from the page she's been scribbling on furiously.

'You okay?' I ask.

She shakes her head. 'Yes. No. I don't know.'

'That's okay. You don't need to know right now,' Cami says, smiling at her.

'Can I share what I've written?' I ask.

'Of course,' Cami says. Rose just nods.

I proceed to read out the list of things I need to stop doing: being a people pleaser, needing the approval of others for my sense of self-worth and so on. When I've finished, I screw the paper up and chuck it into the flames, watching with satisfaction as it catches and disappears.

'That felt surprisingly good,' I say. 'How about you two? Care to share? Or just burn them?'

Cami pulls a face. 'I… um… couldn't think what to write.'

I reach over and grab her paper. 'You bugger, it's a shopping list!' I laugh.

Cami shrugs and looks sheepish. 'My bad. I will have another go. But I'd rather not burn my Tesco's list.'

Suddenly, we become aware of Rose speaking in a low voice, trembling with emotion. 'I drew this,' she says, holding up her page for us to see. She's drawn the dolls' house, but she's drawn it on fire, with flames licking up the walls and out of the roof. The pen strokes are dark and deep, her anger poured into the drawing. You can almost feel the fury coming off the page. The atmosphere in the room becomes serious once more.

'Screw it up, Rose,' Cami says. 'Screw it up and throw it in the fire.'

Rose does as instructed, and we watch as the fire grabs the drawing and obliterates it.

'How do you feel now?' I ask her gently.

'Honestly? Like I've just scratched the surface,' she says. She sounds exhausted.

I can't help wondering if this exercise was a mistake, but we've started now, so we might as well pursue it.

'I know it's hard, but the wounds will only heal once you've opened them to the air, so to speak. You have to get it all out, I think, and then you can start to heal,' I say.

'I know you're right, but it's hard. I've kept this bottled up for so long,' Rose says sadly.

'I know, but that hasn't done you any good, has it? It's been poisoning you from the inside,' Cami tells her.

'Your whole life has been marred by what happened to you all those years ago. But enough is enough. It's time to face it, deal with it and close the door on it. I know it will never leave you, not completely, but wouldn't it be a relief to let go of some of it? To acknowledge the awfulness of it and then try to move forward?'

Rose is quiet for a few moments. 'I have so much anger and bitterness inside me. So much resentment, Mags. I haven't dared open the door to it, for fear it would overwhelm me,' she says.

I nod. 'I know. But you have us now, and you don't have to do this on your own.'

'Mags is right, you're not on your own, and we will support you every step of the way. And you've already achieved so much this weekend,' Cami says.

'I s'pose. Thank you, both of you.'

'You don't have to thank us. We're sisters, that's what we're for,' I say. I'm thinking about the photographs I know Cami has tucked down beside her on the sofa. I just know she's thinking about them too. I take a deep breath. 'Rose... I know you didn't want to come to the funeral... but do you think it might have given you a little bit of closure if you had?'

'Maybe... with the benefit of hindsight, and now that you both know the truth. It's too late now though, isn't it? I don't get to see the bastard burn.'

'Well, maybe not, but this could be the next best thing.' I reach out a hand to Cami and she passes me the photos.

Rose sees what I'm holding and you can't miss the sharp intake of breath. She starts to shake her head. 'No, Mags, no, I can't. I can't look at him!' A sob catches in her throat.

'Okay, okay, it's okay. You don't have to do anything you're not ready for,' I try to soothe. Her chest is heaving as she tries to control her breathing. I look round at Cami, but she doesn't know what to do any more than I.

I wait for Rose's breathing to return to normal before I speak again. 'You don't have to look at the photo, but I'm going to burn one of them. Okay? I'm going to burn it for you, for all three of us.' I flick through the images, and select one of us all in the garden with Ken. Being careful to hold the image away from Rose, I step over to the fire, and toss it in.

I sit back down and watch as the flames lick the photograph. I glance sideways at Rose and find she's staring at the fire with tears streaming down her face. I pull a handful of tissues from the box on the coffee table and hand them to her. 'Let it all out,' I tell her.

'You'd better give me some of those too,' Cami sniffs, and I look round to find her in tears too. Well, that sets me off, and we make short work of the box of Kleenex.

'Shall we run the risk of burning the place down and chuck these on the fire?' I ask, indicating the piles of used tissues, once the sob-fest is finally over.

Cami and Rose nod and I scoop up the crumpled heaps and chuck them in the flames.

'We should make a pact,' Cami says. 'Always to reach out when we feel like crying.'

'Jesus, I'll be on the phone to you every five minutes,' Rose says, and we know she's only half joking.

'It'll get easier. Give it some time,' I say.

By an unspoken agreement, Cami and I don't push Rose any more, and the conversation in the hot tub that afternoon is light and frivolous. We very much want the break to end on a high, and for Rose to be together enough to go home and cope with life for a while longer. That is, until we can arrange for her to see a counsellor, or be all together again.

As we pack the car up, both my sisters express their gratitude.

'Honestly, Mags, it's been brilliant – thank you so much,' Cami says.

'It really has,' Rose agrees. 'Despite all the tears!'

'I'm so glad you both enjoyed it. It's been wonderful spending some proper time with you,' I smile, suddenly feeling a little shy. 'I can't tell you how happy it's made me.'

My sisters pull me in for a hug.

'Honestly,' I continue, my voice wobbling a little as tears threaten, 'you both mean the world to me.'

'Aw! Come on, you dopey dartboard, no more tears,' Cami says, pulling back to take my face in her hands.

I can't help laughing. 'Are you always going to call me that now?'

'Yep,' Cami nods her head vigorously.

'Great!' I groan.

Rose just smiles at us. 'I'm so glad that you both know what happened to me. And that you've both shared your own painful stories. It feels a little less daunting to know you're both on your own journeys to recovery right alongside me.'

'It really does,' I agree. 'No more secrets, eh?'

'No more secrets,' Cami nods.

'Rose?' I ask when she remains silent.

'Well, you know the biggie,' she says. 'I think the rest will have to wait until we can be together again. There are other cans, other worms, but I don't want them on the loose and wriggling around in my brain just yet.'

'Fair enough,' Cami says.

'Okay, but you have to promise to call if you need us – if it ever gets too much? Deal?' I say.

'Deal,' Rose nods. 'Thank you.'

We finish loading the car and I take a final few photos of the cabin and the snow-covered trees. I force Rose and Cami into a few selfies too, and then we say our goodbyes to the place and set off on the road home.

Chapter 19
Sex. Therapy.

Mags

The next few weeks are just life, the usual routine, but with one important difference, and that's the regular contact I have with Rose and Cami. We have a WhatsApp group called Sisters and share something every day, whether it's a funny anecdote or a cry for help.

Unbeknownst to Rose, Cami and I chat separately too, and mainly about her. We're still trying to work out the best way to help Rose deal with the past. Cami had got in touch with her old counsellor when we got home, and asked for a recommendation for someone close to Rose. Rose, in turn, had promised to set up an appointment. Cami and I then nagged her until she did it. She'd had two appointments so far, but said she wasn't ready to talk to us about them yet.

'You don't have to tell us what goes on in the sessions,' Cami tells her in the chat group. 'They're for you, and you alone, if that's what you decide. All that matters is that you're getting the help you need.'

'It has been easier to open up to her than I thought it would be. I think maybe because I'd already opened up to you.'

'That's good. I'm so proud of you. I know it's not easy,' I say.

'She's talking about a course of CAT therapy,' Rose says.

'Hm, I'd prefer DOG therapy, but each to their own,' Cami says, adding a winky face and a dog one.

'Muppet. Cognitive Analytic Therapy.'

'Yeah, I know a little about it,' Cami says. 'It can really help.'

'I don't know much about it,' I say. 'I've done some CBT in my recovery though, which has helped me.'

'The sessions are draining,' Rose says.

'Of course, but as long as you feel like you can go back home and cope for another week, then stick with it,' Cami encourages.

'I think I can. Georgia – the therapist – says I don't actually have to think about whatever I've unpacked in that session. She puts it all in a box and keeps it until next time. It kind of works, although I do occasionally find the odd difficult thought or memory creeping in.'

'That's only natural, and you can always turn to us when that happens,' I say.

'I do want to tell you some of the other stuff,' Rose says. 'One day. When I'm stronger.'

'And we'll be ready to listen. When, or if, that time comes.'

Cami lightens the mood then by sending a picture of a box of puppies. *DOG therapy*, she writes.

I find a meme of kittens with the words *Mad CAT lady starter kit* and post that.

Rose sends a laughing emoji. 'Can I have both?'

Rose

I really want to confide in Cami and Mags about the other stuff that happened to me, but I'm scared they'll judge me. I know

151

that's stupid, because they've confided in me about difficult stuff, especially Mags. Deep down I know they'll be supportive and understanding, but I'm still afraid to take the leap of faith. I love this new-found closeness with my younger sisters, and I don't want to do anything that might jeopardise it.

How do I casually drop it into the conversation that I had three terminations when I was at university? That I had zero respect for my body and had more one night stands than I care to remember. Maybe it would be easier to start with the bulimia? Christ, I was a mess back then. All through uni I was a complete slag. I must've had a horrible reputation. I'd get pissed in the student union and go back with any bloke who showed an interest; back to their crummy student digs, for a quick, often unprotected shag. Then I'd be hit by waves of revulsion and I'd hunt round for my discarded clothes, before making the walk of shame back to my own room, where I'd binge and purge. I probably spent as much time with my head down the toilet as I did in lectures.

It was only luck that I didn't end up with an STD during that time. When Mags had confessed to having PID, I'd felt a stab of guilt. There but for the grace of God. Maybe God thought I'd suffered enough? I couldn't imagine life without my daughters.

It was in my final year of university that I met David, and he was different somehow. I'd tried to pick him up one night in the bar, and he'd rejected my advances, saying I was drunk and to have a little respect for myself. Initially, I'd thought he was a self-righteous twat and told him as much, but his words planted a seed in my brain which germinated and slowly, oh so slowly, began to grow.

I didn't see him for some months afterwards. We were at the garden party of a mutual friend, and I was sober this time. It was summertime and I was wearing my favourite floaty dress and feeling good about myself for once. David spotted me and came over and we spent a happy couple of hours sitting in a swing seat and chatting. I remember feeling a little embarrassed about the time I'd tried to hit on him, and worried he knew all about my reputation, but he gave no indication it was a problem and asked me out for dinner a few days later.

Gradually, over the following months, David taught me to respect myself. He was quiet and self-assured, and in no rush to sleep with me. At first, I was kind of insulted and felt rejected, but I realised he was showing me respect. It was all new to me, this realisation that my body was more than just an object. I suppose, looking back, it was my first proper adult relationship – everything that had gone before was just about sex. And not even especially enjoyable sex. When we did eventually consummate our relationship, David was gentle and considerate. It didn't blow my mind, if I'm honest, but I decided it was better than what had gone before. We'd got engaged after a year together, married after two, and had a honeymoon baby. I was content.

Mags

'I got a punch bag hung in the garage,' Rose says.

We're in one of our now regular video group chats.

'That's great,' I say. 'Hope my picture's not on it?'

Rose laughs. 'No, no photo on it. Yet. The list of candidates is short.'

'Is it helping?' Cami asks.

'Not exactly. I hurt my wrists the first time I used it. Need to get some supports,' Rose grimaces.

'What about boxing gloves?' I ask. 'Would they help?'

'Maybe,' Rose says. 'I'll look into it.'

'I can't picture you in boxing gloves,' Cami giggles. 'Ready to go two rounds with the vicar's wife.'

'Have you met her?' Rose asks. 'She is pretty irritating.'

'Maybe her pic can go on the list?' I suggest.

'Hm, maybe, but she's after Mum, Dad, and you-know-who,' Rose says.

It's the first time you-know-who has been mentioned since the cabin. I jump on the opportunity to ask Rose about her counselling sessions.

'Um... they're actually going pretty well, thanks. Georgia is brilliant – she just seems to get me. And I don't feel judged, or ashamed.'

'That's great,' Cami and I say simultaneously.

'Last time we talked about the fact that *he*'s dead and I didn't go to the funeral – you know, whether it makes it harder to have closure. I told Georgia about the photos you took and she thinks it might be useful to look at them, together though, in one of our sessions. She doesn't think I should look at them on my own, but does think it might help to process everything.'

'I can forward them to you? Or directly to Georgia if that's better?' Cami says.

Rose takes a deep breath. 'Could you send them to me?'

'Yeah, if you're sure you won't be tempted to look at them on your own?' Cami looks worried.

'I can't promise, but I'll try.'

154

Cami nods her agreement. 'Okay, when's your next session? I'll send them just before and then there's less temptation.'

'It's on Tuesday. Thanks, Cami. I can't say I'm looking forward to it; I promised myself I'd never look at his face again.'

'It won't be easy, Rose, but it might help in the long term,' I say. 'You need to confront your demon.'

We ring off soon after, with promises to keep in touch.

Chapter 20
Picture this

Rose

I had my sixth session with Georgia today. We looked at the photographs Cami sent. It was even harder than I'd thought it would be, and my eyes are puffy from crying, my nose swollen from blowing. I debated taking a blotchy-frog selfie to send my sisters, but decided it would only upset them. I knew they'd be worried enough about me as it was.

I'd handed Georgia my laptop and she'd loaded the photos, looking through them before choosing one to show me. When she turned the laptop round to face me, I nearly threw up. It was a photo taken on the day *he* presented me with the dolls' house. Mum had insisted on taking it and I'm scowling at the camera as ever. *He* has his arm round my shoulders, and I shudder to remember how that felt. He looked proprietorial, like he owned me, possessed me. The dolls' house was on the floor in front of us. How I'd wanted to lash out, kick it. Inside I was screaming. I can still hear Mum telling me to smile.

Georgia'd asked me how the picture made me feel? I wanted to say, 'how the fuck d'you think it makes me feel?'

'Look at him, Rose,' she'd pushed. 'Look at his face. If he was here now, what would you say to him?'

I just sat there shaking my head, for ages, refusing to look at him.

'Rose,' Georgia said gently. 'It's safe, you're safe, but you need to look at him. You need to acknowledge him before you can really start to move on.'

'No, I can't, I…'

'Yes, you can, it's time. He hurt you then, but he can't hurt you now. Look at him, Rose.'

And I did. I looked at his face, the face that had hovered above me all those times I lay on his bed while he abused me. And I sobbed and I shook, and I hated Georgia for making me look. 'Why didn't anybody help me? Why didn't my mum see what was happening? Why me? Why?' I wept.

'You were badly let down by the adults in your life, Rose, by the very people who were supposed to protect you from harm. There is no excuse for them, and what was done to you was so very wrong. They stole your childhood, Rose, don't let them steal the rest of your life. And know that nothing that happened was your fault.'

When the sobs finally subsided and I'd managed to get my breathing under control, I felt like crap. But it also felt like I'd cried out another piece of the poison. It felt like a breakthrough.

We sat in silence for a while, I don't know how long. Finally, Georgia spoke:

'Do you think you could look at another photograph? It's up to you. You don't have to.'

I just nodded as I wiped my nose.

Georgia looked at the laptop again. When she turned it around, there was the photo of him, me and my sisters.

'I hated them. Cami and Mags. I hated them for being the

reason I couldn't tell. I resented them, even though I knew it wasn't their fault, not really. And I made their lives a misery with my behaviour, all the rows with Mum.'

'Rose, you have to forgive yourself. You were reacting to a terrible reality, and your feelings were entirely understandable. I'm sure your sisters don't blame you, and you mustn't blame yourself. You're not responsible for other people's happiness.'

I looked at the photo again. It was a little easier. 'I felt like I was screaming on the inside. All the time.' I shake my head. I remember how I felt only too well. 'I used to pray Mum would see that something was wrong; I'd almost try and communicate telepathically with her – think really hard about what was happening to me, so she'd feel it. But she never did. Or, if she did, she didn't care.'

When the session was nearing its end, Georgia asked if I wanted her to delete the email containing the pictures. I thought about it for a minute.

'No, leave it. I might look at the others.'

'Okay, but only do it if you're feeling strong. Remember, you're in control now. No one can make you do anything you don't want to.'

'I might print one out and stick it on my punch bag,' I told her, a little embarrassed.

Georgia just smiled. 'That sounds like a good idea.'

So, here I am, later that night, opening Cami's email. David is already in bed, and the hum of his massager is almost soothing. I take a deep breath and start to click through the photos...

*

'Hey, sis, what's up?' Mags says as her face, and Cami's, appear on my phone screen.

'The photos...' I begin. 'I've been looking through the photos you sent.'

'You okay?' Cami asks.

'I am actually. Now. I sure as hell wasn't earlier, mind you. Georgia got the full blotchy frog. Completely went to bits. I feel much calmer now though – like I made progress.'

'That's great,' Mags and Cami smile. 'You should be really proud,' Mags adds.

'I am, I suppose... anyway, that's not why I phoned.' Two faces look expectantly at me. 'Did *he* know the Lawrences? You know, Anna-May's family. There's a photo of *him* with her – I'm guessing it was taken in their back garden.'

'Um... I think he did – he knew pretty much everyone in the village,' Mags says.

'Yeah, he might have done their garden, I think,' Cami adds. 'He was always helping out with gardening and odd jobs. Why's that?'

'It just occurred to me, after our conversation about whether I was the only one... you know... that he...'

'Oh God, you think he might have abused Anna-May?' Cami says as she realises what I'm trying to say.

I nod. 'She wasn't much younger than me, and looked kind of similar. What if he moved on to her?'

'I dunno, Rose, that's a bit of a leap, isn't it?' Cami says.

'How would he have got her on her own?' Mags asks.

'Well, I don't know, but if he was a family friend...?'

'I suppose it's possible. She looked really young for her age, didn't she?' Cami remarks.

159

I nod. 'But she was an only child, so if he did abuse her, what leverage would he have had to stop her from telling? He couldn't threaten her siblings.'

'All the more reason to discount the theory then, don't you think?' Mags suggests. 'He wouldn't have wanted to risk being found out.'

'But what if he was, and she ran away or something? She could still be alive somewhere,' Rose insists.

'I think that's unlikely,' Cami says.

'Even if it was true, Ken's dead, and his secrets have died with him,' Mags says. I flinch on hearing his name, and Mags sees.

'Sorry,' she says.

Rose shakes her head. 'Don't apologise. Georgia says I need to say his name at some point.'

'He's like Lord Voldemort,' Cami grins. 'He who shall not be named.'

'Ken,' Mags says.

'Uncle Ken,' Cami says.

'Fuck,' I say. 'Ken.' I say the name quietly. 'KEN!' I spit the name out, feeling the venom leave my mouth. 'Bastard, bastard, bastard, Ken!' My heart is pounding in my chest, but I feel like another drop of poison just left my system.

'Well done,' Mags says.

'He's losing his power over you, Rose. I hope you know that?' Cami adds.

And so, with Ken's name on my lips, Anna-May's is forgotten once more.

Chapter 21
Where there's a will

Rose

I haven't stopped trembling since I got off the phone. I get on the phone to Mags and Cami straight away.

'I just got a phone call from Uncle Ken's solicitor.' (It's getting easier to say his name.)

'Oh? What did they want?' Mags asks.

'Has he left you something in his will?' Cami asks. 'Tactless git.'

'You could say that,' Rose says.

'Well?'

'His house. He's left me his bloody house.'

Shock registers on both their faces.

'No! You're joking?' Cami says, aghast.

'Nope. Deadly serious,' I tell her.

'Oh my God!' Mags says. 'Why would he...?'

I raise my eyebrows. 'Because he was a sick bastard, right up until the end?' I suggest.

'But, his sister...?' Mags queries. 'Does she know?'

I shrug. 'Dunno. I s'pose so.'

'Maybe it was his way of trying to make up for what he did?' Cami suggests.

'What? Giving me a permanent reminder of the place it all happened? Nice.'

'Sorry, no, of course. My bad,' Cami apologises.

'I suppose it sort of makes sense. He didn't have any children of his own, and you were his goddaughter…' Mags says.

'What are you going to do with it?' Cami asks.

'Honestly? My first thought was burn it down.'

'Understandable,' Mags says grimly.

'Now? I don't know.'

'Well, there's no hurry is there? Presumably probate will take a while anyway?' Cami says.

I nod.

'Do you think… maybe… you'll go down there? You know, to the house? Might help to lay old ghosts to rest?' Mags ventures.

'I don't know, Mags. The very idea of setting foot in it makes me feel sick. I swore I'd never go back.'

'Maybe speak to Georgia about it? She might suggest it would be a useful part of your healing.'

'The thought of going there at all fills me with dread, let alone going upstairs,' I shudder.

'Of course, and you don't have to decide anything yet,' Cami says.

'I have to come down there to see the solicitor – sign some papers and stuff.'

'Will you see Mum?' Mags asks.

'The idea doesn't fill me with joy, but I suppose I should,' Rose groans.

'We could see her all together. Go out for lunch or something,' Mags suggests.

'That would be good,' I say.

'Safety in numbers,' Cami says with a grim smile.

'Surely she's mellowed with age?' I say.

'Nope,' Cami and Mags say resolutely.

'Not a jot,' Mags adds. 'In fact, I think she's even more sour than ever.'

'Great,' I say, rolling my eyes.

'Don't worry, I'll wear a hat to divert her attention away from you,' Mags says. She fills me in on the nasty comments Mum made on the day of the funeral.

'Spiteful old bitch. You know what? I've got a good mind to give her both barrels. Tell her exactly what I think of her, and what a shit parent she was. Is,' I tell my sisters.

'Part of me wishes you would,' Mags admits. 'I still find it impossible to stand up to her. She only has to open her mouth to reduce me to a small, stupid girl.'

'You can't let her have that sort of power over you, Mags,' Cami says.

'I know, but I don't seem to be able to help it. I wish I was stronger,' Mags says sadly.

'We're all still works in progress,' I sigh. 'But maybe together we can at least pull Mum up on some of the stuff she says. Call her out.'

Mags nods, but I know she's not convinced.

Cami suddenly giggles.

'Sorry, I was just thinking about you owning the house next door to Mum's – you could be the neighbour from hell,' she chuckles.

'Yeah! Or you could rent it out to... I dunno... a real pikey family with twenty-seven children, a Pitbull and two Staffies,' Mags says.

'Who dump mattresses and burnt-out motorbikes in the front garden,' Cami continues.

'And play really loud music at all hours and have all their pikey friends round for parties, drinking and smoking and flicking their cigarette butts in Mum's garden,' Mags adds.

I can't help laughing and admitting that the idea does have some appeal.

'As much as I'd be happy to piss Mum off, I couldn't in all conscience do that to the rest of the street,' I say.

'Yeah, fair point,' Cami admits. 'Back to the drawing board then.'

'I still can't get over the fact he's left you his house,' Mags says, shaking her head.

'I know, me neither,' I agree. 'I haven't told David yet. He'll probably say we should sell it and pocket the cash.'

'Would that be so bad?' Cami asks.

I screw up my face. 'Honestly? Yeah. I hate the idea of having his money. It wouldn't feel right somehow. Like he was trying to compensate me or something.'

'Hm, what about donating the money to charity then?' Mags suggests.

'A children's charity, perhaps?' Cami adds.

'Yeah, maybe. I don't know. I still like the idea of burning it down to be honest,' I tell them.

'Understandable,' Cami says.

'Is there a law against burning your own house down?' Mags asks.

'Good question. Dunno. I s'pose as long as you don't try and make an insurance claim...' Cami says.

'Yeah, if you're not defrauding anyone, surely you can do

what you like?' Rose says.

'I guess so, but please don't go committing arson before you've checked out the legal situation, will you?' Mags pleads.

'Okay, I promise.'

'I bet you had your fingers crossed then!' Cami grins.

I hold up a pair of crossed fingers and laugh.

Mags groans. 'Don't joke about it. I do not want to end up visiting you in prison. You know I'm crap at baking.'

Cami and I look confused.

'To make a cake to hide the file in,' Mags enlightens us.

'I'm sure a shop-bought one would do just as well, Mags,' I tell her.

'I'd probably eat it on the way to the prison anyway,' Mags laughs.

'Well, no one's going to prison so you don't need to rush out and buy a Mary Berry book, okay?' I reassure.

'Good. So, when are you coming down to see the solicitor then?' Mags asks.

'Just got to get cover for David, and then I'll let you know. Can I crash in your spare room, Cams? Just overnight.'

'Yes, of course,' Cami tells her. 'It'll be lovely to have you here.'

'Great, thank you. Well, I'll let you know when I'm coming.'

'I'll book somewhere for lunch when you do,' Mags says, before we say our goodbyes and leave the video call.

Chapter 22
Coming home

Rose

I finally manage to get a carer from the agency who will look after David while I'm gone. It's too short notice to get Bella to help out again. And my other daughter, Jess, is currently swanning around Asia with her boyfriend. David's not especially happy about me leaving him with a virtual stranger, but it really can't be helped. There's no way I can get my head around taking him with me; just the logistics of his wheelchair are a nightmare. We'd once attempted an overnight trip to a supposedly wheelchair-friendly hotel, and it really wasn't. I'd almost tipped him out trying to get him into the restaurant. It was all far too stressful. And Lord knows, I'm stressed enough already at the prospect of going back home.

Home. I haven't thought of Mum's as home for a very long time. Nor the village I grew up in. I couldn't wait to escape from it at eighteen. I'm absolutely dreading the trip, to be honest. Seeing Mum is bad enough, but the house, his house? Just the thought of it makes me shudder. Georgia says it could be a good thing – might lead to another breakthrough. Breakdown, more like.

I'd texted Cami and Mags with the date, and we'd formed

a plan. We'd have dinner together in the evening, I had an appointment with the solicitor the following morning, and then lunch for the four of us before I drove back. I felt exhausted just thinking about it.

*

'Don't not drink on my account,' Mags says as I put the wine list to one side. We're seated in the window of The White Horse pub in town, perusing the menus. I'd arrived at Cami's a couple of hours earlier and chilled out until Mags arrived to collect us for dinner. I suppose she was the natural designated driver nowadays.

'I actually don't feel like drinking tonight,' I say. 'Keeping a clear head for tomorrow's meeting.'

'With the solicitor? Or Mum?' Cami pulls a face.

'Either. Both,' I laugh. 'Although, from the sounds of it, Mum would be better endured under the influence.'

'Under a flak jacket,' Mags grimaces.

I laugh. 'Well, as you've got to face her sober, Mags, I think it's only fair I do too.'

'You might regret saying that,' Mags says.

'Possibly, but I have to drive home afterwards anyway, so…'

'Can you remember the last time we were all with her? You know, at the same time?' Cami asks, frowning.

'Um…' Mags looks thoughtful.

I feel a pang of guilt. 'Sorry, you two, I know I've always found excuses not to come down.'

My sisters both shake their heads.

'Don't be daft,' Cami says.

'You had a bloody good reason to stay away,' Mags says.

'Yeah, well, that bloody good reason is dead, so maybe I don't need to make excuses anymore?' I say.

'Yay!' Mags and Cami smile broadly.

'Right! What's anyone having? I'm starving.'

We spend a few minutes discussing the menu, and I order a bottle of sparkling water for the table. Mags smiles at me gratefully.

'Anyone having a starter?' Cami asks.

The question is redundant really as we always have a main and a pudding.

'Not me, leaving space for pudding,' Mags says anyway.

I smile at how comfortable this is, how familiar it's becoming.

'You look happy, Rose,' Cami says.

'I am, right here in this moment. I am happy.'

'I'm glad,' Cami says.

'I'm still dreading tomorrow, but I am starting to feel a bit stronger. You know, as if I might actually be getting somewhere with all the shit I've been dragging around my whole life.'

'I know regret's pointless,' Mags begins, 'but I do wish we'd got here sooner. I mean, being honest with one another, not suffering in silence the way we did for so long.' She looks wistful.

'I know, Mags,' I say, reaching over and squeezing her hand. 'But the main thing is we're here now. And I'm bloody starving!'

Right on cue, our meals arrive, and we spend an enjoyable couple of hours simply enjoying the food and each other's company.

We're sipping coffees when Mags tells me she's taken the morning off work in case I want company at the solicitor's. I'm touched.

'That would be really nice, thank you,' I smile at her.

Mags looks pleased, and I see a flash of the little girl who was always trying to keep the peace and make everyone happy. I feel tears pricking at the corners of my eyes as I think how much my behaviour affected her. I press my fingers into my eyes to plug the leaks.

'It's been a lovely evening,' I say as we're getting up to leave. 'Thank you both.'

'It has, and you're welcome,' Cami and Mags agree.

We walk back to the car arm in arm, taking up the whole pavement, and Mags drops me and Cami back. 'I'll pick you up about ten twenty tomorrow,' she says as she waves goodbye.

Cami and I are greeted by Jacks jumping up and down excitedly as we open the door. We make a fuss of him before plonking ourselves down in the lounge.

'Nightcap?' Cami asks.

'Um… yeah, okay, why not.'

Cami heaves herself up again and comes back with two tumblers of whisky over ice.

'Cheers,' she says as she hands me one.

'Cheers, sis, and thanks for putting me up.'

'No worries,' Cami says. 'So, how are you feeling about tomorrow now?'

'I'm feeling okay about seeing the solicitor, I think. Sweet of Mags to offer to take me.'

'And Mum?'

'Rather less okay about seeing her.'

'Well, hopefully Mags and I can run interference.'

'Are you going to wear a hat too?' I ask.

'No. But if she's too awful I might tell her my news,' Cami says cryptically.

'And what news might that be?' I ask, furrowing my brows as I try to read her face.

'I met someone.' Cami smiles.

'Oh my God! Why didn't you say something before? I can't believe it! I thought you were off men for good?'

Cami pauses. 'I am.'

It takes my brain a few moments to understand the implications of those two words.

'He's a she?!'

Cami just nods. 'Yep, he's a she.'

'Does Mags know?'

'No, nobody knows, except you now of course. I wanted to sit with it a while, and see how I really felt. If it was real.'

'And is it? Real?'

'Yes, yes, I think it is.'

'Oh my God! I'm so happy for you.'

'Thank you, Rose, that means a lot.'

'It's not someone I know, is it?'

Cami shakes her head, 'No, she's not from around here originally.'

'What's her name?'

'Lydia.'

'Lydia,' I repeat. 'Have you got a photo?'

Cami produces her mobile and passes it to me. On the screen is a picture of my sister with a dark-haired, studious-looking woman wearing glasses and a big smile.

'Oh! You both look so happy,' I say.

'We are.' Cami's voice and expression are softer than I've

ever known them.

'Have you always known then? Is that why your marriages didn't work out? Were you just in denial?' I fire questions at Cami, eager to know everything.

'Woah! Slow down! Have I always known? I'm not sure to be honest. I think I always knew I was different, and that I didn't have a normal attraction to men, but... but I wasn't really attracted to women either.' Cami shrugs her face and shoulders. 'I suppose, knowing what I know now, I must always have been gay. It wasn't until I met Lydia I realised the truth.'

'Wow. When do I get to meet her? What does she do for a living? Tell me everything, I want to know everything!'

Cami laughs. 'There's plenty of time for that down the line, sis. It's early days.'

'I can't wait to meet her. I'm so honoured to be the first person you've told. Are you going to tell Mum?'

Cami grimaces. 'I s'pose I'll have to at some point, but I'm not ready for her to try and take the shine off it just yet.'

'Maybe the shock will be too much for her and she'll keel over and cark it.'

'Hm, wishful thinking.'

'Are we awful? Wishing our own mother dead?'

'Probably, but hey ho.'

Chapter 23
The clause

Mags

I pick Rose up from Cami's as arranged, and we drive the twenty or so minutes to the solicitor's office. Rose seems happier than I'd expected, and I can't help feeling there's something she's itching to tell me.

'You okay?' I ask, turning my head away from the road for a moment.

'Mm hm. I'm fine.'

'Sleep okay in Cami's spare room? Or did Jacks try to come in with you?'

'I slept really well, actually, and Jacks stayed in with Cami thankfully.'

We drive on in silence, but I can feel the furrow between my brows. I just know there's something she's not telling me. I don't have a chance to pursue it though as we're soon pulling into the small car park at the back of the solicitor's. We don't have long to wait in the reception area before the solicitor calls us in.

*

'The bastard,' Rose says.

We're sitting in a coffee shop and she looks ashen.

'Yeah,' I agree, taking a sip of my cappuccino.

'Why would he do that?' I can hear the confusion in her voice.

'I don't know,' I shake my head.

We'd only been in with the solicitor for about twenty minutes. He'd basically told Rose that, apart from a few items listed for family members, she was the sole heir to Ken's estate. What we hadn't been counting on was a clause in the will stipulating that Rose must not sell the house for a period of five years.

'Nothing about not burning it down though,' Rose says, starting to look and sound mutinous. 'I'm buggered if I'm going to let the old bastard tell me what to do. He doesn't get to control me now, or ever again.' As she speaks, Rose's fingers are clenched around the keys to Ken's house. I think if she could've snapped them she would've.

'What are you going to do about going to the house? If you can't face it, I could go round and try to find the things for his family.'

Rose sighs. 'Thanks, Mags. I don't know. I think I need some time to process everything. There's no rush is there? It's not going anywhere. FOR FIVE BLOODY YEARS!' she adds angrily.

I can't help thinking what an ordeal it's going to be seeing Mum with Rose spitting chips. It makes me anxious and I feel that old familiar tightening in my head and chest. Just like old times, I think with a sinking heart. I'm having palpitations and starting to panic. I hope it's not showing on my face. I make my excuses and pop to the loo where I lean on the sink and take a few deep breaths, reciting the serenity prayer, before running cold water over my wrists. I dry my hands and then rummage in my bag for the bottle of Rescue Remedy I always carry, dropping a few drips on my tongue. Next I apply an aromatherapy blend to my wrists and inhale deeply before returning to Rose. She doesn't seem to have noticed anything's amiss – hardly surprising really considering what she's dealing with.

We finish our coffees in silence, killing time until we're due to meet Cami and Mum at a nearby restaurant. Cami has gallantly arranged to pick Mum up. As the hour approaches, I'm filled with more and more dread.

Just before twelve thirty, we push our chairs back, call out a thank you to the staff and leave the coffee shop. It's only a few minutes' walk to the place I've booked for lunch. As we push open the door, I spot Cami and Mum already seated at a corner table. Cami waves. She's probably thinking 'cavalry'. As we approach the table, she raises her eyebrows. I stifle a nervous giggle. No words necessary.

I pull out the chair next to Mum – taking one for the team, I think to myself. 'Hello, Mum. How are you?'

'Magnolia,' she says, before directing her attention to Rose. 'Peony,' she says. Well, that's like a red rag to a bull.

'It's Rose. My name is Rose,' she says through gritted teeth.

Mum harrumphs. 'Not according to your birth certificate.'

'Fuck my birth certificate. And fuck you.' With that, Rose turns on her heel and marches out of the restaurant.

Cami and I look at each other in dismay.

'I... er... I'd better go after her,' I say. 'Sorry.' I address this to Cami. Mum can go hang. 'Wait here. I'll see if she'll come back.'

Mum harrumphs again. 'Don't bother on my account.

Foul-mouthed creature. She can jolly well go back where she came from.'

And that was that. I ran out after Rose and took her back to Cami's, where our middle sister joined us sometime later.

'I thought I'd better get lunch for Mum anyway,' she says. 'Unfortunately, she didn't choke on it. Are you okay, Rose?'

Rose just nods. She went from shaking with anger to crying, and is now just sitting zombie-like staring into space.

I fill Cami in on what happened at the solicitor's.

'What the actual…?' she says incredulously. 'I just can't understand what was going through his head.'

'I know. It's like he's trying to control Rose from the grave. Sicko,' I say.

'I'm so tired,' Rose says when she finally speaks.

'I don't think you're in a fit state to drive home today, Rose,' I tell her.

Cami nods her agreement.

'I don't have a choice – I have to get back for David,' Rose says tiredly.

'Well, we'll see,' I say, getting up and going into the kitchen to make a phone call.

'That's all settled. The carer can stay another night. And so can you,' I tell Rose when I go back into the lounge.

'What? But… I can't. David won't be happy,' she says worriedly.

'Well, right now, I don't really care about David's happiness, only yours.'

Rose leans back and closes her eyes. She looks shattered. The day's events have taken their toll.

'Why don't you go for a lie down?' Cami suggests.

'I think I will,' Rose says, and she heads off upstairs. 'See you both later?'

'We'll be here.'

With Rose out of the room, Cami and I exchange looks and exhale loudly.

'Oof.'

'Oof indeed,' Cami agrees. 'That was fun.'

'They literally can't be in the same room together, can they?'

'Nope. I don't think there's any repairing that relationship.'

'Even if Rose was willing, Mum can't be nice, can she? She knows how much Rose hates her real name.'

'How much we *all* hate our real names. *Cameeellia*,' Cami mimics Mum's voice.

'*Magnooolia*,' I do the same.

'Ugh!'

We chat a bit more about the will then, both agreed that Ken was an utter bastard.

'Maybe we can go round to the house together? Now Rose is staying an extra day,' I suggest.

'Yeah, maybe,' Cami agrees. She then seems to be trying to make her mind up about something. 'Changing the subject, Mags,' she says eventually, and she proceeds to tell me that she's met someone. And her name is Lydia. And she's shocked that I'm not surprised. But I am very, very happy for her.

Chapter 24
The lovely tea set

Cami

Mags went home for a couple of hours after I told her my news. She said she'd come back around teatime and maybe we could get a takeaway for dinner. She didn't seem in the least bit surprised by my announcement about Lydia. Said she'd always wondered if I might be gay. I asked her why she'd never said anything? She'd just shrugged and said she didn't think I was ready to ask myself that question. She seemed genuinely happy for me though. I'm pleased that they both know now. I can't wait for them to meet Lydia.

Rose reappeared after about an hour, looking slightly better than when she left.

'Sorry about earlier,' she said. 'At the restaurant.'

'No apology needed. Mum has a way of pressing all our buttons.'

Rose groans. 'I know, but she literally only had to say my name and I lost my shit.'

'It's probably worse for you. Mags and I see her more often so we're probably slightly more immune to her use of our proper names.'

'I just hate the fact she has that sort of power over us still.

Jesus, I'm nearly sixty and she can still turn me into a teenage banshee.'

I can't help laughing. 'I know it's not funny, but... well... it is actually pretty funny: *Fuck my birth certificate and fuck you*. Classic.'

Rose looks sheepish. 'God, what must the other people in the restaurant have thought?'

'Who cares? They probably enjoyed it.'

'I'm such a dick,' Rose groans.

'Yeah, but you're my dick, and I love you,' Cami says.

'Ew, don't go all gay on me. Anyway, I thought you didn't like dick anymore,' Rose jokes and the atmosphere is lightened. We're still laughing about it when Mags arrives back a while later.

'What are you two cackling about?' she asks.

'Cami and dick,' Rose says, cackling some more.

Mags just laughs and shakes her head. 'I don't think I want to know.'

Over Chinese takeaway, Mags and I broach the subject of the will again, figuring we need to talk about it properly before Rose goes back.

'Let's think about what actually needs doing, and what can wait,' I say.

Rose sighs. 'Can't I just stick my head in the sand and pretend none of this is happening?'

'Sure. I think you might suffocate though,' I tell her.

'Cami's right,' Mags says. 'Ignoring this won't make it go away. You tried that, remember?'

'God, you two are so sensible,' Rose groans.

'You'd better believe it,' Mags says, pulling a mad face.

Rose laughs. 'Alright, alright. Let's make a list. Isn't that what sensible people do?'

I get up and go in search of notepad and pen. 'Okay, first things first... um...'

Rose and Mags laugh. 'Um indeed. Where do we start?' Rose says.

'What about finding the things listed in the will for his sister and her family?' Mags suggests.

'Good,' I say, writing it down at the top of the blank page.

'How do we handle that?' Rose asks. 'Do you think I should just give his sister, wotsername, the keys and tell her to go in and collect stuff herself?'

'Margery. She might already have a set of keys, mightn't she?' Mags says.

I shrug. 'Yeah, maybe. I suppose one of us should phone her really, you know, out of politeness?'

'Bagsie not me,' Rose says, putting her hand up like we did as kids, and grimacing. 'She might be pretty pissed off he's left everything to me.'

'Not everything. She does get a particularly lovely tea set if I remember rightly,' Mags says, pulling a face that would indicate the tea set is far from lovely.

Rose groans again. 'For God's sake. This is hideous.'

'Much like the tea set apparently,' I grin.

'Good to see you two being sensible didn't last long,' Rose says.

'Sorry. Right, back to the list,' I say. 'Um...'

We all laugh.

'What about things like utilities and council tax and stuff?' Mags offers.

'Good thinking,' I say, adding this as point number two. 'I suppose we need to notify them of his death and stuff. I think maybe you don't have to pay council tax for a while.'

'I can't face all this, I really can't,' Rose says. All traces of laughter have left her face.

'You don't have to. Mags and I can take care of this sort of stuff,' I tell her.

'Absolutely,' Mags agrees. 'All you need to do is keep focusing on your recovery, and not letting this bump in the road trip you up. I still struggle sometimes, when things get tough, but I have my little coping mechanisms,' she says, thinking back to the coffee shop episode earlier.

Rose rubs her temples. 'It's hard.'

Mags and I nod. We know.

The list rather grinds to a halt after two points, and conversation drifts to my recent revelation. I'm so thrilled both my sisters know about Lydia, and are entirely accepting. I share more photos and answer their million and one questions. I'm loving this new closeness. I never want to go back to the way things were before.

We're all yawning our heads off by ten thirty, and Mags heads home after hugging me and Rose tightly.

'Love you both,' she says, kissing us on the cheeks and waving as she walks to her car.

'Love you too!' Rose and I shout after her.

I can't remember us ever doing this before. It feels good.

Chapter 25
The house

Rose

I sleep fitfully and my dreams are full of flashbacks. I wake in a cold sweat more than once. When would I be free of him? I stand in the shower for ages, letting the hot water revive my tired body. I feel old. Old and tired.

I find Cami in the kitchen making coffee.

'Morning,' she says. 'You're up early. Sleep okay?'

'Morning. Yes. And no.'

'Oh dear, sorry to hear that,' Cami says, handing me a mug of coffee.

'I was dreaming, you now, about back then.'

Cami looks sad.

'I was back in the house, his house, and I kept running from him, running and running, but I could never get away,' I tell her, cupping my hands around my mug.

'I can't imagine how awful it was for you,' Cami says. 'It will get easier, I promise. Confronting what happened is the only way to move through this. I know the house thing is a huge blip, but you will get there.'

I nod. 'I know you're right. It's bloody hard though.'

'I can't help wondering if you should go to the house, today, with me and Mags. Confront those nightmare images head on, in daylight.'

The thought terrifies me and I feel close to tears. 'I don't know if I can face it, really, I...'

'It's okay. You don't have to, I just thought it might help lay the ghosts to rest.'

I think for a few moments. 'I want to be strong, Cami, really I do. And I don't want to leave you and Mags to deal with everything. Can you ask Mags if she'll come?'

Cami picks up her phone and calls Mags.

'Hey, sis, you up for pulling a sickie today?' she asks.

I can't hear Mags' response, but Cami tells her to come round when she's ready. Cami then makes a phone call of her own, sounding pathetic as she blames a dodgy Chinese. Mags arrives about forty minutes later.

'Dodgy Chinese?' she winks at Cami.

'Great minds,' Cami says.

'Sounds like one of my internet dates,' Mags says, laughing.

By ten o'clock, we're pulling up outside the house. I just hope Mum doesn't spot Mags' car. I definitely don't feel up to seeing her two days in a row. Or ever.

We sit in the car for a while, just looking at the front of the house.

'I suppose we might need to think about getting someone in to keep on top of the garden?' Mags says.

Cami produces the notepad she had last night, and adds Garden Upkeep to the rather pathetic list we'd started.

'It pisses me right off that this is going to start costing me money,' I say.

'Mm, I was just thinking the same thing,' Cami says.

'Could you get a tenant in?' Mags asks. 'The solicitor didn't say anything about that.'

'Yeah, maybe. I think I need to don my big-girl pants and phone Margery, don't I? Get her thoughts on the matter,' I say, not relishing the prospect.

'Might be best coming from you,' Mags agrees.

Cami writes Phone Margery at the top of the page, above number one.

Silence overtakes us once more. Finally, Mags speaks. 'So, are we going to brave it?'

I feel two pairs of eyes turned on me expectantly.

'Oh Christ! Come on then.' I undo my seatbelt and climb out of the car, making old-lady noises as I do. 'Mags, you need to get a different car.'

Mags just makes a face that says, *er no I don't*, and we assemble on the pavement in front of the house.

I can feel myself trembling and my heart rate quickening. I let Cami and Mags lead the way.

'Here, Cami, have the key,' I say, passing it to her. I don't trust my shaking hand to do the job.

Cami opens the front door and steps inside the hallway. Mags turns to me. 'You okay?'

I just shake my head. The rest of me is already shaking, and getting worse. My heart feels like it could burst out of my chest any second, and it hurts to breathe. 'I can't, I can't, I just can't.' The next thing I know, Mags is hugging me and I'm sobbing and sobbing and can't stop. I'm nine years old again, and I'm terrified.

'Shh, shh, it's okay. He's gone. No one's going to hurt you,' Mags says, continuing to hold me until the sobs subside.

Cami comes back out and hands me some tissues from her handbag. 'Better out than in,' she says.

'The crying or the house?' I ask.

Cami just smiles. 'Do you think you can go in now?' she asks gently.

I take a deep breath and nod. 'I think so.'

Cami takes my hand and leads me over the threshold, like a frightened little girl. My breath catches again as I take in the old familiar hallway. It's obviously been repainted over the years, but it is essentially the same, with the telephone table and oval mirror on one side, and coat stand on the other. Seeing his coats hanging there sends a shiver down my spine.

'It's just a house, Rose,' Mags says. 'There's nobody here except us, and nothing that can hurt you. Okay?'

I nod and let them lead me through into the lounge. The panic in my chest increases. 'Open the curtains, please open the curtains,' I hear myself say. Mags hurries over and pulls them back to let daylight in. I take a deep breath and look around. It looks different and I'm relieved to see that the three-piece suite has been replaced.

Then they lead me through the kitchen and into the conservatory.

Mags

When we took Rose into the conservatory, I thought she was either going to pass out or run out. Her hand flew to her mouth and she just made this awful choking sound. Cami and I both held her hands and we could feel her whole body shaking.

'I'm going to open the back door,' I said, letting go of Rose's hand. 'Let some fresh air in.'

I opened the door to the garden and then looked around the conservatory, trying to remember how it had looked when we were children. From my recollection, it looked just the same: the same old cane furniture and lots of plants. Casting my mind back to Rose's confession about what happened to her in this room, I could imagine the horror she was feeling at being back here.

'Do you need to sit down?' Cami asked her.

'Mm. Not here.'

We went back into the lounge and squeezed together on the sofa. Rose leaned her head back and closed her eyes. My eyes met Cami's and I saw reflected in them the same pain and feelings of helplessness I was experiencing. How do we help her?

Chapter 26
The ballerina

Cami

It had been blatantly obvious that making Rose go upstairs was a seriously bad idea, and we'd left the house without really dealing with anything.

'What about the things for Margery?' Rose had said, looking defeated.

'It doesn't matter – there's no rush,' I'd told her.

'I have to phone her…' Rose had started.

'No, you don't. In fact, I definitely think you shouldn't,' I'd told her.

'I agree,' Mags had said. 'I think either I or Cami should do that.'

'I'll do it,' I'd volunteered.

Rose and Mags had both smiled gratefully at me. And that's how I come to be dialling Margery's number. I take a deep breath and wait for the call to be answered, half hoping it won't be.

'Hello?'

'Hello. Margery?'

'Yes.'

'Hello, it's Cami, Camellia… I lived next door to Ken as a girl.'

'Oh, yes, I remember. You have two sisters, don't you?' She sounds nice, normal. Not like the sister of a paedophile at all.

'Yes, that's right. Um… I'm sorry for your loss.' I'm wishing now that I'd spoken to her at the funeral. And I'm actually not sorry at all. Well, I suppose I am sorry for Margery. Presumably she didn't know her brother was a paedophile.

'Thank you. I think I saw you at the funeral, didn't I? With your mother? And one of your sisters?'

'Yes, that's right, with Mum and my sister Mags.'

'Of course, Mags. Ken was godfather to one of you, wasn't he?'

'Um… yeah, my eldest sister, Rose.'

'I thought she would have been there… at the funeral,' Margery says.

'She couldn't make it, unfortunately,' I say through gritted teeth. 'Her husband is in a wheelchair,' I add by way of explanation.

'Oh dear, I'm sorry to hear that. A pity she couldn't make it though – I know Ken did a lot for you girls and your mother.'

Oh, you don't know the half of it, I think to myself, anger rising in my chest. It pisses me off that I have to protect Ken's memory and I have to remind myself I'm actually doing it to protect Rose. I quickly change the subject. 'So… um… I don't know if you know about the will?' I hold my breath.

'No, not yet. I have an appointment to see the solicitor tomorrow.'

Crap. I wonder if what I'm about to tell her is privileged information or something, and that I should wait for the solicitor to inform her? *Sod it.* In for a penny. 'Oh, okay, well, I might as well tell you – Ken left the house to Rose.'

There's silence on the other end of the line.

'Oh,' Margery says eventually. 'Oh, well, that is rather a shock, I must say.'

'I'm sure,' I say, while thinking it's not as shocking as what took place in the house.

'Well, I suppose Rose was the closest thing he had to a child of his own,' Margery concedes.

I can't help wondering if she never questioned her brother's unmarried state or lack of offspring? Surely she must've wondered? But then, we three sisters had managed to keep huge secrets from each other for decades. I decide to give Margery the benefit of the doubt.

'Is Rose going to sell the house?' Margery asks.

'Well, no, not yet. I don't think she's really made up her mind what to do with it yet to be honest,' I say, thinking this is turning into the least honest conversation ever. I don't feel I should give Margery any more details. 'I expect the solicitor will fill you in on the details when you see him tomorrow. Perhaps, if I give you my number, you could give me a ring to discuss things further?'

'Well, yes, I suppose so. But shouldn't I speak to Rose directly?'

'No!' I say rather too quickly. 'Er... no, Rose has asked me to handle things for her, you know, with her husband and everything...'

'Well, okay then. Let me get a pen and something to write on.'

I give Margery my phone number and we say our goodbyes. I heave a sigh of relief that the worst bit is over and at least she knows about the house. It could've gone a lot worse.

I open WhatsApp to let Rose and Mags know I've spoken to Margery and that she's calling me back after she's seen the solicitor. Rose had headed home soon after the visit to Ken's house, saying she needed to be on her own, and the drive would do her good. Mags and I had tried to persuade her to wait a while, worried that she'd spiral again, but she'd insisted she was okay. She had seemed strangely calm when she left, but you couldn't help feeling it was the calm before the storm. We'd made her promise to let us know the minute she arrived home.

'Have you heard from Rose?' I'd rung Mags about three hours after Rose had left. Her journey home shouldn't have taken any longer than this.

'Nope. Starting to worry. I take it you haven't heard either?'

'No. Could just be traffic?' I'd said.

'She might have stopped at the services?'

'Yeah, I expect that's all it is. Let me know if you hear from her.'

'Of course, and ditto,' Mags said.

It was another hour before Rose let us know she was home, by which time Mags and I had imagined all sorts. Rose just said she'd stopped on the way, to think. When asked what about, she'd simply said, 'stuff'. Neither of us pushed her.

*

Margery was true to her word, and phoned me after she'd seen the solicitor.

'I wondered if I might go to the house to collect the things he bequeathed me and the family?' she says.

I thought for a moment about what Rose would want, but decided I should just deal with it myself. 'How about I meet you there?' I suggested. 'Rose left the keys with me.'

'Yes, that would be fine,' Margery agreed and we arranged to meet at the house after I finished work.

I arrive at the house before Margery and go in to wait, turning the lights on and mentally noting that the house is warm – the heating must be on a timer. I'm studying the display panels on the boiler when I hear a voice call out.

'I'm in the kitchen,' I yell, fiddling with the timing pins. I figure I can reduce the number of hours the heating's on for each day, thus saving Rose some money.

'That's a good idea,' Margery says as she enters the kitchen. 'I should just put it on for long enough each day to stop the pipes from freezing.'

'Yes, that's what I thought. Be with you in a sec.' Reasonably confident that I've set the heating to come on for an hour in the morning and an hour at night, I turn away from the boiler to greet Margery properly.

'Sorry to meet you under these circumstances,' I say.

'Oh, that's okay. It is what it is. We just have to deal with it, don't we?' Margery smiles. I'm relieved there's no confrontation in her voice.

'So, shall we hunt for these things then?' I say, digging around in my bag for the list the solicitor had given us. 'Oh, and Rose says if there's anything else you particularly want – you know anything with sentimental value – please just take it.'

'Oh, that's kind of her, thank you. I don't suppose there'll be much of interest – my brother wasn't the sentimental type, and I kept most of our parents' bits and bobs when they died.'

'Okay, well… shall we start with the tea set? I think I spotted that in the glass cabinet in the lounge.'

We locate the china and Margery fetches bubble wrap and a cardboard box from the hall. 'Thought we'd be needing these,' she says.

When we've exhausted the downstairs rooms, I lead the way upstairs. It's the first time I've been up here, and I shiver as I cross the landing. Margery notices. 'Are you alright, dear?' she asks.

'Someone just walked over my grave, I think.' Well, I can't exactly tell her the real reason, can I? I pause, unsure which door to open.

'This one's Ken's bedroom,' Margery says, taking charge and opening the bedroom door.

I follow her in reluctantly. I can't shake the awful feeling. This was where it happened. Where the sick bastard repeatedly raped my sister. My beautiful, innocent sister. I force myself to look around the room. I assume it looks different all these years later. I'm relieved not to see an old-fashioned feather quilt on the bed. Instead there's a regular duvet in a navy-and-white striped cover.

Margery is opening drawers and rummaging through Ken's belongings.

'Here's his watch,' she says. 'Would it be okay to take that? I don't s'pose my boys will want it, but it would be nice to have something personal.'

'What? Oh, yeah, of course, that's fine,' I tell her. I just want to get out of this room, but Margery hasn't finished and has pulled out a small wooden box from one of the drawers.

'What's this?' she says, holding up a fine silver chain. She steps over to me and shows me a pendant with a tiny silver ballerina in a pink tutu on.

The implications of finding such an item in Ken's bedroom are, of course, not lost on me, and I'm hit by a wave of nausea. 'Oh, er, I don't know. Maybe he found it somewhere and kept it in case he located the owner?' I suggest, shrugging. 'Probably put it away and forgot all about it.'

Margery stares at the necklace for a few moments longer before saying, 'You're probably right. Not one of yours or your sisters' then?'

'No, I don't think so – I don't recognise it.' It occurs to me that it could've been a present for Rose that he didn't get round to giving her. Whatever the case, I just want to get out of the bedroom and out of the house. 'So, is that everything then, do you think?' I prompt.

Margery puts the necklace back where she found it and looks around the room. 'Yes, yes, I think so.'

I heave a sigh of relief and lead the way downstairs.

'We didn't find his computer, Cami dear,' she says, just as I'm about to offer to carry the box to her car. 'I know he had one of those laptop ones. Did you see one anywhere?'

'No, no, I didn't, um… well, I can let you know if it turns up,' I say, trying to hide my impatience. The last thing I want to do is begin another search of the house. 'Here, let me carry the box for you.'

I pack Margery and her lovely tea set off and go back inside to turn off the lights and lock up. I just want to go home and take a shower. I feel somehow unclean after being in Ken's bedroom. I make a mental note to mention the pendant to Mags next time I speak to her.

Chapter 27
The laptop

Mags

I just had a weird conversation with Cami. She and Margery – who sounds like a nice old dear – found a girl's necklace in Lord Voldemort's bedroom. Pretty odd. From Cami's description I don't remember it being Rose's. She wasn't into ballet, but I suppose a ballerina is a fairly generic girly thing, like unicorns or love hearts. It has got me wondering though... I've read enough books about psychos who keep trophies of their victims. Part of me's relieved they only found one thing. What if they'd found a whole hoard of mementoes that couldn't be explained? Cami also mentioned a missing laptop. Probably just as well Margery didn't find that, bearing in mind our suspicions about what Ken might have on there.

I try to put the mystery of the necklace to the back of my mind, but I can't shake the feeling that I'm missing something. I phone Cami back.

'Hey, you. Hope you've recovered from your visit to the house. Can I borrow the keys tomorrow? Something about that necklace you found is bugging me.'

'Yeah, of course. You might as well keep them for now. I'm in no hurry to go back there. What is it about the necklace? I didn't recognise it.'

'I'm not sure... just a nagging feeling about it. Probably nothing, but seeing it might help me remember. Shall I look for a computer while I'm there?'

'Up to you, Mags. Can if you want.'

*

The next day I decide I do want, and I let myself into Ken's house determined to unravel the mystery of the necklace and find his laptop. Cami'd described where I'd find the little box and I have no trouble locating it. I sit down on the bed to open it, but jump up when I realise where I'm sitting, feeling a little shudder run down my spine.

'No wonder Rose wants to burn this place down,' I mutter to myself as I close up the bedroom and head downstairs.

Back in the kitchen, I take out the silver chain and study the ballerina. Her skirt is dotted with little pink diamantes. There's definitely something familiar about it, some memory I can't quite get hold of, an intangible wisp of a thing. I put the necklace back in the box, frustrated that I can't recall where I've seen it. I put the box in my handbag and turn my attention to finding Ken's laptop.

'Right, if I was a dirty old pervert, where would I keep my computer? Come on, you old bastard, where is it?' I ask Ken's ghost. 'You didn't know you were going to pop your clogs, did you? So you didn't need to hide it... Crap. It's in your bloody bedroom, isn't it?' I jog back up the stairs and go reluctantly into the bedroom once more. There are mahogany bedside tables either side of the bed, but only one has items on it. I go round to that side, crouch down and peer under the bed. There, on the floor, just tucked in under the bed is a silver laptop. 'Gotcha!' I retrieve the machine and leave the room once more. 'I can see why you needed a shower, Cams,' I mutter.

I lock up gratefully and head home with my finds.

Later that evening, I'm sitting in my lounge with the ballerina necklace on the table in front of me; I still have no recollection of where I've seen it before. I've just cleaned the laptop with antibacterial wipes and I can feel an expression of distaste on my face as I think about the man it belonged to.

'Right, Lord Voldemort, let's see what we can see, shall we? Christ, I'm losing the plot, keep talking to myself. Maybe Cami's right and I should get a dog.'

I open the laptop up and press the power button. Nothing. Arse. The battery's flat and guess who didn't look for a charger? I think about going back to look for it, but I really don't want to be in the house on my own after dark. I close up the laptop with a sigh.

*

I don't have a chance to go back to Ken's house until after work the next day and, as I let myself in once more, I shudder involuntarily. I'm not a superstitious person but, if I was, I might believe Ken's ghost was in residence. I just want to find the laptop charger and then I'm out of here. After a fruitless search of the lounge and kitchen, I find the cable plugged in next to Ken's chair in the conservatory. I push the image of him sitting there looking at God-knows-what on his laptop out of my head when it pops up unbidden. At least I didn't have to go up to his bedroom again.

It's a relief to close the front door and get back to my car.

I put the laptop on to charge as soon as I get home and message Cami to say I found it. She messages straight back: *Okay, let me know if you manage to get into it.* Part of me is sincerely hoping I don't.

Later that evening, once I've had dinner and cleared up, I try turning the laptop on and am rewarded with a sign-in screen. As predicted it's password protected. I try the obvious old-person, easy-to-remember ones to no avail. I guess I'm not really surprised.

Okay, Ken, let me inside that mind of yours... what would your password be? Nothing too obvious, but easy to remember...

Peony_Rose. Nope.

PeonyRose. Nope

Imafilthyoldperv.

This was getting me nowhere. I message Cami again.

Best guesses for his password?

Oh God. Dread to think. Have you tried Rose's name?

Yep, first thing I tried.

Date of birth?

Yep, tried all the obvious things.

Um... thinking...

Wondered what the noise was.

I feel like it would be something to do with Rose, don't you?

Yeah, I do. But what?

Saturday? Saturday girl?

I'll give 'em a go... Nope.

Okay... what about dollshouse?

Nope. Hang on, I'll try a capital D. Nope.

What about a number? Can you think of a meaningful number?

I'll try birth years and house numbers. Hang on. Oh my God,

Cami, I'm in. Dollshouse63 — Rose's birth year.

Shit. I mean, yay, but shit. I'm worried what you might see on there.

Ew. Me too. I feel unclean just touching this thing.

D'you want me to come round?

No, don't be daft. I'm a big girl.

Okay, well, here if you need me.

Thanks, Cams. Catch up soon.

The screen in front of me has filled up with icons. Nothing looks unusual at first glance. I click on File Explorer and watch as it loads. I'm aware that my heart rate has quickened slightly. I spend the next forty minutes trawling through files, emails and pictures. And then I ring Cami.

'Any joy?' she says as she picks up.

'Well, yes, and no, I think is the answer to that question.'

'Oh?'

'Mm... No in that I didn't find any child porn or anything sinister like that, but there is a password-protected file called "Bank" I couldn't get into.'

'Okay, so that could be where the dodgy stuff is?' Cami says. 'Can you tell anything about the file? Size, or anything?'

'No. To be honest, Cami, I don't really know what I'm looking at.'

'I'd probably be the same. We're not the computer generation, are we?'

'Nope. Anyway, the thing that I did find was the necklace...'

'Necklace? Oh, what? You mean the ballerina one?'

'Yeah. In Pictures I found copies of a lot of the same photos we had of him and us, and ones from the funeral too. He must've scanned them in or something. Anyway, there was that one of Ken with Anna-May we saw – I didn't really study it before, but my subconscious must've taken in that she was wearing that necklace. Or an identical one.'

'Holy crap. Really?'

'Mm hm. I'm trying not to jump to conclusions, but it's a hell of a coincidence, isn't it?'

'Yeah, it is. I mean, it's a pretty standard girly necklace… but…' Cami pauses.

'But it's pretty suspicious that we found the necklace in the bedroom of a paedophile and a missing girl had one exactly the same,' I finish for her.

'Yeah. Shit. That's a hell of a can of worms, Mags.'

'I know. We have to go to the police, Cami, don't we?'

Cami doesn't answer right away.

'Oh God, Mags, I don't know. If we go to the police, then inevitably it will have to come out about Rose. I don't know if she's strong enough for the abuse to be made public knowledge. The girls would find out their mum was a victim. The knock-on effect could be really damaging.'

'Oh, hell. We can't do nothing though, can we? We can't just ignore this.'

'No, I know, but let's not rush into anything. No one's in danger if we leave it a bit longer – Christ, Anna-May went missing decades ago.'

'Do you think she ran away because of what he was doing to her? Assuming he *was* abusing her,' I ask.

'Honestly? I don't know, but that would be the best-case scenario,' Cami says grimly.

'God, what a nightmare,' I groan.

'Yeah, I almost wish we hadn't found that sodding necklace.'

'I know. But we did. It could have her DNA on it, couldn't it? Still? After all these years?'

'I suppose so. If it really is hers. This might sound awful, Mags, but I care more about the wellbeing of our sister than I do about a girl who went missing a lifetime ago, and is probably, let's be honest, long dead.'

'I know, I know, but her poor parents...' I insist. I can't quite let go of the idea that we should be going to the police.

'You really think it's going to help them to find out that their daughter might have been the victim of a paedophile? A dead one at that. There can be no justice now, Mags. Ken can't be punished. All that would happen is those still living would be hurt.'

I can see Cami's logic, but I still feel horribly uneasy. We agree to do nothing for now, and say our goodbyes. I can't settle for the rest of the evening and, not for the first time in recent weeks, I could really do with a drink.

Chapter 28
Sleep on it

Rose

I just got off the phone with Cami. She told me Mags recognised the necklace as being Anna-May's. The implications of that are just starting to sink in.

Was she his victim too? It can't be a coincidence, can it? The necklace, I mean. And if she was, then... then... I could have prevented it. Fuck. I didn't think about girls who might come after me. I didn't *let* myself think about them. I saved my sisters and, when it finally stopped happening, I tried to save myself. Admittedly, I did a pretty shit job of that. But if I'd told someone what he was doing to me, it would probably have saved Anna-May, and maybe other girls too.

Christ, what a mess. As if I wasn't screwed up enough. This is a real headfuck. And, if Anna-May is dead, then I basically killed her, didn't I?

I asked Cami what she and Mags are going to do and she said nothing. Yet. She said they wanted to give me time to think. But I know ultimately they'll want to do the right thing and go to the police. If there's any chance of finding out what happened to Anna-May and getting closure for her parents, I know they'll want to take it. And I know that's the right thing to do, but what about me? It's one thing my sisters knowing what happened to me, but everyone? I don't know if I'm up to that.

And what about Anna-May's parents? Will they blame me for whatever happened? This is all so bloody unfair. And that old bastard isn't even here to face the music. He's still ruining my life from beyond the grave. He got away with it. All of it. He died with everyone still believing he was one of the good guys. I need to speak to Cami and Mags.

'Hey, you two,' I say when the WhatsApp video call connects.

'Hey, you,' two voices answer.

'So, this is a right old mess, isn't it?' I say glumly.

'Yep. What are your thoughts?' Mags asks.

'Muddled. I don't know. I'm torn, to be honest. I know what the right thing to do is…'

'Go to the police with our suspicions?' Cami finishes.

'Yes, but is there any way we can do that without revealing what happened to me?'

'Honestly, Rose, I don't think there is. It's bound to come out one way or another,' Cami says.

'I agree. And it would look worse if you hadn't said something up front,' Mags adds.

'Shit. I suppose I already knew that. I'm just so scared.'

'I know, and it's not fair. Any of it,' Mags smiles sadly.

'It's bloody not,' I say.

'I just think we have a moral obligation to go to the police,' Mags says.

'Mags is right,' Cami agrees. 'I know it sucks, Rose, and we won't do anything without your agreement, but…'

I'm trying hard not to cry.

'It might not be as bad as you think though. With the support of your counsellor, and all the progress you've made,' Cami continues.

'She might even say it would help with your recovery,' Mags suggests.

'I know you're both trying to help, to make me feel better, but I feel sick to my stomach at the thought of people knowing.'

'People that matter – the ones who know and love you – won't see you any differently,' Cami says.

'We both know that's not true, Cams, but thanks for trying,' I reply.

Cami pulls an apologetic face. 'I'm sorry, Rose, there really is no easy way forward, and nothing we can say to make it better.'

Mags pulls a matching face.

'Bloody hell! This is a nightmare. Just when I think I'm starting to heal, I'm gonna have the stitches yanked out again and I'll have to start the process all over again. And the girls, my girls, how can I tell them?' The tears are flowing now at the prospect of telling my daughters about the abuse.

'The girls are mature, intelligent young women, and they'll understand. Yes, of course, they'll hurt for you, but I really believe your relationship with them is rock solid,' Cami says.

'I agree with Cami. You've done such a great job with Bella and Jess. I'm sure they'll be one hundred percent supportive,' Mags adds.

'I can't bear the thought of them seeing me differently, and of people pitying me,' I say through the tears.

'People aren't going to forget the Rose they've known for forty-plus years because of something that happened when you were a child,' Cami insists.

'I'm scared though. I'm so scared.'

'We know. Wish we could hug you right about now,' Mags says.

'Whatever happens, you're not on your own and you can lean on us as much as you need to,' Cami says.

'Thank you, both. Can I sleep on it?' I ask.

'Yes, of course, take as much time as you need,' Cami says.

'Okay,' I sigh. 'I'll speak to you both soon. I'm now off to have a very large gin.' I realise what I've said. 'Sorry, Mags, that was tactless. You could probably do with a very large gin right now too. Please don't let me derail you.'

We say our goodbyes and end the call.

Mags

I phone Cami straight back.

'Well, this sucks,' I say.

'Bloody does,' Cami agrees. 'It's all so unfair on Rose.'

'I know. Just when she's doing so well with her counselling. I wanted to ask, did you tell her about the laptop, and that password-protected file?'

'No. I thought the necklace was bombshell enough. The idea that there might be evidence of her abuse on there felt like too much.'

'Good move. She'll have to know sometime though.'

'One step at a time, Mags, I think.'

I sigh. 'Rose was right about one thing. I really could use a drink.'

'I bet. Are you doing okay though?'

'One day at a time, that's all I can focus on.'

'You're doing great, double dee,' Cami says, laughing.

'Sod off. Anyway, don't know about double dee, but I could do with a double G and T,' I say, laughing too.

'Did you have a go at cracking the password for the locked file?' Cami asks, getting the conversation back on track.

'Yeah. No joy. If it does contain what we suspect, I guess he would've gone a lot less obvious.'

'Hm. We might never crack it, but I'm assuming the police would?'

'Yeah. I just wish we could know what's on there before it gets to the police – you know, so we can prepare Rose.'

'It might not even be stuff that relates to Rose. Might just be stuff off the internet, you know, general stuff.'

'Yeah, hopefully that's the case. God, that sounds terrible.'

'It's okay, I know what you mean. It would be the lesser of two evils.'

'Thinking about it logically, Rose was abused in the 1970s, so there's unlikely to be any digital evidence of it, is there?'

'Hopefully. God, I don't think I could handle seeing pictures of Rose on there.'

'Me neither. Just have to wait and hope.'

'Oh well, nothing more we can do now, I s'pose, except wait and see what Rose says.'

'Yep.'

We say our goodbyes and hang up. I head to the fridge and the bottle of Coke. I'm well aware that the gremlins in my head are screaming to be fed.

Before I turn in for the night, I spend a bit of time trying random passwords to open the file on Ken's laptop. No joy and I close the thing down with a sigh. I have a really bad feeling about what's going to happen next.

Chapter 29
Call the police

Rose

Sleep eludes me again, as it does so often of late. I toss and turn for an hour or more, before resorting to a sleep hypnosis thing on YouTube. It promises to make me fall asleep in minutes, so I can't understand why it therefore runs for just over an hour.

When I wake the next morning, I realise I don't remember much of the recording at all, so it lived up to its promise. And now all I can think about is what's on the rest of it? Has anyone ever stayed awake long enough to find out? Maybe I should listen to it during the day? Maybe not when I'm driving though, eh? Just in case.

Anyway, I'm grateful to the man who helped get me to sleep. I think he might become a regular night-time visitor. It's been a long time since I had a man in bed with me. I don't often let myself think about the rest of my life. And the rest of David's life. I don't think it really bothers me that I might never have sex again, but it does bother me that I might never have that closeness again. Mind you, since the menopause, I'm as dry as a desert and probably about as appealing. At least I never have to worry about David leaving me for a younger woman.

As I plod downstairs to make tea and unlock the back door for the carer to come in, I force my thoughts back to the matter in hand: what to do about the necklace. I really wish they'd never found it, and that Mags hadn't recognised it. Blissful ignorance would have been entirely preferable. I know what the right thing to do is, but the right thing isn't always the easy thing, is it?

I take my tea back up to bed and try to rally my thoughts, but they simply go round in circles and get me precisely nowhere. Eventually I give up and get up, frustrated that I'm no closer to knowing what to do.

The carer's been by the time I'm showered and dressed, and David is sitting at the computer in the study. He spends most of his days there now, sat in his wheelchair. I don't often let myself think about what his life's been reduced to. I wonder if he thinks about the fact that he'll probably never sleep with a woman again? God, how depressing this all is. If this is it for the rest of my life, I honestly don't know if I want to bother. What's the point?

I can feel myself spiralling and I know I have to do something about it, but it's getting harder every time. The bulb in the light at the end of the tunnel has blown. There's been a rock-fall too, and I can't even see the entrance today.

Deciding it's too early for gin, I make coffee for me and David. I give his shoulder a squeeze and kiss the top of his head when I take his in. I'm guiltily aware that I rarely show him any sign of affection these days.

To ease my guilty conscience a little, I make a lemon drizzle cake which has always been David's favourite. He seems pleased when I put a piece in front of him after lunch. I must make more of an effort.

While I'm in this trying-to-do-the right-thing mode, I message my sisters.

Before I change my mind, you're both right, we have to tell the police about the necklace. Let's talk tonight. Xx

I'm not expecting to hear back from them as they're both at work, and am surprised when two messages of love and support ping back almost immediately. It's reassuring to know they really are there for me and have got my back.

I struggle to settle to anything for the rest of the day. I'm terrified by the thought of what's to come. David's in bed by eight thirty and I settle myself into my chair in the lounge for the call with Cami and Mags.

'Yo,' Mags is the first to speak when the video call connects.

'Yo,' I reply.

'Yo yo,' Cami responds.

'Muppets,' I say. Neither of them denies it.

'Had time to think?' Mags asks.

'Sadly, yes. In between eating lemon drizzle cake,' I sigh.

'And? What did you conclude?' Cami asks.

'That I really love lemon drizzle cake.'

'Muppet,' Cami says. 'What else?'

'Well, cake generally, I suppose,' I reply.

'Oh God, it's going to be one of those conversations, is it?' Mags groans.

I just nod.

'Seriously, though, have you thought about what you want us to do about the necklace?'

'Um, yeah, pretend you didn't find it? Bury it in the garden? Chuck it in the sea?'

'I wish it was that easy, Rose, but Margery saw it too. What if we ditched it and then she told someone about it?' Mags says, pulling an I'm sorry face.

'Arse,' I say.

'Rude,' Mags says.

'Not you, dopey.'

'Don't you start with the dopey dartboard thing too!' Mags says, laughing.

'Back to the matter at hand, muppets,' Cami says. 'What are we going to do?'

We spend the next fifteen or so minutes concocting a plan of action and say our goodbyes. I would quite like to either leave the country now, or hide under my duvet until it's all over. I settle for another large piece of cake.

Cami

Sometimes I hate being the sensible sister. I suppose Mags will always be the baby, even now, and she has enough to deal with trying to stay clean and sober. And, I have to admit, I'm in a pretty good place right now, with Lydia in my life. I've told Lydia everything about Rose and the necklace and our suspicions. Rose and Mags don't know that though. I'm not sure they'd approve of me confiding in someone outside the family. But I trust Lydia completely, and I want our relationship to be based on trust and honesty. My two marriages never stood a chance, looking back. I wasn't being honest with myself, let alone with anyone else. Well, I won't make the same mistakes again.

I've phoned the main police station and have an appointment

to go in and speak to a detective this afternoon. Mags has dropped the laptop and necklace round to me and I know what I have to say. I've never been in a police station before and I'm feeling a little anxious about the whole situation. Lydia offered to come with me, but I was worried that would get back to Rose. I feel bad about lying by omission to her and Mags, but I will tell them at some point, when this has all worked itself out.

I arrive at the police station in good time, and a uniformed officer greets me at the front desk. She makes a call and tells me to take a seat, someone will be down to collect me soon. I take a deep breath and sit on one of the hard plastic chairs opposite the desk. I don't know why I'm so nervous.

It's only a couple of minutes before a be-suited man appears through a door to my left and crosses the lobby to greet me.

'Mrs Lawson?' he smiles and extends his hand. 'DS Peters.'

'Yes, that's me. Do call me Cami though,' I say, shaking his hand. He has a firm grip which is somehow reassuring. I relax a little. I feel like I'm in safe hands.

'Cami, of course. This way,' he gestures towards the door and I follow him as he swipes his badge to open it and leads me up a flight of stairs. We go through an open-plan office with half a dozen or so people at their desks, and then DS Peters opens a door to an interview room. It's like the rooms you see on TV, sparsely furnished with table and chairs, and I feel my anxiety rising again. I shouldn't be in a room like this.

DS Peters is clearly reading me. 'Please, don't worry, it's just the quietest place to talk, without phones ringing and so on. Can I get you a cup of tea? Glass of water?'

'No, no thanks, I'm fine,' I say, shaking my head. I just want to get this over with now.

'Okay, have a seat,' DS Peters says, gesturing to one of the chairs, which I'm relieved to see aren't bolted to the floor.

DS Peters sits down opposite and smiles at me. He places a manilla folder and a notebook and pen on the table in front of him. I hadn't even noticed he was holding them before. 'Right, so I understand you've got some information regarding an old missing person case, Cami?'

'Um, yes, well, it might be nothing of course, but…' I babble nervously.

'Take your time, Cami, just start at the beginning.'

'Well, I suppose it started when we found the necklace.' I suddenly remember it's in my bag and I rummage in the side pocket, producing the necklace which is now in a small polythene bag. I pass it across the table. 'I'm afraid we did touch it – me, Mags my sister and Margery. Sorry. We didn't realise what we were looking at then.' I'm babbling again.

DS Peters smiles. 'Don't worry, you haven't done anything wrong, Cami. Keep going.'

I have to give him credit at this point. He really is very good at calming me down. 'Sorry,' I say again. 'So, anyway, when Mags saw the necklace, she thought she recognised it from somewhere. And somewhere turned out to be around the neck of a girl who went missing when we were kids.'

'So, that would be Anna-May Lawrence, the girl you told my colleague about on the phone?'

'Yes, yes, Anna-May. I think she was fifteen when she disappeared, and they never found a body. It was 1978, or thereabouts. I expect you know all about it anyway?' I realise that the detective probably wasn't even born when Anna-May disappeared as I say this.

'Yes, it was the summer of 1978. I have the original missing person file,' he says, indicating the file on the table. It's not a particularly thick file, it has to be said. 'So, tell me where you found the necklace.'

'Um… in the house of our old neighbour… my sister's godfather. He died recently and we, his sister Margery and I, were looking for things mentioned in the will. The necklace was in a box in a chest of drawers in his bedroom.' I pause, wondering if I'm making sense.

'So, this neighbour, this man…'

'Ken. Ken Abbott.'

'Ken. Why were you surprised to find such an item in his house? What made you suspicious?'

I can feel my heart rate quickening as I feel the moment of awful truth approaching. I can only delay it for so long.

'Well, you see, he'd never married or had children. And he didn't have any nieces, only nephews, so we couldn't think of a reason for him to have it. Especially not in a chest of drawers in his bedroom.'

'Okay, but you mentioned he was your sister's godfather? Could it have been for her?'

'Well, yes, we did consider that was a possibility, but then when Mags, that's my sister, saw it she thought she'd seen one just like it somewhere, and…' DS Peters interrupts. 'So, Ken was Mags' godfather?'

'Oh, no, no, he was Rose's godfather. Sorry, this is all sounding rather confusing.' I spend the next couple of minutes explaining the family dynamics.

'Right, I'm with you. So, going back to Mags, how did she come to realise the necklace could have been Anna-May's?'

I explain about the photographs then, and the one with Anna-May. 'They're on his laptop. Here, I brought it with me.' I reach into my bag for a second time and pull out the laptop. 'I brought the charger too. I assume you'll want to keep it for now?'

'Yes, we'll certainly want to take a look.'

'We... um... we guessed his password to get into it,' I admit. 'I hope that's okay?' I say sheepishly. 'I've written it down for you,' I say, passing him a yellow Post-It note.

'Saves us a job,' DS Peters says, taking the piece of paper and sticking it on the file. 'Dollshouse63. Can you tell me what the significance of that is?'

'Er... well, yes, Rose was born in 1963, and Ken gave her a dolls' house for her birthday one year.'

'They must have been very close? For his password to relate to her.'

I can see how DS Peters made detective. He's very good.

'Um, yes, you could say that.' Come on Cami, you're going to have to tell him sooner or later. I can't help protecting Rose for as long as possible though.

'There is a file on the computer which is locked and we couldn't crack that one. It's called Bank.'

'So that could simply be financial records.' He looks at me quizzically and I can feel him trying to read me. 'But you don't think so, do you, Cami?'

I shake my head. 'No, I don't.' I take a deep breath. 'I, we, think it might be child pornography. You see, Ken Abbott was a paedophile.'

If DS Peters is shocked, he doesn't show it. 'That's quite an allegation. What makes you think that?'

It's now or never. 'Because I found out recently that he started abusing my sister Rose when she was nine years old.' I realise my hands are shaking. No going back now though.

'Take your time, Cami. I know this is hard.'

'Sorry, it is still so raw, and Rose doesn't want people to know, so it's hard, you know?'

'Of course, I totally understand. I have to ask you this, Cami, and I don't want you to take it the wrong way, but do you believe Rose?'

'What? Yes, yes, of course I do! Why on earth would she make up something like that?'

'I'm sorry, but I had to ask.'

'It all makes so much sense now – our childhoods and why Rose was the way she was back then. She kept it secret all these years, until after Ken died.' I fill DS Roberts in on more of the gory details, concluding with the fact that Rose inherited the house.

'So, that's why you came to be in his house, I see.'

I nod. 'And if you'd seen the state Rose was in when she went back into the place for the first time, you'd never have asked if she was telling the truth. She's only now getting the help she needs to come to terms with what happened to her, and this thing with Anna-May has rather derailed her. She's worried about everyone knowing, especially her daughters. Is there any way she can be kept out of it? The investigation, I mean?'

'I can't promise that. We will need to speak to Rose at some point. It might be better if she told her daughters herself, in case it has to come out as a result of our investigation.'

'I thought you might say that,' I sigh.

DS Peters smiles at me, sympathetically. 'So, if I'm

understanding you correctly, you think Anna-May might also have been abused by Mr. Abbott and that he's involved in her disappearance somehow?'

'Yes, that's what we're thinking. Anna-May even looked a bit like Rose back then, you know, if he had a type.'

'He never touched you or Mags?'

I shake my head vehemently. 'No, and we have Rose to thank for that.' I explain about Ken's threats to hurt me or Mags if she told. 'And she never did.' I can feel a lump in my throat as I think about what Rose endured all those years to keep me and Mags safe. 'Sorry,' I say, 'I think I have a bad case of survivor's guilt.'

'It's okay. I understand. We will need to have access to Mr. Abbott's house, of course. And we will need to speak to both your sisters, and to Mr. Abbott's sister.' He looks back through the notes he's been making. 'Margery.'

'Oh, will you? Margery doesn't know about any of this. Can't she be kept out of it. For now, at least?'

'I'm sorry, Cami, I don't think that's going to be possible.'

I put my face in my hands and rub my eyes. 'No, I see. God, what a mess.'

'You've done the right thing, coming to us. I do think you should get Rose to tell her daughters the truth though. It'll be better coming from her.'

I exhale. And nod.

'Okay, so I just need contact details for everyone involved now. And do you have the keys for the house? Or would you prefer to be at the property when we go in to search it?'

'Um… oh God, I don't know. Perhaps I should be there in case my dear mama spots you. She still lives next door.'

'No problem, I can give you a call to set that up. It'll probably be in the next day or so.'

We wind up the interview soon after, and I shake hands with DS Peters once more. 'Thanks for your time. And patience. It's all been a bit of a shock as you can imagine.'

'No problem, Cami. You did great. Let me show you the way out and I'll speak to you soon.'

Chapter 30
The bonfire buddleia

Mags

Why is it that anything to do with the police makes me feel automatically guilty? Like when you're driving and there's a police car behind you, you always feel like you're doing something wrong, and suddenly start driving like you're on your test.

I'm waiting in my car outside Ken's house for the police search team to turn up and I've actually just checked my coat pocket for drugs. For God's sake, Mags, get a grip. Cami'd rung me in a panic because something had come up at work and she couldn't make it. I really wish she'd just given them the keys. I haven't dared look across to Mum's. I'm just hoping she doesn't look out the window. God knows how I'll explain what's going on if she does. Although there's a part of me that wants to tell her exactly what *is* going on, and what *was* going on all those years ago right under her nose. With any luck, it might be the death of her. Christ, I am so going to hell.

I don't have long to wait before two cars pull up: an unmarked one, and a white van with 'Forensic Investigation' on the side. Well, bugger me, that's a bit of a giveaway. I take a deep breath, stick a smile on my face, and get out of the car, to be greeted by a very good-looking man who I estimate to be in his late thirties.

He looks a little surprised to see me, expecting Cami as he was.

'DS Peters? Hello, I'm Mags. Cami couldn't make it after all, so I'm afraid you've got me.'

'Mags. Hello. Thanks for coming,' he says, smiling at me and shaking the hand I've extended.

Cami hadn't mentioned how drop-dead gorgeous he was, but then I suppose he was the wrong sex for her to notice such a thing these days. His handshake is reassuringly firm – something Cami had informed me of. He meets my eyes steadily, and I feel a little flutter of attraction deep in the pit of my stomach. I let go of his hand and turn towards the house, eager to conceal the flush I can feel on my cheeks. *Pull yourself together, Mags, you're old enough to be his... well... much older sister*, I think to myself.

I lead the way to the house and unlock the front door. It's cold inside and I shudder involuntarily.

'Could you show me where you found the necklace, Mags?' DS Peters asks.

'Yes, of course, upstairs,' I say, leading the way. 'I wasn't the one who found it, of course, that was Cami. And Margery – his sister.' I open the door to Ken's bedroom and feel another shudder. DS Peters notices. Cami'd said he was perceptive.

'Sorry, I know this must be hard for you, Mags. Finding out what happened to your sister.'

'Yes, it is. Very.' I go to open the chest of drawers, but he stops me.

'Sorry, I know your fingerprints are already all over the

house, but if you could try not to touch anything today? We will be taking your fingerprints and those of your sisters to eliminate them from our findings in due course.'

'Oh, yes, of course. Sorry.' I gesture towards the drawer. 'It was in there, inside a little wooden box.'

'Okay, thanks,' the policeman says, opening the drawer with gloved hands and sifting through the contents. Finding nothing of interest, he closes the drawer once more. 'So, Cami mentioned that you found Mr. Abbot's laptop, and that you also recognised the necklace as being Anna-May's?'

'Yes, I found the laptop under the bed. I didn't realise the necklace was the same as Anna-May's until later – it just looked familiar, you know? It was only when I saw the photo later on.'

He just nods.

'And you unlocked the screen and found the file called Bank, is that right?'

'Yes, well, with Cami's help, I suppose.'

He nods again. He's making me nervous now.

'Did Mr. Abbott ever touch you, Mags?'

I'm taken aback at the question. 'No, no, never. Just Rose.'

'Sorry, had to ask,' he says, smiling gently. 'And you had no reason to doubt Rose's story?'

'No. Absolutely not. Not for a second.'

'Okay.' There's that smile again. 'Right, well, if you want to wait downstairs in the lounge. Don't s'pose there's any chance of a cuppa?'

'Um... I'd have to get some milk. I expect there's coffee if you don't mind it black?' I'm kicking myself for not thinking about bringing milk.

He turns that smile on me again, and I find myself offering

to go and buy some. I trot downstairs, check for teabags and sugar before heading out to my car. There's a supermarket a few minutes' drive away. I make a mental note to buy biscuits too. Thankfully, there's no sign of Mum as I leave the house.

When I get back to the house, DS Peters is in the lounge talking to a man in white coveralls. They stop talking as I enter the room and I can't help wondering what they were saying. For some reason, I find myself wanting this younger man to think well of me. For God's sake, Mags, this way lies trouble.

I boil the kettle and make tea, and put out the biscuits on a plate. Then I take a seat on the sofa, nursing a mug of tea and wishing it was something stronger.

Occasionally, DS Peters comes in and asks me a question about the house.

'What do you think you might find?' I ask him after one such visit. 'I mean, after all this time?'

'Maybe nothing, but you never know. People can be careless when they think no one suspects them of any wrongdoing. And if he was a paedophile, it's unlikely that he just stopped scratching the itch.'

I nod. 'That's what we thought. That's why we think there must be stuff on his computer. And there might have been other girls, mightn't there? I mean, apart from Rose.'

DS Peters shrugs and raises his eyebrows. 'We shouldn't speculate at this stage, but we're certainly keeping an open mind.'

'So, what happens next?' I ask.

'Well, we need to try and establish if the necklace really was Anna-May's, so we'll be speaking to her parents and getting a DNA sample. We have to pray there's trace contact DNA on the necklace for a comparison.'

'Could there be? Even after all this time?'

'It's entirely possible. DNA doesn't degrade on surfaces for a very long time, and if the necklace had been worn next to the skin over a period of time, we might strike gold.'

'Well, silver,' I chip in.

DS Peters looks momentarily puzzled. Why did I have to say that? 'Ah! Yes, the necklace is silver, isn't it?' he says, finally.

'And what if there's isn't any DNA? What then?'

He shrugs again. 'It's going to be difficult after all the time that's elapsed, but we'll do everything we can.'

I nod my head slowly, thinking of Anna-May's parents, of Rose, of all the lives which are about to be turned upside down. Again.

DS Peters interrupts my thoughts.

'We're going to take a look around the garden, Mags, and search the shed. Would you mind coming out with us? It would be useful to know if there have been any obvious changes over the years.'

'Yes, of course, although I'm not sure how reliable my memory will be after all this time.' I put my mug on the table and follow the police officer through to the garden.

We stand on the patio just outside the conservatory and I let my gaze travel round the garden. At first glance, it looks pretty much the same as I remember: the central lawn, bordered by flowerbeds, leading to a few fruit trees at the far end. I close my eyes and try to cast my mind back. I can feel eyes on me, and I open my own to find DS Peters watching me.

'Okay?' he asks.

I nod. 'This bit's the same, the patio,' I say, gesturing around me. 'Maybe if we walk round?' I start to walk slowly up the garden, looking around as I go. 'It really doesn't look that different from the way I recall it.'

We continue up the garden. I stop at the back edge of the lawn. To the left is a greenhouse and to the right a shed.

'I think the shed is new. I mean, there was always a shed there, but this looks like a different one. The old one was smaller, I think. The greenhouse looks the same.' I walk a little further on. 'There was always a compost heap there,' I say, pointing to the left-hand corner behind the greenhouse. 'And the bonfire...' I begin, turning to the opposite corner and walking a few feet further on. 'There was always a bonfire here. Ken was always having bonfires. I remember Mum telling him nothing would ever grow there.'

Growing out of the blackened earth now, however, is a buddleia, a butterfly bush.

Chapter 31
This way be dragons

Mags

The search winds up soon afterwards. The forensics guy had a look in the shed and conferred briefly with DS Peters on the lawn, before packing up to leave. As far as I could see, they didn't take much from the house – just a few of those evidence bags you see on the TV shows. I can't help wondering what's in them.

DS Peters thanks me for my time. 'We'll be in touch if we need anything else,' he says, before shaking my hand and giving me another of those winning smiles.

'No problem,' I tell him, smiling back. 'Call me anytime,' I add, the words escaping my lips before I have a chance to stop them. 'Way to sound desperate, Mags,' I mutter to myself as I watch DS Peters leave.

As I rinse the mugs, I think again about what will happen now. What if they prove the necklace *did* belong to Anna-May? Then what? Would it all have to come out? Everything that happened to Rose. 'God, what a nightmare,' I groan.

With the mugs dried and put away, I take a quick tour of the house to see what state it's been left in. It all looks tidy enough though; the only real signs of the forensic search are several areas with a dusting of charcoal-grey powder over them. When I check the bedroom, I see several of these on the bedside cabinet and the chest of drawers in which we'd found the necklace. I remember what DS Peters had said about taking our fingerprints to eliminate them. While I didn't relish the prospect of being fingerprinted, I'd be quite happy to have another opportunity to see the attractive young policeman. An image of a disapproving Cami pops into my head. 'Yeah, yeah, I know!' I'm fully aware what my sisters think of me and the opposite sex.

I stick my head in the bathroom; more of the grey powder here, and a toothbrush conspicuous by its absence from the holder by the sink. Concluding the police must have taken it to test for DNA, I wonder again what else they took. With Ken having been cremated, there was no other way of getting his DNA, I suppose.

As I'm locking up the front door, my phone pings with a text message from Cami.

Hiya. All done? How'd it go?

Yep, all done. No problems. Don't know what, if anything, they found.

Sorry to have lumbered you with it.

No worries. It was fine. I'm thinking of DS Peters as I write this.

Good. I wonder what will happen next?

Dunno. I s'pose they'll be in touch soon enough.

Yep. Was it DS Peters?

It was indeed. You didn't tell me what a bit of alright he is.

Down girl! Cami writes. I can almost see her rolling her eyes.

What? I'm only human. Doesn't hurt to look.

Hm. As long as that's all you do. I know what you're like.
I don't know what you mean, adding a winking face.
He's too young, Mags. And too policeman-y.
Don't worry, I'm not about to throw myself at him.
Good. Right, I've got another meeting to get to. Well done today.
Thank you. Speak soon.

I start the engine just in time to see Mum come out of her house and look over in my direction. I quickly look away, hoping she hasn't spotted me, and pull away from the kerb.

Rose

Try as I might, I can't keep what's happening at *his* house out of my mind. And that's where I feel like I'm going. Out of my mind. The prospect of everyone finding out what happened to me all those years ago is almost unbearable. Almost. I bear it because what other choice is there? The thought of my own daughters knowing hurts my heart. I can't bear the thought of them thinking differently of me; seeing me differently. I suppose it might help them understand why I was so protective of them growing up. Why I still am really. When Jess had said she was going travelling I had felt sheer panic. I worried about her constantly, despite regular, reassuring calls. Watching *The Serpent* on iPlayer probably hadn't been the best idea either. I regularly had nightmares about her being drugged, or robbed, or worse.

Maybe, if there is a silver lining to this bloody great black cloud, then my daughters understanding me a little better might be it. I wasn't just a neurotic, over-protective parent for no reason; I had a very good reason. And now it might be coming back to haunt not only my sleeping hours, but my waking ones too.

I know the police search was happening today. I haven't heard from Cami or Mags. I expect they're trying to protect me from it, but I can't leave it all to them, as much as I might like to. It simply wouldn't be fair. I've already caused them so much pain. I have to share the burden now, and not add to the great weight of emotional baggage already heaped on their shoulders. My recent run-in with our mother was a stark reminder that my sisters still suffer at her hands. And tongue. Another glimmer of the silver lining for me, perhaps.

I'm fully aware that I have decisions to make concerning the inheritance. I'm so angry *he* seems to be having the last laugh. Safe beyond the grave, immune from the shame and punishment that should have come to him in life. If only I'd been stronger, braver, and told someone. Could I have saved other girls from the horrors I endured? Would Anna-May still be here? Raising a family of her own somewhere, safe and happy and living a good life. I know deep down that's not the case. In the moments when I'm totally, painfully, honest with myself, I have to admit that she is dead, whether at his hands or those of another. I suppose we'll never know, and I will have to live with the guilt for the rest of my life.

Don't go down that path, I tell myself. There be dragons. David saves me from going any further, calling from the downstairs loo.

'Coming!' I call. I find him naked, having stepped out of his shorts and now unable to get back into them. I clean him up and help him into them once more. *This is my life now*, I think with a sigh.

Once David is settled back at the computer I phone Mags, deciding I need to be proactive and face things head-on, dragons or not. I need to take back whatever control I can, and keeping myself informed of proceedings is part of that. Mags answers on the second ring.

'Hey, Rose. How goes it?' she asks.

'Oh, you know, same shit different day. Literally in this case as David just got stuck in the loo again.'

'Oh dear! How's his physio going? Any improvement?'

'Slow. There really doesn't seem to be much, if any, improvement anymore. I'm not sure he'll actually get much better now,' I say sadly. It's a painful admission to make out loud.

'Sorry to hear that. It can't be easy for either of you.'

'No, but I'm kind of resigned to it now I think. He's the father of my beautiful girls and I owe him this. I think he deserved, deserves, better, but this is our lot. Just got to get on with it.'

'You both deserved better, Rose. Don't give up hope.'

'It's hard to have hope, Mags, especially with this can of worms that's been opened, not knowing what's going to come out. Other than worms,' I say grimly.

'I know. I wish we could do more to help, Cami and I. You know we'll do whatever we can though, don't you?'

'Yes, I do, and I'm so grateful, but I can't leave it all to you two. I have to do my share. That's why I'm calling really, to find out how the police got on at the house today.'

'Oh, okay. It was fine, honestly. I don't know if they found anything of interest – they didn't seem to take much away. I reckon they took a toothbrush. For DNA testing I s'pose. They will want our fingerprints at some point, you know, to eliminate us from things. You might be able to go into your local police station to do it. Sorry, I should've asked,' Mags says.

'Don't apologise, Mags. I think I might come down there soon and face this thing head-on, and speak to the police. It feels like I'm just putting off the inevitable otherwise.'

'That's a good attitude to have, I think. Take back the control.'

'Exactly what I thought. I'm buggered if I'm going to let *him* control me any longer. I refuse to let him have the last word.'

'Good for you! When do you think you'll be down?' Mags asks.

'Just as soon as I can arrange cover for David,' I tell her.

We wind up the call soon after, with promises to speak soon, and I get straight onto the care agency. It's time to take this dragon by the horns.

Chapter 32
The calm before

Cami

Rose is due to arrive today, and I've prepared my spare room for her. Mags is going to join us for dinner tonight and I've got a pork and cider casserole in the slow cooker. I'll do some mashed potatoes later. I think we're going to need comfort food.

I spoke to Rose a couple of days ago and she sounded strangely calm. I can't shake the feeling that a storm is coming though. Mags has arranged for us to go in to the police station tomorrow. They're going to take statements from us, and our fingerprints and DNA. I feel quite anxious about it. This isn't something normal people do. Thinking about it though, I suppose our family never was normal. We just have to get through it, and we will. Stronger together.

Rose asked if Lydia would be joining us for dinner, but I really don't think this is the right time. I haven't admitted to Rose and Mags that I've confided in Lydia, and I don't want to spend the evening treading on more eggshells than is necessary. The bloody worms everywhere are going to be bad enough. Anyway, I don't think I'm ready to share Lydia yet. I want to enjoy our blossoming relationship without the taint of my family for as long as possible. I had to tell her everything though. I had to explain the scars on my legs. Thankfully, Lydia is incredibly understanding and supportive. I'm honestly not sure what I'd've done without her these past weeks. I feel bad that Mags doesn't have someone she can lean on though. I almost feel guilty for being happy. I'm so proud of how Mags is handling her recovery and being single. I just hope she doesn't blow it by chasing after a certain policeman. She says she won't, but she was rather eager to phone him to arrange for us to go into the station. Time will tell, I suppose.

Mags

Dinner with my sisters tonight. As much as I'm looking forward to us all being together again, I'm nervous. Rose sounded too calm somehow when I last spoke to her. I have a bad feeling that it won't, can't, last and that at some point something's going to blow. The thought of what might happen makes me anxious, tense, and makes it all the harder to stay sober. Several times a day I find myself wishing I could have a drink or something to take the edge off. My Coke consumption has gone up dramatically. At least I'm not snorting it up my nose though. It takes all my resolve to resist and I'm scared it might all become too much for me to cope with. I want to be strong, for Rose, and for myself. I know I only have one shot at getting this right. If I falter, I know there'll be no getting back up. I have to stay clean and I follow my daily rituals as if my life depends on it. Which it does, I suppose.

DS Peters is in my thoughts way too much, which is also a worry. In the past I would have acted on the attraction, buoyed up by one substance or another. Now it's just something else I have to resist. I can't deny how much I'm looking forward to seeing him again though, even under these awful circumstances. He's the only bright spot on this dark and depressing landscape. Besides, he probably isn't attracted to me anyway. I ignore the little voice in my head asking when did that ever stop me? Focus on Rose, focus on Rose.

Rose

I feel strangely calm as I drive south. I suppose it's some sort of coping mechanism; one of many employed over the years. Just got to get through it and hope I come out the other side vaguely intact. Knowing that David depends on me now has become oddly comforting and I'm focused on the bigger picture of getting home to him again. Home. It's not where I'm heading now. Home, I can now admit, is with David. For better or for worse. No point railing against the cruelty of the fates. This is the hand I've been dealt and I just have to play it out. I no longer have aspirations for more. Not for myself. All my hopes and dreams now rest with my daughters. They will do better. Fare better. They will, must, thrive. Otherwise what has been the point of my life? If they are happy, my life has not been for nothing.

I let my thoughts drift for the remainder of the journey and I'm barely aware of the miles passing. Before I know it, I'm parking the car outside Cami's and ringing her doorbell.

'Hello, you,' Cami says, pulling me into a hug. We stand on the doorstep for some time, arms wrapped tightly around one another. Eventually, Cami lets go of me, reaching out for my overnight bag. 'Here, let me take that,' she says. I follow her into the hall where she puts my bag at the bottom of the stairs to go up later. 'Come into the kitchen and I'll make a cuppa.'

I pull out a chair and sit down at Cami's kitchen table which is a smaller version of my own large scrubbed pine one. The same but different, like us.

'How're you feeling?' Cami asks.

'Okay I s'pose. Bit tired now I've sat down, to be honest.'

'That's understandable. You sounded quite upbeat on the phone when we spoke though.'

'Yeah, I'm trying to be more... not positive exactly... but, I dunno, brave?' I say, shrugging.

'You're bound to be up and down. It's only natural,' Cami says from where she's filling the kettle at the sink.

'I s'pose. I just want to get tomorrow over with and go home and try to forget what's happening to be honest, but I'm determined to face up to this.'

'Good for you,' Cami says, sitting down opposite me and reaching over to squeeze my hand where it rests on the table. 'You're doing great, sis, really. We'll get through this. Just remember you're not alone.'

'I know, and I'm grateful, really I am, even if I don't always show it. I know I can be a cow.'

'Hey, me too. Not our fault. We have cow genes, they're bound to surface from time to time.'

'Mags is never a cow though, is she? I can't remember a time when she wasn't just trying to please everyone.'

'Maybe she was adopted?' Cami says.

'Lucky cow,' I say, and we both laugh, the atmosphere lightened once more.

'She has a bit of a crush on the policeman in charge of the investigation,' Cami says, getting up to make the tea. 'Bit of a worry when she's been doing so well. I am concerned that she's vulnerable at the moment.'

'God, I feel like that's my fault too,' I groan.

'No! Don't be daft. None of this is your fault, Rose, and you must keep that in your head – you were the victim in all of this.' Cami must see the expression on my face change at her use of the word victim. 'Sorry,' she says. 'But you know what I mean. You were just a child. The only blame should go to Ken. Well, and to Mum, for being an all-round shit mother.'

'She really was, wasn't she?' I agree, sighing.

'Yep,' Cami says, nodding her head sadly. 'I really wish she'd been the sort of mum you could have gone to and confided in. Even if she couldn't see what was going on right in front of her nose, you should have been able to tell her what was happening.'

I sigh again. 'So many regrets, Cami, so many things I wish I'd done differently. I thought I was doing what I had to to protect you and Mags. But I fucked up both your lives anyway.'

'Ahem! What did I just say?' Cami reprimands.

'Sorry.' I can't help myself. I feel such overwhelming guilt.

'Don't make me ahem you again,' Cami says, putting down a mug of tea in front of me. 'Where's that positive mental attitude I heard on the phone?'

'Well, I'm positive I'm mental and got an attitude,' I shrug.

'Hey, you and me both,' Cami laughs.

'Mags is just mental, without the attitude.'

'Yeah, strange how different she is in some ways. Maybe being the youngest has something to do with it.'

'Yeah, maybe. It'll be nice to see her later. What time's she coming round?'

'Straight after work, so about six. We can have a nice relaxed evening, glass of wine or two...' Cami stops herself, and grimaces. 'Oops,' she says.

'Mags doesn't expect us to not drink,' I say.

'No, I know, but it feels a bit mean anyway. She's fragile. It doesn't seem fair to put temptation in her way.'

'On top of the policeman too.'

'Unfortunate turn of phrase there!' Cami grins.

'You don't think she would, do you?' I ask.

'Um... no, I don't think so. Certainly not while there's an active investigation going on.'

'Afterwards?' I ask, pulling a face.

Cami just raises her eyebrows.

'Let's abstain tonight,' I say.

'Yep. Good idea. All for one, and all that.'

We sit in silence for a while, both clearly lost in our thoughts.

It's me who breaks the silence. 'Does abstaining tonight mean we have to now?' I ask sheepishly.

Cami laughs. 'I was just thinking exactly the same thing. We are bad people.'

'Yeah, but I'm happy with that if it means I can have a glass of wine.'

'Are you even going to bother with your tea?'

'There's a joke in there about tea and total, but I'm too tired to put it together.'

'Wine it is then,' Cami says, getting up and going to the fridge. She's soon back at the table with a bottle of New Zealand Sauvignon Blanc and two glasses. 'Sorry, Mags,' she says as she pours it out.

We take our glasses and the bottle through to the lounge and make ourselves comfortable. Whether consciously or not, the conversation switches to safer topics: war, politics…

The sound of the doorbell takes us both by surprise.

Cami looks at her watch. 'Shit. It's almost six, that must be Mags. I haven't done the potatoes. The wine! Bugger. You get the door and I'll get rid of the evidence.'

I can't help laughing. 'We haven't done anything wrong, Cams.'

'No, I know, but, you know…' she says, half out of the room, clutching the now empty bottle and glasses.

'Yes, sadly, I do,' I agree, heaving myself off the sofa and going to greet our younger sister.

I plod to the front door and open it to a smiling Mags. She holds out a supermarket bag. 'I brought wine,' she says.

Chapter 33
Sauce

Mags

I arrived at Cami's right on time but it almost felt like they weren't expecting me or something. I'd proudly handed Rose the bottle of wine I'd bought for them, and Rose had laughed. It wasn't until they explained the whole 'let's abstain for Mags' sake' thing that I understood why. It made me feel kind of uncomfortable to know they must have been talking about me and my 'problems'. I just know that DS Peters' name will have come up too. I suppose all I can do is prove to them I've changed. I'm not the same, weak, girl I was. I'm in control. Just about.

We'd actually had a nice evening in the end though. Rose and I had sat at Cami's kitchen table while she peeled potatoes, and we'd stayed there to eat the casserole. There had been an awkward moment when Cami'd realised she'd cooked with cider and I could see the panic on her face. To be honest, I had the same moment of panic. I'd avoided things cooked with alcohol for over a year, and was anxious about the effect it might have on me. I honestly didn't know how it was going to make me feel.

'Doesn't the alcohol burn off during cooking?' Rose had asked.

'Not completely I don't think,' Cami had said. 'I'm so sorry, Mags, I just didn't think.'

'Please don't apologise. I'm just sorry to be a nuisance,' I'd said.

'You're not a nuisance,' both my sisters had said simultaneously.

'That's nice of you both to say, but I am. A bit. You can admit it,' I said.

'Yeah, okay then, you're a bloody nuisance,' Cami had joked. 'Seriously though, I am sorry, and you're absolutely not.'

'We all need to stop apologising for ourselves,' Rose said. 'Honestly, let's just acknowledge that we're none of us perfect, but that's okay, and stop saying sorry.'

'Hear, hear,' Cami agreed.

'I'll try,' I'd said, but I wasn't convinced I could actually break the habit of a lifetime. I'd already had to break so many, I wasn't sure I had the capacity to add anything else to the list.

'Going back to the sausages...' Cami had begun.

'Does Lydia know?' I'd asked, grinning. I needed to lighten the mood. It was what I did.

Rose laughed with me.

'Oh, ha ha, very funny,' Cami had said. 'Seriously, the sausages...'

Well, that set me and Rose off laughing all the more. Cami raised her eyebrows at us, tutted like a disapproving parent and turned away to attend to dinner. When she turned back to us, she'd speared a sausage on a fork and was taking a big bite.

'Ow, ow, ow... hot, hot, hot!' she'd said, fanning her mouth with her free hand.

'I don't think Lydia has anything to worry about,' Rose said, snorting with laughter.

Cami told us both to eff off at that point, in between gulps of cold water.

'Sorry, Cams,' I said, trying to regain my composure. 'You were saying, about the sausages...' I can't risk making eye contact with Rose at this point.

'I was going to say, I could do you more of a sausage and mash type plate, without all the sauce.' Cami realised too late what she'd said. 'Don't!' she warned us.

'That sounds perfect, thank you, Cami,' I said, stifling more giggles.

'Yeah, she's been off the sauce for a year already,' Rose chipped in.

Cami'd ignored that and busied herself serving dinner. It had felt really good to be happy and laughing together, thoughts of what lay ahead temporarily forgotten.

Rose

I sleep surprisingly well after dinner with my sisters, in spite of the looming police interview. Mags picks us up at ten fifteen in the morning to drive us to the police station.

'You look nice,' Cami says to her. Mags blushes. She does look as though she's made a special effort with her appearance. No prizes for guessing who that's for.

'Thanks. Not too much, is it?' she asks, looking down at herself and smoothing the lines of her floral wrap dress, which she's wearing over knee-high leather boots.

It is a bit much, to be honest, but Cami and I both say of course not. No point denting her already fragile confidence. No doubt Mum would've said something horrible. The cow genes at work again.

We drive the few miles to the police station in silence, none of us wanting to voice what we're probably all thinking. We arrive in plenty of time and are met by DS Peters.

'Thank you for coming in,' he says. 'We'll try and make this as painless as possible.'

I just smile and nod. A lump seems to have developed in my throat. I think Mags mutters something like 'you're welcome, thank you'. She probably blushes too. We follow DS Peters through the door and up a flight of stairs into an open-plan office. I'm starting to feel anxious now, my bravado deserting me.

'Have a seat,' DS Peters says, gesturing to three chairs in front of a desk. He then sits down behind it, smiling reassuringly at us.

I look at him properly for the first time. Mags was right, he is very attractive.

'I know this is nerve-wracking,' he says, 'but it's really nothing to worry about. One of my officers will take you each to have your fingerprints taken, and then a quick swab for your DNA. Then I'll be taking your statement, Rose,' he says, nodding in my direction. 'I've assigned other detectives to interview you, Mags, and you, Cami. It should all be done and dusted in a couple of hours.'

Mags cracks a rather feeble joke about dusting for fingerprints at that point, and I cringe inwardly for her. She really does have a thing for the handsome policeman. He just smiles. He's probably used to women falling at his feet. He does have a very nice manner though. Somehow makes you feel everything's going to be all right. Except it isn't, is it? Not in my case. My dirty laundry is about to get a very public airing. Something I've spent my whole life avoiding. I groan inwardly at the prospect of what's to come.

A uniformed female officer comes and gets Cami first. I smile at her as she gets up, and Mags squeezes her hand. This is a weird experience. Mags disappears next and I'm left alone with DS Peters.

Mags

Cami and I are waiting back at DS Peters' desk when Rose finally reappears. Her body language screams exhaustion, and her face does the same. She looks as though she's been crying. We get up and pull her into a hug.

'You okay?' Cami asks.

Rose nods. 'Just about.'

'Well done for getting through it,' I say, giving her another squeeze.

'I feel absolutely shattered,' Rose says quietly.

'Well, that's not surprising. You've been through the wringer.'

'Come on, let's get you out of here. Home for a cuppa,' Cami says.

'I think I might need something stronger than tea,' Rose says. 'Sorry, Mags.'

'Ahem!' Cami and I exclaim in unison.

'Sorry,' Rose says again.

Cami and I can't help laughing, and even Rose manages a smile.

'Listen,' I say, 'you've got to stop tiptoeing around me where alcohol's concerned. It just makes me feel awkward when you try and avoid mentioning it. Or drinking it, for that matter. I'd really rather you just acted normal around me.'

'What is this *normal* you speak of?' Cami says, an exaggeratedly quizzical expression on her face.

'Yes, I don't think I'm familiar with this concept,' Rose says, matching her expression.

'Don't be dicks,' I say, laughing. 'You know what I mean. Normal for us.'

'Ah! Normal for *us*. This I comprehend,' Cami says, nodding sagely.

'Yes. For normal, read utterly dysfunctional,' Rose adds.

It's at this moment I realise DS Peters has arrived back and is watching us, a bemused expression on his face. I feel my own face flush as I wonder how much he overheard of the exchange with my sisters. It matters way too much that he has a good impression of me. I don't want him to know the truth about me and my tawdry past.

'Are we free to go then?' Cami asks, regaining her composure faster than I.

'Yes, you're free to go, ladies. Thank you all for coming in today. We'll be in touch if we have any additional questions, but that's it for now. Let me show you out.'

'Thank you,' I say, smiling shyly at him. God, he makes me feel sixteen again.

Once outside again, we all take a deep breath in.

'Oof. Glad that's over,' I say.

'Mm,' Cami agrees. 'Not the most fun experience.'

'I've had smear tests more enjoyable, to be honest,' Rose says, grimacing.

'Well, it's done now. Let's get back to Cami's and compare

notes,' I say, taking Rose's arm and heading to the car.

Once safely back at Cami's, we settle ourselves in the lounge.

'How was it for you then?' Cami asks me first. I think we're putting off asking Rose, whether consciously or otherwise.

'Not too bad really. Just asked about Ken and the house and what I remembered from back then. I explained that, as the youngest, my memories were probably a bit unreliable and not very useful. I had no idea he was anything more than the man who brought us sweets and took us places. They asked about Anna-May, but I really don't remember her much at all. I'm not even sure I do remember her as anything other than the girl who disappeared.' I pause then. 'Then they... um... they asked about Rose, you know, what happened to her. But obviously I could only tell them what you told us, Rose. I don't think I was really very much help at all,' I say apologetically.

'You were just a little girl, Mags, you've nothing to be sorry for,' Rose says, smiling gently. 'How about you, Cams? Thumbscrews? Good cop, bad cop?' Rose says, winking, trying to make it easier for us.

'Pretty much the same as Mags, I guess. I told them he gave me the creeps a bit, but that I didn't have any real reason to suspect him of anything.'

'Did they ask if you believed me?' Rose asks.

Cami and I look at each other, both obviously uncomfortable at the question.

Cami responds first. 'They did, and I told them categorically that I believed you.'

'Me too,' I nod vehemently.

'Thank you,' Rose says quietly. 'I wish you hadn't had to go through this. Any of it.'

'It's okay, Rose. We wish you hadn't gone through the horrors you endured. We're in this together now though,' Cami says.

'Absolutely!' I agree.

'I did tell them you changed a lot back then; that you were really angry a lot of the time, and that everything kind of made sense after we found out what had happened. I hope that's okay?' Cami says.

Rose nods sadly. 'Of course. I told them the same thing. And I told them I made your lives a living hell too, always fighting with Mum.'

I feel my chest constrict. 'You didn't tell them about… um… about… you know… my drinking and stuff?'

'No, Mags. Nor about Cami's scars. I still want to protect the two of you if I can. There's going to be enough collateral damage as it is. DS Peters told me they'll have to speak to Mum, not only as our parent, but as his neighbour,' Rose says.

'Oh crap. Didn't think about that,' Cami says.

'Crap indeed,' Rose says, raising her eyebrows. 'He asked me if I want to tell her myself, you know, before they speak to her.'

'Ouch,' I say. 'What are you going to do?'

'Change my identity? Leave the country?' Rose says.

'Do you want me to speak to Mum for you?' Cami offers, grimacing at the prospect.

Rose shakes her head, 'No, that's really sweet of you, but I can't ask you to do my dirty work, either of you. I said I'd sleep on it and let them know tomorrow. DS Peters promised they wouldn't do anything until after they hear from me. He really is a very decent human being.'

'He really is,' I agree, smiling at the thought of him.

'Down girl,' Cami says, grinning at me.

'I know, I know, I'm down. Can't blame a girl for looking though.'

'I know I looked,' Rose says, 'and I'm old enough to be his mother.'

'You won't be surprised to hear I'm totally immune to his charms,' Cami says.

'Well, let's hope he can charm the old battle-axe. Seriously, Rose, what are you going to do?' I ask.

'I seriously don't know,' Rose groans. 'I feel like it's my responsibility to tell her, but I would rather chew my own arm off. I think I'll decide in the morning. Don't suppose I'll be getting much sleep tonight.'

Chapter 34
The confrontation

Rose

As predicted, sleep eluded me as I went over and over whether I should be the one to speak to Mum about the police visit, and the reason for it. I felt sick at the prospect, but still somehow duty-bound to tell her myself. God knows why when she'd been such a lousy mother. I didn't owe her anything, but still some part of me persisted in wanting to protect the woman who'd given birth to me.

I plod downstairs where I find Cami in the kitchen nursing a cup of coffee.

'Morning,' she says. 'Get any sleep?'

I shake my head. 'Not a lot. Spent the time Googling how to get a fake passport and the best destinations for ex-pats with a slightly dodgy past.'

Cami nods. 'Time well spent, when the alternative is confront you-know-who about you-know-what.'

'Yup. I thought so.'

'Have you made a decision?' Cami asks.

'Yeah, I'm gonna bite the bullet.'

'That might be less painful,' Cami says, pulling a face.

'Feel like I have to. It's my mess, my responsibility.'

'That's a brave attitude, but no-one would blame you for letting the police tell her.'

'Maybe not, but I think it's important she hears it from me. Maybe there's a part of me that wants to confront her with it. See her face when she finds out, you know? Is that awful?'

Cami shakes her head. 'Not at all. You have every right to be angry with her, Rose. She let you down.'

'She let all three of us down.'

After breakfast with Cami, I shower and get dressed, ready for battle. I can't decide if I should phone Mum to tell her I'm coming round, or just turn up.

'Maybe just turn up unannounced,' Cami suggests. 'That way she can't make an excuse and say she's going out.'

'Yeah, maybe. I know full well I'll spend the drive over there praying she *is* out.'

'Are you sure you don't want me to come with you?' Cami offers, not for the first time.

I shake my head. 'No, thank you. It's sweet of you, but I wouldn't wish this on my worst enemy.' I pause. 'Thinking about it, she *is* my worst enemy.'

Cami winces. 'Poor you. I wish you didn't have to do this.'

'You and me both. Just need to get it over with now I've made my mind up.' I'm pulling on my coat as I speak. Cami follows me to the front door. 'Wish me luck,' I say.

'Good luck. Be strong. Don't let her get to you.'

'I'll try,' I say, not sounding in the least convinced I'd succeed.

'Just remember you're in control, of the situation, and how you respond to the old cow.'

'That's just it, though, I'm not in control where she's concerned. Look at what happened in the restaurant,' I sigh.

'That was the first time you'd seen her in ages though. Maybe prepare yourself for her to call you Peony.'

'Ugh. Yes. Right, I'll see you later. If I haven't been arrested for murder,' I say grimly.

'Justifiable homicide, I reckon,' Cami says, hugging me goodbye. 'See you in a bit.'

On the short drive to my childhood home, I become aware of my heartbeat increasing as the miles decrease. There's a niggling pain in my temples and a feeling that I might forget to breathe. I wonder if this is how Mags feels when she needs a drink? Or how Cami used to feel before she cut herself? Thinking of my sisters and the pain they've both endured gives me a fraction more resolve.

All too soon, I'm pulling up outside the house. I don't turn to look at the house next door; I can't risk destroying what little equanimity I've maintained on the drive over. Taking a deep breath, I undo my seatbelt, open the car door and heave myself out. I'm still silently praying that Mum will be out. No such luck. I press the doorbell and soon see the silhouette of my mother through the stained glass of the front door. I can't help recalling the number of times I'd smashed the glass, slamming out of the house as an angry teenager.

The door opens. I take a deep breath.

'Hello, Mum.'

'Peony. What are you doing here? Are your sisters okay?' She looks surprised. Not pleased. Just surprised.

Another deep breath. Silently count to ten.

'I... um... I was in the area and I... er...' I stammer, twelve years old again.

'For goodness sake, spit it out!' she spits.

'Can I come in?' I ask, thinking I shouldn't have to ask to be invited in by my own mother, but not wanting to continue this charade on the doorstep.

She makes a sort of harrumph noise, but gestures for me to go in all the same. I lead the way into the kitchen, the scene of so many of our fights. I recognise the same hideous floral table-cloth from my childhood. The niggling in my temples is getting worse and I'm having palpitations now too. The thought that I might suddenly have a stroke pops unbidden into my head. That would be one way of getting out of this, I think grimly. Then who would look after David?

I hover next to the table, not knowing whether I should sit down or not.

I'm still dithering when Mum speaks again.

'Well?' she says. 'To what do I owe the honour?'

'Sit down, Mum, please. Do you want a cup of tea? You're gonna need one,' I mutter under my breath.

'I don't need to be told to sit down in my own house, thank you very much,' she says, folding her arms mutinously and standing resolutely with her back against the work surface.

I close my eyes for a moment, trying to maintain my composure. 'Okay. Don't sit down then. You won't mind if I do though,' I say, pulling out a chair at the end of the table, next to a blousy display of Magnolias on the tablecloth. Mags' face pops into my head. I draw strength from the thought of her, and of Cami, whose floral namesake is also represented on the surface in front of me.

'There's something I need to tell you,' I say finally.

Chapter 35
Fair warning

Rose

'I have to tell you something, Mum,' I repeat. I look up at her, her thin mouth drawn in an unattractive line across her gaunt, hard face. She doesn't speak. 'I have to tell you that the police will be coming to talk to you in the next day or so.'

I watch the expression on her impassive face change to one of sneering distaste. 'What trouble have you gone and got yourself into now?'

I swallow back the painful ball of anger starting to grow in my throat. Why must she always think the worst? Of me, and my sisters: her daughters.

'Oh, you know, just the usual: bit of armed robbery and some arson,' I say, my voice dripping with sarcasm. I regret the words the instant they're out. I mustn't rise to the bait. Don't give her the satisfaction, I reprimand myself.

She tuts. 'I suppose you think that's funny?'

'No, not really,' I sigh, thinking it's actually a darn sight funnier than the actual truth I'm about to hit her with. 'Please, won't you sit down, Mum?' I urge again.

She remains stonily silent and unmoving.

'Okay then,' I begin. 'The police will be coming to talk to

248

you about Uncle Ken…'

'Why on earth would they be coming to talk to me about him?' she interrupts. 'Poor man's barely cold in his grave.'

I resist pointing out that he was cremated. 'It's about something that happened years ago. Something involving him.' I pause. 'And me.'

I see a flash of something I can't read in her face. Fear? Confusion? I don't know.

'Well?' she urges.

'This isn't easy…' I begin again.

'Nothing you could have done would surprise me, my girl,' she says nastily. How could her claiming me as her own sound so repugnant?

I'm fighting tears now. 'It's not something *I've* done. It's something that was done *to* me.' I watch her face, but she has regained control of her features and I can't read anything there. 'It's what *he* did. What Uncle Ken did. *To* me. And not just once. Many, many times. So many times. Right next door. Right under your nose.' I can feel tears streaming down my face now. The dam has burst and there's no stopping the stream of words spilling out of me. Years and years of pent up pain and heartbreak come gushing out. 'He hurt me, Mum, he hurt me so much, and you didn't stop him. Why didn't you stop him? You should have known, should have seen, what was happening to me. What he was doing to me. For years and years, and I couldn't tell you what he was doing to me because he threatened Mags and Cami. Why didn't you protect me? You should have protected me.' I'm sobbing now, a snotty, gabbling mess of pain, barely coherent. I don't even know if she's taken in what I've been saying.

249

When I finally look up, clearing my vision with a wipe of my sleeves, her face is seething with a barely controlled rage; her expression one of hatred and disgust.

'You nasty, foul-mouthed creature!' she screeches finally. 'Get out of my house! How dare you come here and make those disgusting accusations? Get out!'

She doesn't believe me. Something breaks in me, when I didn't think there was anything left to break. Some part of me turns to ice. Another to fire. My own mother thinks I'm a liar; that I would make up something like this, something so horrific.

I shake my head slowly. 'Oh, they're disgusting accusations, all right, but they also happen to be true. What he did to me was beyond disgusting. It was depraved and perverted. He was sick. But you? What's your excuse? What's your excuse for being such a nasty, bitter old cow? For failing your daughters at every turn? Hey? Answer me that. What did we do to deserve such a hateful creature for a mother?'

What little colour she had in her grey complexion has faded. But I can't stop now the floodgates have opened. I want my words to hurt her. I want the wounds to cut deep. As deep as the wounds I've borne all my life. As deep as the scars on Cami's legs, and as deep as the pain I see in Mags' fathomless green eyes when she thinks no-one is looking.

'You were a crap mother, you know that? When did you ever show us love? Hm? Even the merest hint of affection? Show us that we were wanted, that we mattered? I'll tell you when. Never. That's when. You're a hateful old tartar – always have been, probably always will be. It's no wonder Dad left you. It's just a shame he didn't take us with him. If you hadn't driven him away, maybe Ken wouldn't have preyed on me.'

She's shaking now, but I can't stop. I don't want to stop. This has been a long time coming. 'Maybe if you'd been a better mother, you'd have seen what was happening right under your nose. Didn't you ever wonder why I changed? Why I got so bloody angry? Why I cut off my hair? If you'd felt any sort of maternal love, don't you think you'd have asked yourself those questions? And then asked me? But you didn't, did you? No, and he kept on doing it to me. He raped me, over and over again. I was nine years old and he raped me. Ten. Eleven. Twelve. Thirteen. And he got away with it. He didn't get punished for what he did to me, and now it's too late.'

Still she says nothing, but she's unfolded her arms and is holding on to the back of a chair, supporting herself. I feel no remorse at any pain I'm causing her. As far as I'm concerned, she had it coming.

'I probably wasn't his only victim either. Remember Anna-May Lawrence? The girl who disappeared. They think she might have been one of his victims too.'

She has the decency to look shocked at this revelation. It's another barb to my heart that she apparently cares more about somebody else's child than her own. She starts to shake her head at me.

'You're a nasty little troublemaker, Peony. Always were, always will be. I should wash your mouth out with soap and water. I won't listen to any more of your filthy lies. Ken was a good man and I won't have another word said about him, may he rest in peace. I think you should leave now. And don't bother coming back. You're not welcome here anymore.'

'Oh, that suits me just fine. I'd be quite happy if I never had to set eyes on you again. I didn't have to come here today. I could've let the police tell you what was going on. For some reason, I thought you deserved to hear it from me. What a fool I was. I won't be making that mistake again. As far as I'm concerned, you're no longer my mother.' With that, I push my chair back, stand up and start to make my way to the front door. I pause at the bottom of the stairs as a thought strikes me.

Chapter 36
The bonfire

Rose

I head upstairs and open the door to my old bedroom. The room is just the same as when I left it to go to university nearly forty years ago. I shudder as the chill air hits me. Crossing the room, I touch the radiator and find it cold. A money-saving measure no doubt.

Standing in the corner of the room is the object I'm interested in: the dolls' house. I had thought, hoped, I would never lay eyes on it again. The last mention of it had been when Mum suggested, in a rare moment of generosity, I might like it for my own girls. I had declined for obvious reasons.

There's a layer of dust, like snow, on the roof. I open the door and peer inside. It's still filled with the dolls and furnishings added over the years, including the dolls whose hair I cut off. I slam the door shut again and put my arms around the house, hefting it up and leaving the room, kicking the door shut behind me.

Mum is standing at the bottom of the stairs, a look of confused anger on her face. I ignore her, barging past on my way to the back door. I can feel Mum following me.

'What are you doing? Where are you going with that?' she demands.

I don't answer her, but instead put the dolls' house down long enough to unlock and open the door, before heading into the back garden. I don't look back to see if I'm still being followed, but I can no longer feel her presence.

About halfway up the garden is the gate between this garden and Ken's. I put the house on the lawn and draw the bolt back on the gate. By standing on tiptoe I can reach the matching bolt on the other side, and gain access to the garden I haven't set foot in for so very long.

I try to ignore the trembling which has started in my tummy, and walk the thirty or so feet to the top of the garden. It's still obvious where Ken used to have his regular bonfires, but there's now a shrub growing on the patch of scorched earth, which I recognise as a buddleia.

I drop the dolls' house unceremoniously on top of the plant.

'Bugger!' I exclaim aloud, turning on my heel and storming back up the garden and through the gate. I find Mum in the kitchen, where she's on the phone.

'You have to come now. Your sister's here and she's gone completely mad,' she's saying. I raise my eyebrows, wondering if it's Mags or Cami who's been unfortunate enough to get her call. I couldn't care less to be honest. Shrugging, I turn my attention to the matter at hand. Finding what I want next to the cooker, I head back up the garden.

Taking one of the matches out of the box, I strike it and toss it in through one of the tiny windows. I'm rewarded with an instant flicker as the flammable fabrics inside catch. Within seconds the flames are fanning out of the upper storey windows and licking up the roof as the fire spreads. I imagine the plastic dolls melting as toxic fumes hit my nostrils. I step back from the fire as the heat intensifies, becoming aware of my heart pounding in my ears as adrenaline courses through me.

I'm staring, transfixed, at the flames, lost in thoughts of I don't know what, when Cami's voice breaks through.

'Yo! Firestarter!'

I blink and turn to see my younger sisters walking towards me.

'Don't s'pose you brought marshmallows?' I say, grinning at them.

'Unfortunately not. Had we known you were having a bonfire…' Mags says.

'Spur of the moment thing,' I tell them. 'Seemed like a good idea.'

'Freaked the mother out,' Cami says.

'Which one of you got the call?' I ask.

'Both of us!' Mags informs me.

'Sorry.'

'Don't worry about it,' Cami says.

'Do we take it you told her?' Mags asks.

I nod, and pull a face.

'That good, huh?' Cami says.

'Yep. She called me a filthy liar and threatened to wash my mouth out with soap and water.'

'Jesus!' Cami exclaims.

'Oh my God!' Mags says, shaking her head in disbelief. 'How could she think you'd make something like that up?'

'She really is a piece of work,' Cami says sadly. 'I'm sorry, Rose.'

'It doesn't matter, really it doesn't. I'm done with her now, and she basically told me never to darken her doorstep again. Suits me fine.'

'Can't believe she threatened to wash your mouth out with soap – just like when we were girls,' Mags says.

'I'd like to have seen her try,' I laugh. I feel slightly manic. I'm not sure if it's the adrenaline or the toxic fumes.

'Did she ever actually do it to you when we were kids?' Cami asks. 'I know she was always threatening to.'

'Only once. Well, she tried. I scratched her arms and she called me a little vixen,' I tell them. 'She didn't try again after that. Still threatened to from time to time.'

We stand around the fire in silence for a while, like some sort of coven, just watching the dolls' house burn. The fire has reached down to the buddleia and is smoking as the greenery burns. I feel a moment's remorse at burning the shrub, but figure it will grow back anyway. I watch with satisfaction as the roof caves in, sparks flying into the air.

'This is actually quite cathartic,' I muse.

'I bet,' Cami nods. 'Burning it, and everything it represents.'

'Kind of like Ken being cremated,' Mags adds.

'Yeah. A bit sorry I missed that now,' I say.

'We enjoyed it on your behalf,' Cami says.

'Yeah. Although I wish we'd known then what we know now. Could really have enjoyed it then,' Mags adds.

'And taken marshmallows,' I chuckle.

We slip into silence again and watch as the walls come down, sending another flurry of sparks into the air. Cami and Mags slip their arms into mine and lean their heads on my shoulders. I realise I'm actually glad Mum called them so they could share this with me. It feels momentous somehow.

Mags eventually breaks the silence. 'How are you feeling now, Rose?'

'Um… pretty good, I think, all things considered. I realise that I no longer care what *she* thinks,' I say, nodding towards next door.

'Well, that's good. Anything else you want to burn?' Cami asks.

'That,' I say, nodding towards Ken's house and grinning. I can't help laughing at the looks of alarm that cross the faces of my sisters.

'Don't worry, I'm not actually going to do it,' I reassure them. I wait for their expressions to turn to relief before adding 'probably'.

'Are we gonna get out of here then?' Cami asks.

I look at the fire which has died right down now. There's no risk to the surrounding area if we leave it. 'Yep, let's go.'

We head back up the garden and through the gate. Mags leans over and re-bolts it. We find Mum sitting at the kitchen table. There's a glass of what I assume to be sherry on the table in front of her. I bite back the urge to say, 'it's not Christmas, is it?' She can't meet my gaze when I look at her. 'Bye then, Mum. See ya later,' I say with a backwards wave of my hand as I leave the room. 'Much later,' I add, probably out of earshot.

I wait in the hall for Cami and Mags to join me. Hopefully this is the last time I'll ever be in this house. In *her* lifetime anyway.

We reconvene back at Cami's, having all arrived in separate cars.

'What did the old bat have to say for herself then?' I ask.

'Not a lot. She was actually pretty quiet,' Mags says.

'Unusually so, really,' Cami adds. 'She seemed kind of defeated.'

'Resigned. Or something,' Mags says. 'Definitely subdued.'

I try to process this. 'Do you think she knew?'

'About you? What happened?' Cami asks.

I nod. 'Yeah. Do you think she's feeling guilty?'

Mags and Cami shrug their answers.

'I think she did. At some level. She must have,' I say.

'Maybe,' Cami says hesitantly. 'Maybe she couldn't face admitting it to herself.'

'You think she actually has a conscience then?' I ask, raising my eyebrows.

'I honestly don't know, Rose. She'd have to be a monster to feel nothing, no remorse or anything. If she did know, that is,' Cami says.

'Mm. Maybe it was too painful to admit it. Easier to pretend it wasn't happening,' Mags offers.

'Well, whatever the case, I'm done with her for good,' I tell my sisters. 'And I'll make damn sure she never has a relationship with my daughters. She doesn't deserve them, and I don't want them poisoned by her.'

Mags and Cami don't say anything. I can't help wondering if they're a little shocked by my mutinous attitude. So be it; this is about self-preservation.

Chapter 37
The fall

Mags

Rose seemed strangely liberated after burning the dolls' house, like another layer of emotional pain had been peeled away to reveal fresh skin underneath. I could totally understand, of course, but it didn't have the same effect on me.

All I could think of as I watched the flames was how much I'd loved to play with it, and how envious I was of Rose back then. I thought she was the luckiest girl in the world to own such a beautiful thing. I'd almost hated her for her neglect, and sometimes abuse, of it. She didn't deserve it, that's what I'd thought. I would have treasured it, cared for it, loved it.

Now that I know why she hated it, now I understand, I just feel immense guilt. I misjudged my big sister. I was so very wrong about her. I'm trying to be rational about it, remind myself I was just a child and had no way of knowing what was happening to Rose, but the guilt is weighing heavily on me. I'm struggling to forgive myself for getting it so wrong. I know Rose bears me no ill, that she would say there's nothing to forgive, but I can't shake the feelings of guilt gnawing at my insides.

The need for something to dull the pain is worse than it's

been in a while. I'm terrified I might give in this time. Give in to the screaming voice in my brain, demanding something to silence it, to numb it. When I left Cami's, hugging my sisters goodbye, I drove around for hours, too scared to stop moving, for fear I'd end up buying alcohol. When I finally went home I couldn't settle to anything, pacing and anxious, my nerves in tatters. I felt as though ants were crawling over my skin and I scratched my arms raw. I couldn't stop the screaming. I tried to meditate to no avail. I couldn't still the noise, stop the ants' unceasing march. I tried phoning my sponsor. No answer. I started to leave a garbled message about being on the edge, needing help. I need help. I have to ask for help.

Cami

I miss the text from Mags, not finding it until more than an hour after she sent it. I'd gone for a soak in the bath after dinner and not taken my phone in with me. The message read simply, *Help*, and my heart constricted with panic.

I dialled Mags' number at once, but it rang and rang and went unanswered.

'Hey, Mags,' I said to the voicemail. 'Sorry – just picked up your text. Hope you're okay. Call me when you get this.'

Padding downstairs in my dressing gown, I find Rose in the lounge watching television.

'Have you heard from Mags?' I ask her.

Rose looks up, shaking her head, 'No. Why's that?'

'She texted the word help about an hour ago, and now she's not picking up. Just wondering if we should be worried?'

'Oh. That doesn't sound good.'

'Do you think we should go round there? Make sure she's alright,' I ask.

'Um, yeah, maybe. Let's try phoning again first.'

I press Mags' contact in my mobile again, and again it goes to voicemail. I shake my head at Rose, who's already getting out of her chair.

'I'll get dressed,' I say, hurrying upstairs where I throw on jeans and a jumper, pushing the feeling of nausea in my throat back down with a swallow.

When we arrive at Mags', the house is in darkness, and the sick feeling returns. Her car is parked outside, so it's pretty safe to assume she's home. Checking my watch, I see that's it's just after nine, so too early for her to have gone to bed, surely.

We ring the bell and wait. Nothing. The house is silent. We ring again, and knock. Nothing. Rose pushes open the letterbox.

'Mags!' she calls. 'Mags! You there?' We knock again but still nothing.

'I'll try phoning. See if we can hear her mobile.'

With the letterbox open, we can hear the faint ringing of Mags' phone. The sick feeling in my stomach is increasing.

'She might just have fallen asleep on the sofa or something. I'm sure she's okay,' Rose says, putting her hand on my arm.

I shake my head. 'No, something's wrong. I can feel it. I'm going to try round the back.'

Rose follows me around the side of the house and through the low wrought-iron gate. We reach the lounge patio doors first, finding them locked.

'Kitchen,' I say, walking the few feet to the back door and trying the handle. 'Bugger. Locked.'

'What do we do now?' Rose asks. 'Is there a spare key anywhere?'

'I think there's one at Mum's, bizarrely, but I don't fancy going round there at this time of night.'

'No, me neither,' Rose agrees, shaking her head vehemently.

'I'm gonna break in.'

'What?! Are you sure? Isn't that a bit drastic?'

'Maybe. I don't know. What if she's hurt or...' I begin.

'Or passed out drunk?' Rose finishes.

'Yeah, or that. We have to do something.'

Rose nods.

I look around, using the torch on my mobile, for something heavy, settling on the hedgehog boot-scraper by the back door.

'Stand back,' I tell Rose. I take aim at the glass panel in the door, turning my head away as I swing. Glass shatters into the kitchen and I pull my coat sleeve over my hand to reach in and unlock the door.

Turning lights on as we go, we make our way through the house. We don't have to go far. We find Mags lying on the floor in the lounge, in front of the sofa, a puddle of pale vomit under her head.

'Oh my God, Mags! Oh, Mags,' I hear my voice cry out, quickly by her side.

'Shit. Is she okay? Is she... is she breathing?' Rose is by my side, reaching out for Mags' wrist, then her neck. 'She's got a pulse. Turn her over on her side,' she instructs.

I help Rose manoeuvre Mags onto her side. 'Mags, can you hear me? Can you open your eyes?' I can feel myself falling apart, panic overtaking me. Thankfully Rose is calm and taking control.

'Call an ambulance,' Rose says. 'Tell them it's a suspected overdose.'

I dial 999 and wait for them to ask which service.

'Ambulance. Ambulance. Please. My sister…'

I put the call on loud speaker and Rose and I answer the operator's questions between us as best we can, checking Mags' mouth and making sure her airways are clear.

'The ambulance is already on its way,' the calm voice on the other end of the phone assures us. 'I'm going to stay on the line until they arrive. Just keep talking to Mags, and tell me if anything changes, okay?'

'Okay,' Rose says. I'm crying so hard now that it's hard to speak.

It feels like a lifetime before the sound of the siren reaches my ears. I'm sitting on the floor, cradling Mags' head in my lap, oblivious to the sticky wet of her vomit seeping through my clothes.

Rose gets up to admit the paramedics who quickly assess the situation.

'Do you know what she's taken?' one of them asks, while they examine her.

I just shake my head, feeling helpless, and scared.

'Paracetamol, I think,' Rose says. 'And probably alcohol.'

I look up at Rose in surprise. I can feel a question on my face.

'I found this,' she continues, answering my question, and holding out the blue-and-white box of paracetamol. 'It's empty. I don't know how many she took though, or if it was full to start with. And vodka. Possibly a half bottle.' My face registers another question. Rose ignores me.

The paramedic nods, all the while continuing to assess Mags.

They're talking to her, trying to rouse her, while they fit an oxygen mask over her mouth and nose and take her blood pressure.

'We're going to get Mags into the ambulance now so we can assess her further, okay?'

'Okay,' I hear Rose say. I just nod mutely.

The other paramedic brings a stretcher in and Rose and I watch helplessly as they load Mags into the back of the ambulance. The neighbours have come out to see what's going on. Bloody ghouls, I think, ignoring their quizzical looks. I resist the urge to tell them to fuck off, as much as I want to, to protect Mags from prying eyes.

'Is she going to be okay?' I ask, finally finding my voice, before the doors of the ambulance close.

'Her vitals are strong,' the paramedic says, with a smile I assume is meant to be reassuring. I don't feel reassured. I just feel terrified. 'The fact that she vomited is a good thing,' he adds with another smile. 'We're going to insert a cannula which will speed things up when we get to the hospital. You can follow us there if you want.'

I nod, 'Yes, yes, we want. Please look after her.'

Rose puts her arm round my shoulders. 'She'll be okay, Cami. She's in good hands. Come on, let them work and we'll follow in the car.'

I let Rose lead me back into the house where I sit trembling on the sofa while she hunts around for Mags' keys. A few minutes later and we're sitting in the car waiting for the ambulance to leave.

'How are you so calm?' I ask, still trembling and tearful.

'With everything I've been through since David's stroke,

I've kind of had to be. I've learned to trust the professionals, and that panicking just makes everything worse,' she shrugs.

'It's just as well as I have apparently turned to jelly. How did you know she'd had alcohol? I get the paracetamol, even though I didn't spot the box, but what about the vodka?'

'There was an empty bottle on the floor, just under the sofa. Must've rolled there.'

'Do you think she's going to be okay?'

'Yeah, I do. Like the paramedic said, being sick was a good thing – it stopped at least some of the stuff she took from getting into her system.'

Just then, the blue lights start to flash on the ambulance once more, and it pulls away from the kerb. With Rose at the wheel, we pull out to follow, covering the fifteen-minute drive in silence.

Chapter 38
The relief

Mags

I wake up in the hospital, with no recollection of the previous night, the journey here, or what has happened since my arrival. What I do know is that I have a pounding headache and my mouth and throat feel awful, and there's a drip stand next to me with two bags of liquid, one clear and one bright yellow, feeding down tubes into a cannula in my arm. Cami and Rose are asleep in chairs either side of me.

'Cam...' I start to say, but only a croak comes out. I clear my throat and try again. 'Cami. Rose.'

Two pairs of eyes spring open and a second later, two pairs of arms are awkwardly trying to hug me.

'Oh thank God!' Cami says. 'You scared us!'

'I'm going to get the nurse,' Rose says, squeezing my hand before she leaves the room.

'How are you feeling?' Cami asks. 'We were so worried when we found you.'

'What happened?' I ask, still feeling decidedly groggy. 'I can't remember, I...'

'Don't worry about that now. Let's just get you checked over,' Cami says, wrapping both her hands round one of mine.

Rose comes back in then, with a nurse following closely behind.

'Can I have some water?' I ask when the nurse has given me the once over.

The nurse nods and Cami passes me a cup of water, which I sip gratefully from, wincing slightly as I swallow.

'Your throat will be sore for a couple of days,' the nurse says. 'We had to insert a tube to administer activated charcoal last night. Just try and take regular sips of water.'

I wince again. This time it's not from the pain in my throat, but from embarrassment as I begin to realise what must have happened. 'I'm sorry,' I say. 'For the trouble I've obviously caused.'

Cami and Rose protest at once. I just shake my head and wipe away the single tear that's rolling down my cheek, which is flushed with shame.

'Someone will be in to take your blood pressure shortly, and the doctor will be round to assess you a bit later,' the nurse says before leaving the room.

'I'm so sorry,' I say to my sisters again.

They both shush me at once.

'We had a deal, remember?' Cami says. 'No more apologising for ourselves.'

'This is a little different though, let's be honest,' I say, 'and I *am* sorry I scared you both.'

'What happened?' Rose asks.

Cami glares at her, clearly still worried about my mental state.

'It's okay, Cami,' I reassure her. 'Really.' I close my eyes for a moment, trying hard to recall the previous evening.

'You don't have to talk about if you don't want to,' Cami says.

'No, it's okay. I owe you both an explanation. Such as it is. I remember being in Ken's garden, and watching the dolls' house burning, and afterwards how much better you seemed, Rose… and I was glad. I was happy for you, but…' I hesitate, not sure I want Rose to hear the next bit.

'It's okay, Mags, you can tell us anything,' Rose says.

'It just brought back so many memories of when we were kids, and how jealous I was of you after you got the dolls' house. Now, knowing what it symbolised to you, I was overwhelmed with guilt and regret and… well… it hurt so much, and I simply wanted the pain to stop. Like it did that day in your bedroom when I found the vodka that first time. So, I went to the corner shop and bought a small bottle of vodka. I just sat looking at it for ages. Then I took the lid off. Part of me wanted to pour it down the sink. That part of me tried to phone my sponsor, but she didn't answer. The weaker part decided one wouldn't hurt. After one there was no going back. No putting the lid back on the bottle. I just sat and cried and drank. I vaguely remember having a headache – probably from all the crying – and I know I took some paracetamol…' I break off, pressing my fingers into my eyes which are tender and tired. I feel Cami's fingers curl round my own.

'You're doing great, Mags, but you can stop any time,' she says.

Rose clearly has other ideas. 'Were you trying to kill yourself?' she asks.

'Rose!' Cami exclaims.

'We need to know, Cams. For whatever decisions we make next, we need to know if Mags is suicidal.'

'She's right, Cami,' I say. I don't speak for a while as I try to assess my current state of mind. 'I don't think I was trying to kill myself,' I say finally. 'I think I just wanted to stop the pain. I don't believe I took too many painkillers on purpose. I probably got drunk and forgot what I'd taken.' I feel so ashamed in the cold light of day. As if Rose didn't enough on her plate without me falling spectacularly off the wagon.

'Well, that's good then,' Cami says, smiling at me. 'Just a blip.'

'Hell of a blip,' I grimace. 'I'm mortified.'

'Draw a line under it, Mags. It happened, and you can't change that, but you can control what you do next,' Rose says.

'I know you're right, but I feel so stupid. And weak,' I say.

'You have to forgive yourself,' Cami tells me. 'Not just for last night, but for everything. We've all made mistakes, Mags, and God knows we had reason enough for most of them, but it's time to move on.'

'Cami's right. You've always been your own harshest critic. It's time to be your number one fan,' Rose says.

I shake my head. 'I don't know how. I know I've always looked to other people – well, men if I'm honest – for approval and my sense of self. I don't know any other way.'

'Then it's time to learn,' Cami says, smiling at me. 'Look on this episode as the end of the old you. Time for a new Mags, one who loves herself and doesn't need the approval of anyone, least of all a man.'

We're interrupted by someone coming in to check my blood pressure. I take the opportunity to ask about the yellow liquid feeding into my arm.

'That's got stuff in to help your liver. The doctors will

probably want to do some more tests to check for any liver damage. How are you feeling now?'

'Um… embarrassed,' I say.

The nurse chuckles. 'Apart from that. How are you feeling physically?'

'Tired. Bit of a headache, and my throat's sore. Okay though, considering.'

'That's good. I'm just going to take some bloods and the doctor will come and see you when they've got the results. Okay? Any questions?'

The nurse proceeds to take an armful of blood, after which I slump back on the pillows with a groan.

'I can't believe I was so stupid. What a dick. I really wasn't trying to kill myself though, honestly. You do believe me, don't you?' I ask my sisters, feeling concern on my face to match theirs.

'We believe you,' Cami says. Rose says nothing, just smiles at me. I can tell she's not convinced.

'You don't have to stay if you've got things to do,' I tell them. 'I'll be fine, and hopefully I'll be able to go home later.'

'Well, I do need to ring DS Peters,' Rose says. 'Tell him I've spoken to the old cow.'

'I still can't believe how awful she was to you,' I say, shaking my head.

Rose shrugs. 'It was pretty much what I expected. She has a pretty low opinion of me.'

'Maybe when she's had time to digest the information, she'll realise she's misjudged you?' I say.

'I do love how you always try to think the best of people, Mags. Even after everything that's happened,' Rose says, a wry smile on her face.

'God, I know, I'm hopelessly naive. I can't seem to help myself.'

'We wouldn't have you any other way,' Cami says. 'It's kind of endearing really.'

'It is,' Rose agrees. 'You have a sort of innocence about you. I'm afraid I'm a complete cynic.'

'I think I'm somewhere in between,' Cami says, chuckling. 'I'll assume someone's nice until they prove otherwise. Which is pretty much always, sadly.'

'It's funny how we're all so different, isn't it?' I say.

'Different flowers from the same garden,' Cami smiles.

'I really am so grateful to have you both,' I say. 'Thank you for rescuing me. I promise it won't happen again. No more blips. I never want to feel like this again, or to put you through it.'

'Good!' Rose says. 'We'll hold you to that.'

'Will you phone when you have your results?' Cami says. 'And if you need picking up.'

'I will. I might just try and snooze for a bit while I'm waiting.'

'Good idea. Right, we'll see you later,' Rose says, leaning over to kiss my cheek.

A thought suddenly strikes me. 'Um… you won't mention to DS Peters about me being in hospital, will you? I'm sure you wouldn't anyway, but…' I can feel myself blushing.

Rose laughs. 'I won't tell the sexy policeman anything, don't worry. Not that you should care what he thinks.'

'I know. I can't help it. I just don't want him to think badly of me.'

'You're definitely a work in progress, Mags.'

I scrunch up my face. 'Baby steps. I'm going to speak to my

sponsor when I get home, and go to some meetings.'

'That's good,' Cami smiles.

'I honestly think I'm going to be okay though. I don't want either of you to worry I'm going to slip up again.'

'Well, we're going to worry, but maybe that will make you think twice before you pop to the corner shop!' Rose says, going all big sister on me for a moment.

'Funnily enough, I think it will. I never want to let either of you down again.'

'It's not about letting us down, Mags. Do it for you,' Cami insists.

'Well, if doing it for us works, I'm actually all for it,' Rose adds.

'Yeah, I s'pose. Just don't do it for DS Peters!' Cami laughs.

'Spoilsport!' I say, sticking my tongue out at her.

'Yeuch! Have you seen the state of your tongue?' Rose grimaces.

I cringe. 'It does feel a bit furry now you come to mention it.'

Cami rummages in her handbag and produces a packet of chewing gum and hands me a piece.

Cami and Rose wave their goodbyes then, and I'm left with my thoughts and my shame. I am mortified at what's happened, but I realise there's no point beating myself up about it. I know that the best way to make up for it is to ensure it never happens again. I'm determined to prove to my sisters that the wheels are firmly back on the wagon, and are staying there.

With that thought in my head, I close my eyes and let sleep claim me.

Cami and I drive home yawning our heads off. We'd barely had any sleep, not nodding off until the early hours of the morning, too worried about Mags to do so until we knew she was going to be okay. Coffee is the first order of the day when we get back to the house and we sit at Cami's kitchen table cradling our mugs.

'Do you really think she's going to be okay?' I ask.

'Um… actually, I do, yeah,' Cami says, nodding. 'I really think this might prove to be a blessing in disguise.'

'How so? Did she need a reason to change the lounge carpet?'

'Ew, I'd forgotten about the carpet. We'll have to go round and clean up before Mags gets home. She doesn't need her nose rubbed in that.'

'As much as I'd like to stay and help scrub Mags' carpet, I really do need to get back to David. I'm just going to phone the police station and then head off. Sorry.'

Cami sighs. 'No problem. I'm sure you'll have your share of unpleasant scrubbing to look forward to anyway.'

'Oh what glamorous lives we lead,' I chuckle.

'Don't we just.'

We sit in silence for a while. I can feel my eyes growing heavy and my body sinking tiredly into the chair.

'Right, I need to get up and get on before I nod off,' I tell Cami.

'Yep. Me too. I'll get round to Mags'. Will you just lock up when you leave?'

'Will do. Let me know later how Mags is, and what the test results show.'

'Uh huh. I hope she hasn't got liver damage,' Cami says worriedly.

'To be honest, with her history it's a miracle her liver hasn't already packed up. Hopefully one blip won't make too much difference.'

'Hopefully,' Cami says, holding up crossed fingers.

Cami hugs me then, before rummaging in the cupboard under the sink for cleaning supplies. I heave myself up and wave her off before making a quick call to DS Peters, packing my overnight bag and hitting the road. It's actually a relief to be heading home to David, and whatever scrubbing awaits me.

Cami

I'm mid-scrubbing in Mags' lounge when my mobile rings. I pull my rubber gloves off, push my hair away from my face and look around for my mobile.

'Hey, Mags, everything okay? Can you come home?'

'Hello. You alright? You sound out of breath,' Mags says.

I don't want to tell her that I'm trying to get her vomit out of the carpet.

'Yep, all good. What did the doctor say?'

'Well, by some miracle, my liver apparently isn't in too bad a shape, and I can come home as soon as they've done the paperwork.' I can hear the relief in her voice.

'Oh, thank goodness! That's great news. Do you know what time I can collect you?'

'Um… not sure yet. Shall I call when I'm ready?'

'Yes, okay. Or I'll come when I'm done here and keep you company.'

'Thanks, Cami. I'll see you in a bit.'

I end the call and exhale with relief. Mags having liver damage would really have been one too many things to cope with at the moment. For us all. I quickly text Rose to let her know. I don't wait for a reply as she'll still be driving home. Pulling my gloves on, I return to the job of cleaning and disinfecting the carpet. I've already disposed of the vodka bottle and the packaging from the paracetamol. It doesn't take too much longer to finish the unpleasant task and soon all trace of last night's misadventure is gone.

I pop home for a shower and a change of clothes before heading to the hospital. Mags is sitting in a chair, looking much brighter than when I'd left her a few hours earlier.

'You look better,' I tell her.

'Feel it,' Mags says. 'That vitamin drip thingy worked wonders. My throat's still sore, but I figure it'll be a good reminder to never ever do this again.'

'Yes, I think we've all had enough drama for three lifetimes. I'm all for a quiet life now.'

'You'll be glad when all this business with Ken is resolved and you can get on with your new life with Lydia. I can't wait to meet her,' Mags smiles.

'We all will. Rose needs closure, although she did seem stronger and more positive this visit, I thought.'

'Mm, I thought that too. She seems to have found some sort of acceptance or something,' Mags agrees.

'Just hope the police investigation doesn't bring it all up again.'

'Would you not mention bringing stuff up, please?' Mags says, fake vomiting.

A nurse comes in and catches her mid-mimic, and we both laugh.

'I see you're feeling better. I've got your discharge letter,' the nurse says.

Mags thanks her shyly, still embarrassed at the events of the previous night.

'Well, just don't let it happen again. Ask for help before you get to that stage, eh? We don't want to see you back in here again, okay?' the nurse says.

'Okay,' Mags nods.

We leave the ward arm in arm and head to the car park.

'Do you want to stay at mine tonight?' I ask as I open the door for Mags.

'That's sweet of you, Cams, but I'll be fine at mine. Honestly. I promise you don't have to worry about me.'

'Not worried, just thought you might like the company.'

'I think I need to go home. Face up to whatever carnage I left last night. I need to stand on my own two feet. Starting now.'

'Oh, er... well, I've dealt with the carnage. And it wasn't really carnage at all, honestly. The lounge carpet is just a bit damp still.'

'Oh God! I'm so ashamed. Was I very sick? Jesus, I didn't wet myself did I?' Mags sounds horrified.

I can't help laughing. 'No, you didn't wet your pants, but you were a bit sick. It's fine. Anyway, throwing up probably prevented you from being more seriously ill, so I'm delighted I had to clean it up.'

'Thank you so much. I promise you'll never have to do it again,' Mags sounds contrite.

'I'll hold you to that.'

Chapter 39
The lion's den

Cami

After I dropped Mags home, I couldn't settle to anything. Try as I might, I couldn't shake the worry of her being alone after what had happened. I had picked up the phone to call or text half a dozen times, but had stopped myself, knowing that I had to trust her.

Rose rang to let me know she'd arrived home safely.

'Glad you're back. David alright?'

'Yes, he's fine. I think he actually quite enjoys the fuss the carers make of him. They're a darn sight more attentive than I am.'

'It's easy when you're not there all the time. And being paid for it!' I tell her.

'Yeah, I s'pose so. I am determined to be more encouraging though; get him up and doing his physio more regularly, and get him out and about.'

'That's good. Just remember to look after your needs too. You can't look after someone else if you don't look after yourself. And keep up with your counselling sessions, won't you?'

'Yes, I've realised how important those sessions are – I'll definitely keep going.'

'And I'm always here if you need me, don't forget that.'

'Likewise. Oh, before I forget, I spoke to DS Peters briefly about them going to see Mum. He wanted to know if one of us wanted to be there when they go round. I didn't know what to say. I said probably not, but that I'd check with you and Mags. What do you think?'

'Oh God, we can't ask Mags. She'd probably jump at the chance to see the handsome DS Peters again, but I really don't think she should be around Mum at the moment, not in her fragile state. If anyone could drive a person to drink, it's our bloody mother.'

'Hm. How would you feel about being there with Mum?'

'After the way she treated you, I don't think I want to be anywhere near her quite frankly,' I say.

'Shall we just leave it to the police then?'

'Yeah, why not. She'll probably be all sweetness and light without us there anyway.'

'I'll be glad when this investigation is over. I feel like I'm so close to moving on with my life, but it's always there in the back of my mind, waiting to bite me on the bum when I least expect it.'

'I bet. Hopefully it won't be too much longer. I don't suppose there's much chance of them getting anywhere after all this time.'

'I keep thinking about his laptop and that file you told me you couldn't open. I can't bear the thought that he has images or anything in it. I'm still quietly hoping that no one else will have to know what happened to me.'

'I don't know how much the police can tell us. I'm happy to speak to DS Peters if you want – see if I can find out anything.'

'Thanks, Cami. That would be good,' Rose says.

I make a note on the calendar to call DS Peters the following morning. I can't resist one text to Mags before I go to bed, just to check she's okay. I'm relieved when her reply pings back almost immediately.

I'm fine, Cams, promise. Early night and start afresh tomorrow. Thanks for being there for me. Love you. xx

Her last two words give me goosebumps. We so rarely say them to each other. We so rarely had them said to us.

Love you too. Glad you're okay. Sleep well. xx

Then, as an afterthought, *Call me if you need me. Anything. Anytime. xx*

I hope she doesn't take offence, or think I don't trust her to be on her own, and I'm chewing anxiously on my thumbnail as I await her response.

Thank you. I will. Night night. xx

I'm feeling slightly more relaxed as I plod up the stairs to bed.

The next morning I phone DS Peters to let him know they can go ahead and speak to Mum without one of us being there. If he's surprised, he doesn't let it show in his voice. I suppose in a normal family, it would be strange to let an elderly parent undergo a police interview without being there to support them. Ours is not a normal family. I suspect DS Peters already knows this.

I take the opportunity to ask about the investigation in general, and the laptop in particular.

'Obviously I can't say too much about an investigation that's still ongoing, Cami, but you can let Rose know that there was nothing on the laptop. The file marked banking was just that,' the police detective says.

'Oh, thank you, that is a relief!' I say. 'It's all awful enough as it is.'

'I know it's difficult. I'm sure you and Mags are supporting Rose through the ordeal though.'

'We're doing our best, certainly, but it's been such a shock finding out what happened to her.'

'I can imagine. We'll do everything in our power to make this whole thing as painless as possible, but I can't promise Rose's abuse won't come out.'

'Thank you, we appreciate that. Rose knows it's a possibility. When will you be going to talk to Mum?'

'Later today, I think. I'll take a female officer with me. Anything I should know before I go?'

I raise my eyebrows. 'Take riot gear?'

DS Peters laughs. 'I see.'

'Seriously, she'll probably be as nice as pie,' I tell him.

'Okay, well thanks for your call, Cami. I daresay we'll speak soon.'

'No problem, bye.'

I follow up the call with one to Mags.

'Morning, Cami. I'm fine!' she says, laughing down the phone.

'Sorry, I'm not checking up on you, honest.'

'No, I know. And I appreciate your call, really I do. I know it's just because you care.'

'I do. I can't help worrying,' I admit.

'Understandable after what happened, but I think it actually did me good, as mad as that sounds.'

I don't mention the fact that I voiced the same thought to Rose. 'Really?'

'Mm hm. It made me realise that I do want to get better. To be better. To live better.'

'That's great, Mags. I'm so happy and relieved to hear you say that.'

'A fresh start. A bit like the one you gave that patch of carpet in my lounge. I need to shampoo the rest of it now to match,' Mags laughs.

'It's good to hear you laugh,' I tell her. I suddenly remember my conversation with DS Peters. 'Oh, while I think about it, the police didn't find anything dodgy on Ken's laptop. The file marked banking actually was banking.'

'Oh, that is good news. Does Rose know? She'll be so relieved. I know the idea of there being physical proof of what happened to her was eating her up.'

'I'll phone her next.'

'Did DS Peters say anything else?' Mags asks.

'If you're asking did he ask about you, then I'm afraid not,' I say.

'Hey, a girl can dream,' Mags says, laughing again. 'But actually I meant about the investigation.'

'No, not really. They obviously can't say too much. He did say they're going round to talk to Mum today.'

'Oh God. Did you warn him to wear a flak jacket and not get too close?' Mags says.

'Funny you should say that...' I begin.

More laughter echoes down the line. 'I daresay she'll be sweetness personified. Two-faced cow.'

'I think DS Peters is probably a very good judge of character and he'll see right through to her frozen core,' I say.

'Do we need to be there? At Mum's. When they go round?' Mags asks.

'No, we decided against that. Probably better for everyone involved, don't you think?'

'Yeah, you're probably right. It's just…'

I know where Mags is going, and I jump in. 'She doesn't deserve our support or our loyalty, Mags. She may be our biological mother, but she's never been a mother to us.'

I hear Mags sigh down the phone. 'I know. I don't know why I persist in wanting to protect her. Sod it. Let them give her the thumbscrews.'

'That's the spirit,' I laugh.

'I would like to be a fly on the wall though, if I'm honest. Wouldn't you? Hear what she says to the police about back then. About Ken, and Rose.'

'Hm, yeah, maybe. I just don't think it's a good idea, so I guess we'll never know. Anyway, glad you're doing okay. I'd better ring Rose and let her know the news about the laptop. Speak to you soon. Take care.'

'Thanks, Cams, I will. You too.'

Mags

After speaking to Cami, I try to focus on something other than the police visit to Mum, but I can't shake the feeling that one of us should be there with her. Whatever else she is, she *is* our mother, and she shouldn't be subjected to a visit from the police at her age without some support. I wonder briefly if it's really my attraction to the detective fuelling this idea, clouding my judgment, but I decide to go. I pull a brush through my hair, but don't bother with any makeup as a way of convincing myself I'm there for Mum, not to impress DS Peters. Besides, he probably hasn't given me a first look let alone a second.

On the short drive to Mum's, I wonder if I'm some sort of

masochist. I must be to be venturing into the lion's den after what had happened the night before last. But I feel strong, stronger than I have done in a while, bizarrely. This feels like the right thing to do, and God knows I'm the queen of trying to do the right thing. For other people, if not for myself.

I let myself in at Mum's, calling out as I always do, and finding her in the kitchen washing up the breakfast things. She obviously hasn't heard me. 'Morning, Mum,' I repeat.

'Oh! Magnolia. What do you think you're doing, creeping up on me like that? Are you trying to give me a heart attack?'

I resist the urge to say yes. 'I did call from the hall, Mum, you can't have heard me.' She looks older somehow since I last saw her. More frail. Smaller, sallower.

She sort of harrumphs. 'What are you doing here, anyway?'

'Can't I just come and see you without having a reason?' I ask, already knowing the answer. She glares at me. 'Cami says the police are coming to talk to you today, and I thought you might like someone here with you,' I tell her, hoping she'll be grateful, but knowing deep down she won't.

'Whatever for? I'm quite capable of dealing with the police on my own, thank you very much.'

'Silly me,' I sigh, before she has a chance to call me it herself. 'Shall I make us a cup of tea? I'm not sure what time they're coming.'

'Waste of everyone's time, I'm sure. That sister of yours is a troublemaker. I'll soon put the police straight on a few things. That poor man...' she starts.

I'm just waiting for her to add 'not even cold in his grave', but we're saved by the bell.

Chapter 40
The lion tamer

Mags

I open the door to a surprised DS Peters.

'Oh, hello, Mags,' he says.

'Hello. Sorry, I know Cami said no-one would be here with Mum, but it didn't feel right, so…'

'So, here you are,' DS Peters finishes. 'I'm glad you are. It's better for us to be honest.'

I feel my face flush with no makeup to hide behind. 'Um… Mum's in the kitchen. I was just about to put the kettle on,' I say, leading the way.

'Thank you,' DS Peters says. 'This is DC Havilland,' he continues, introducing the female officer accompanying him.

I turn back and smile a hello.

'Mum, the police are here,' I say as we enter the kitchen. She turns to us from her place at the sink, drying her hands on a tea towel, with a look on her face that says she's ready to do battle and a mouth open with a retort on her tongue.

'Hello, I'm DS Peters. And this is my colleague, DC Havilland.' The policeman gets in first and disarms her as I knew he would. He reaches out a hand to Mum and smiles his winning smile.

Fifteen-love, I think to myself.

Mum takes the offered hand, 'How do you do. Can I get you a cup of tea, officer… Peters, did you say?'

'Yes, tea would be lovely, and yes, it's Peters. Thank you for agreeing to see us.' *Thirty-love.*

'Of course,' Mum says, busying herself filling the kettle and getting tea things ready. 'Although I'm afraid you will have had a wasted journey. Ken was the loveliest man you could ever meet.' *Thirty-fifteen.* 'Magnolia, where are your manners? Show DS Peters and… the other one… into the lounge. Then come back for the tray.'

I feel like a small child again, being ordered about by her, being criticised by her. Why had I come? Would I never learn? I mumble 'this way' under my breath and lead the two officers through to Mum's sitting room.

I carry the tea tray in for Mum. She's used her best china and there are cubes of sugar in the bowl, with a small pair of tongs balancing on the top.

'Shall I be mother?' she simpers. I fight the urge to smash the tray on the floor and scream at her, taking a deep breath and putting the tray carefully on the coffee table, where Mum proceeds to pour tea for DS Peters and herself, completely ignoring DC Havilland and me. I sigh and pour the female officer a cup, raising my eyebrows by way of an apology. She smiles at me.

Sitting back into my chair, cradling my cup and saucer, my gaze settles on DS Peters as he continues his charm offensive on Mum. She's simpering at him sickeningly. I can't blame her though. He really is an exceptionally attractive man. At one point he glances over at me, almost as if he can feel my eyes on him, and I look away shyly, feeling a blush on my cheeks. He smiles at me before returning his attention to Mum.

'So, Mrs Clarkson, I know your daughter, Rose, has told you a little of what we want to talk to you about. It's just an informal chat at this stage. Obviously the alleged abuse took place a long time ago and Mr. Abbott is not here to defend himself.'

I bristle a little at his use of the word alleged, but keep my gaze firmly directed into my teacup. I know he probably has to use certain terminology at this stage of the investigation, but it irks nonetheless. I feel his eyes on me again, almost as if he is reading my mind and trying to send a silent apology.

Mum interrupts him. 'Yes, *Peony* told me, and let me tell you, there was no abuse and that's all there is to it. She's always been a liar, that one. I apologise that she's wasted your time. And mine,' she adds, her lips pursing briefly in distaste before she remembers just how attractive the young policeman is, and lifts them once more.

I can feel my heart rate increasing, pounding in my ears, and my hands clenching on the fragile china cup. How fucking dare she? I grit my teeth and swallow the angry bile in my throat back down. I raise my eyes to DS Peters' face, wondering how he'll respond to her flat-out denial. He smiles at her.

'I know how painful it must be to contemplate the idea that someone hurt one of your daughters,' he begins. Playing to her maternal streak? I can't help a small pfft escaping my lips. Doesn't he realise her's is about as wide as a cotton thread? 'However, we have to take any accusation of abuse seriously. I'm sure you understand that?'

Mum's back to simpering again. 'Of course. You're only doing your job, dear. But you've had a wasted journey. Ken was never anything but decent and kind to Rose, to all the girls, and to me. She should be ashamed of herself, dragging his good name through the mud. And him not here to defend himself. He should be allowed to rest in peace. Poor soul.' She tuts and shakes her head.

My jaw is clenched so tightly that it's painful now. If she says he'd be turning in his grave again I might just lose it. I think you've met your match DS Peters. Still not ready to admit defeat, he persists.

'So you never saw anything... inappropriate... in Mr. Abbott's behaviour to Rose? You never saw him touch her in a way that made her uncomfortable?'

'Never! And you'll never hear me say otherwise,' Mum says.

I feel my brows furrow at her words, which seem a bit strange.

'What about Rose's behaviour back then? Did her behaviour change? Did she seem angry or unhappy?' DS Peters pushes.

'Of course she did – she was a teenager. They're all moody. All those hormones. It had nothing to do with Ken. My goodness, he was her godfather. The very idea...' Mum tails off, shaking her head to add emphasis.

'Why did Rose burn the dolls' house that Mr. Abbott gave her?'

I look up at DS Peters in surprise on hearing the question. I guess Rose must have told him what she'd done.

Mum looks flustered for a moment, caught off guard. 'Why does that girl do anything?' she blusters. 'Attention seeking I expect. Looking for a bit of sympathy, no doubt. Thinks she's hard done by having to look after her husband in a wheelchair. Poor man. What did he do to deserve being lumbered with her for a wife?'

That's it. I can't listen to any more of her lies and vitriol. I silently replace my cup and saucer on the tray and walk out.

'Are you okay, Mags?'

DS Peters' voice breaks my trance. I don't know how long I've been standing at the kitchen sink, letting it support me as I stared out into the garden.

'Oh, yeah, I guess. I just couldn't listen to that anymore,' I say, nodding in the direction of the lounge. 'How can she say those things? About her own daughter? She's just hateful.'

'I'm sorry. I know how hard this must be on you and your sisters,' DS Peters nods. 'I know it's no consolation, but I want you to know that I believe Rose. It's just difficult...'

I nod, 'I know.' I want to ease his discomfort, to let him know I understand his position. 'It just hurts that our own mother doesn't believe us. How could she think we'd make up something like this?'

'I'm afraid she's not going to budge, so we're going to leave it for today. It may be that we will have to interview her formally further down the line though. Depending on where the investigation takes us.'

I nod again, a sigh escaping my lips. DS Peters turns to leave, but hesitates. 'One more thing, Mags. You'll recall the file marked Banking on Mr. Abbott's computer? We found that he made monthly payments to your mother for many years. Having checked with his bank, these payments started in 1972.'

I feel the blood drain from my face as I realise the possible implications of what I've just heard. '1972? The year Rose turned nine. The year the abuse started... oh my God!' My hand goes to my mouth as a sob tries to escape. 'You think it was hush money, don't you? She knew. And he paid her to keep her mouth shut.' I make no attempt to quash the tears bubbling in the corners of my eyes.

'I'm sorry, Mags, but it is a possibility,' DS Peters says, looking apologetic.

'It's not your fault,' I tell him.

'No, but it's another blow, I realise that.'

'Yeah, just when I think my opinion of her can't sink any lower,' I say, dabbing at my eyes with a tissue I've pulled out of my pocket. 'Did you ask her about it?'

'Yes. She said it was just the kind act of a friend and neighbour who knew she was struggling financially after your father left. She didn't see anything strange about it as he was also Rose's godfather and saw it as a way of supporting her.'

'A likely story,' I say, a small laugh of disbelief escaping my lips.

DS Peters rests his hand briefly on my arm. 'I'll leave it up to you whether or not to tell Rose about the payments. Take care, Mags. Do get in touch if anything comes up. We'll show ourselves out.' With that he turned to leave.

I don't know how long I stood there after he'd gone. Mum didn't come back into the kitchen, which is probably just as well. By the time I made up my mind, I was coldly calm.

Cami

'Oh my God!' I can't believe what Mags just told me. She'd arrived a couple of minutes earlier, flushed and breathless, confessing she went round to Mum's for the police interview.

'I know, right?' Mags says, raising her eyebrows. 'What do you reckon? Think he paid her off? Paid her to look the other way?'

I close my eyes for a moment. 'That is such an abhorrent thought, but I really can't see any other explanation.' I feel sick at the idea of our mother basically selling her oldest child to a paedophile. 'What did she say when they asked her about it?'

'Oh, some rubbish about him being a good Samaritan in her time of need,' Mags pooh-poohs, with a wave of her hand.

'Jesus. It's unbelievable. Should we tell Rose?'

'We can't, Cami. God, can you imagine what that would do to her?'

'But what if it comes out later? And we'd kept it from her?'

'We'll just have to cross that bloody burning bridge if and when,' Mags says.

'I s'pose so. It just keeps getting worse, doesn't it?' I groan.

'Yep, but we can't undermine what little equanimity Rose has found. Not if we don't have to.'

'How did you leave things with Mum?'

Mags grimaces.

'What?' I push her.

'I... um... I told her I don't have a mother anymore.'

'What? Shit! You didn't?! Did you?' I can't believe what I'm hearing.

Mags nods. 'Yep. Told her she wouldn't be seeing me again. Even remembered to retrieve my spare house key on the way out.'

'Wow,' I'm shaking my head in disbelief at the idea of my baby sister, the people pleaser, doing such a thing. 'Wow,' I repeat.

'I know. The worm has turned. No more Mrs-Nice-Mags.'

'Well done, you.'

'Long overdue. It's about time I grew up, isn't it? I'm tired of the old Mags, frightened of her own shadow and worried what people think of her. No more,' Mags says, shaking her head.

'I'm proud of you,' I smile at her.

'Thanks, sis. I'm pretty proud of me too, as it happens,' Mags grins. 'The old cow can rot in hell as far as I'm concerned.'

Chapter 41
Cold hands

Mags

It was a couple of days after Mum's police interview that I got the call. It was from her other neighbour, a nice lady about Mum's age called Pamela who'd lived there with her Yorkshire terrier for a decade or more. She was on friendly enough terms with Mum. As much as anyone could be anyway. I don't think they popped round to each other's houses for coffee and a chat, but they looked out for one another as older ladies living alone might.

'Oh, hello, Pamela, how are you?' I say, feeling my brow furrow as I wonder why she's calling.

'Hello, dear. I'm fine, thank you. I'm sorry to bother you – I'm sure it's nothing – it's just, well, I haven't seen your mother for a couple of days and… well, I usually see her hanging the washing out on a Tuesday…' she says, her words tailing off in a sort of unspoken apology for worrying me.

'Oh, okay, um… have you been round and knocked on the door?'

'Yes, dear. No answer. I peeped in through the windows and the letterbox, and called out, but nothing. I do hope she hasn't had a fall or something.'

'I'm sure it's nothing to worry about. Probably just taken to her bed with a cold or something. You don't have a spare door key do you?'

'No, I'm afraid not. I did suggest it once, you know, with us both being on our own, but your mum didn't seem to like the idea. She is a very private person, I know.'

'Did you try the door? She doesn't always lock it.'

'Yes, I did, but it was locked. So was the back door.'

'Mm, well, don't worry, we'll pop round and check on her. Thanks so much for the call.'

'Of course, no problem at all. What are neighbours for? Would you be a dear and just knock on my door and let me know she's alright?'

'Yes, of course. Thanks again. You take care.'

Bugger. I hit Cami's mobile number and wait for her to answer.

'Hey, Mags,' she says brightly. 'Wassup?'

'Our bloody mother. Pamela from next door just rang to say she hasn't seen Mum for a couple of days and is worried. I said one of us would go round and check on her, and then remembered I don't have a door key anymore – I dumped it unceremoniously on the kitchen table when I walked out on her the other day.'

'Oh for God's sake. What a pain in the arse. I can't go round until after work though, unless you want to collect the key?'

'Not really. It's only been two days since I said I was done with her.'

'Hm. I wouldn't put it past her to be doing this on purpose. She'd know full well that you'd be the one to get the concerned neighbour on the phone,' Cami says.

'That did cross my mind too. Send me on a massive guilt trip in her direction. Conniving old witch.'

Cami sighs. 'I'll go round later. I don't want her to get her claws back into you.'

'Are you sure? Do you want me to come with you?' I say, mentally crossing my fingers that she says no.

'No, it's alright.'

'Thanks, Cami. I owe you!'

'Big time,' she agrees, only half joking.

'Oh, one more thing, could you just poke your head next door and let Pamela know after you've seen Mum? Put her mind at rest.'

'Yep, sure. Must go. Speak later,' Cami says.

'Bye, Cami, and thanks.'

Cami

I get to Mum's at around six fifteen. The house is in darkness. The lights are on next door at Pamela's and I see the curtain twitch as I approach Mum's house. I lift my hand to wave. I expect the poor old dear has been worrying and looking out for one of us all afternoon. I'll be able to put her mind at ease soon enough, I think, lowering my hand and digging in my bag for Mum's front door key.

Letting myself in, I call out as I close the door.

'Hi, Mum, it's Cami.' No answer. The house is silent except for the low hum of the boiler in the kitchen. Assuming that she's not sitting downstairs in the dark, I take the stairs, calling out again as I go. Still no answer. For the first time I start to wonder if she really is ill, or has slipped over in the bathroom or something.

'Mum,' I say as I push open her bedroom door. No response. Maybe she's sleeping. The curtains are open and there's just enough light coming in the window from the streetlight to make out her shape in the bed. I go to her side and switch on the bedside lamp.

She looks pale and still lying in the bed. 'Mum,' I say once more, putting my hand on hers where it lies on top of the eiderdown. Her hand is cold. 'Mum?' I move my hand to her shoulder, shaking her slightly. 'Mum? Wake up. It's Cami.' Nothing. As realisation dawns, I feel a shiver run through me and tears well in my eyes. She's cold. She's dead. She's gone.

Mags

I grab my car key and shrug into my coat as I leave the house, on some sort of autopilot as I drive the short distance to Mum's. Cami's words are going round and round in my head. 'She's gone. Mum's gone. She's gone, Mags. Can you come? You need to come,' she'd garbled down the phone. She'd hung up before I really had the chance to respond. What did she mean, Mum was gone? Packed her bags and gone? What? Where?

Realisation only dawns when I pull up behind a police car and ambulance at the house. Oh my God. She's not gone. She's dead. I feel the colour drain from my face, and the warmth from my veins, as tears fill my eyes.

Cami meets me in the hall and pulls me into a hug. Neither of us speaks. We know exactly what the other is feeling. Words are unnecessary. We only break apart when a paramedic comes down the stairs.

He smiles sadly at me as he passes. I smile back, not knowing what to say.

Cami leads me through into the kitchen where a police officer is on the phone. I smile at him too. I feel oddly numb.

'Sorry about that,' the police officer says as he ends the call.

Cami introduces me as her younger sister.

'Hello, Mags. I'm very sorry for your loss. As I was saying to Cami, as your mother's death was unexpected, we are required to notify the coroner. They may well order a post-mortem to determine the cause of death.'

I nod at him, still mute and trying to process what's happening. Cami squeezes my hand. 'Can I see her?' I ask, finally finding my voice.

'Yes, of course, if you're sure,' the officer says.

I just nod. Cami leads me by the hand and we go upstairs together. I pause outside Mum's bedroom door, taking a sharp intake of breath. 'Is she okay, is she, I mean…?' I can't find the words. I don't need to.

'It's okay. She's peaceful. She just looks like she's sleeping,' Cami smiles reassuringly at me, squeezing my hand again.

There's another paramedic by the bed when we enter the room. She looks up and smiles sadly at us, before closing up her bag and turning to leave. Then we're alone with her. With Mum.

'I don't know why I'm crying,' I say, wiping the tears with my sleeve. 'She was not a nice person. Why am I crying, Cami?'

Cami shrugs. 'I did too. Whatever else she was, she was our mother, Mags. I'd say tears are a fairly normal response.'

'I s'pose. I don't really know what I feel though.'

'You don't have to know. There are no rules for this situation.

I think whatever you feel is right. For you. I expect we'll go through a whole gamut of emotions over the coming days and weeks.'

'I feel sad. I think. Not sad that she's dead. Sad that she wasn't a nicer person when she was alive. Sad for me. For us.'

Cami nods. 'I know what you mean. Feels like she wasted her life being bitter and cold.'

'Yeah. I would have done anything to feel loved by her. Wanted,' I say sadly.

'We should phone Rose to let her know,' Cami says.

'God, yes, we should. What happens now? Will someone collect her... the body, I mean?'

'Mm hm, the coroner's office step in now.'

I shudder at the thought of them cutting her open. 'I wonder if they'll find a heart...?' I say quietly. 'Heartless. She was heart-less, Cami.'

'I know. We deserved better.'

'We did. We really did.' I pause. 'I s'pose we'd better make that phone call.'

Rose

Ding dong the witch is dead. I can't believe it. My first thought when Cami and Mags told me was that she'd taken the easy way out, before the police investigation dug any deeper into our childhoods and found out what a shitty neglectful parent she was. I'm not going to lie, I'm glad she's dead. Does that make me a bad person? I really don't care if it does. Like mother like daughter, eh? You reap what you sow in this life, and she got what she deserved – dying alone, with no family at her side because she'd driven them all away. Even little Mags had had enough of her.

Chapter 42
Orange is the new black

Mags

They found a heart. They didn't say it was small and shrivelled, or a block of ice, just that it stopped beating and they don't really know why. Nothing especially unusual was found in the post-mortem for a woman of Mum's age apparently. It was as if she'd just laid down and died.

Cami and I were busy making funeral arrangements and putting off asking Rose if she was actually going to come down for it.

'She should be there, don't you think?' I say.

'Yep. Even if she's there for all the wrong reasons – it'll help give her closure,' Cami agrees.

'I put the death announcement thing in the local paper. Kept it simple – died peacefully at home type thing. Details of the funeral in case anyone actually liked her enough to want to come and pay their respects.'

'I s'pose some of the neighbours might want to come. Poor old Pamela next door was actually quite upset.'

'Probably just made her aware of her own mortality,' I say. 'Did Mum even have any proper friends?'

Cami shrugs. 'Kind of sad, really, isn't it?'

'Yeah. What are we going to do about a wake? Do we have to do the whole tea and sandwiches thing? I'm not sure I could bear making polite conversation and people trying to find nice things to say about Mum.'

'I know what you mean. It's all a bit hypocritical, the whole don't speak ill of the dead thing, isn't it?'

I nod. 'Just a lot.'

'Let's do what's right for us.'

'No wake then.'

'Suits me fine.'

Rose

I'm wearing orange. Mum always said it looked awful on me, so it seems only fitting to be wearing it to her funeral.

I'm driving down on my own. When I'd asked David if he wanted to come, he'd declined without a moment's hesitation. I think he's still self-conscious about being in a wheelchair, which I can totally understand. To be honest, I'm glad I won't have to worry about meeting his needs when the day's going to be enough of an ordeal anyway. When Cami'd asked me if I was coming to the funeral, I hadn't answered her right away. But then I'd thought about how I'd regretted not going to *his*.

'Yes, I'll come,' I'd sighed down the phone to Cami, and now here I am on the motorway, alone with my thoughts, which are complicated to say the least. After a few miles, I turn up an eighties radio station and try to shake my thoughts away.

The rest of the journey is uneventful and a couple of hours later I'm pulling up in the crematorium car park. I undo my seatbelt and lean my head back with a sigh, trying to release some of the tension that's built up in my neck and shoulders. I close my eyes and try to corral the thoughts stampeding round my brain. A tap on the car window makes me jump a short while later. I open my eyes to see the faces of my sisters smiling at me.

'Hello, you two,' I say as I open the door. I'm pulled into an awkward hug by two pairs of arms.

'Hello,' Cami and Mags say in unison.

'How are you doing?' Cami asks.

I shrug my answer, and they both nod their understanding.

'Strange day,' Mags says. 'Just got to get through it the best we can.'

'Yep. And we will,' Cami says, squeezing our hands. 'Stronger together.'

'Stronger together,' Mags and I repeat, like some sort of mantra.

'How long 'til she gets here?' I ask.

Cami looks at her watch. 'About ten minutes. Not long.'

I nod. 'Do you think it's okay that we didn't follow the hearse? Did the funeral people think it was a bit odd?'

'Of course it's okay. And it doesn't matter what they think. This is about doing what's best for us. God knows we've done little enough of that in our lives,' Cami says.

I smile sadly. 'Hm. I s'pose. I just want it to be over, to be honest. I'm dreading it.'

Cami and Mags nod. They know.

'It'll be over soon enough. Then we can get on with our lives,' Mags says.

'Apart from the small matter of the police investigation and Ken's ruddy house,' I say.

'God, yes, apart from that,' Mags says, smiling a sad apology.

'We've still got to deal with Mum's house too,' Cami adds.

'Can't we just burn them both down?' I ask, only half joking.

'No, you pyromaniac you,' Cami laughs.

'Just a thought,' I shrug.

'Think of something nice to do with your inheritance,' Mags suggests.

'Like what?' I ask.

'I dunno. A world cruise or something?' Mags says.

'Yeah, maybe. Once this whole shitstorm has died down. It's hard to look forward at the moment.'

'It'll be over soon, I'm sure,' Cami says.

'Hope so, although I can't imagine anything being resolved after all this time. Feels like a whole lot of pain for nothing,' I say.

'Not nothing, Rose,' Mags says fiercely, gripping my arm with both her hands. 'Not nothing. Don't ever say that. We're glad you told us. However painful it's been, you should never have had to carry that burden on your own.'

'Absolutely!' Cami agrees. 'I only wish you could've told us sooner.'

I can feel tears pricking the corners of my eyes. 'I… I'm sor…'

'No! Don't you dare say you're sorry! We understand why you couldn't tell us before, totally,' Mags says.

'Now, wipe those tears away,' Cami says. 'We're going to hold our heads up high today and get through this. Nice dress by the way,' she adds, raising her eyebrows and nodding in the direction of my very orange dress, which is clearly visible under my coat.

I can't help laughing. 'Right back at you!' I say, nodding at Cami's red dress.

'Thank you, kindly,' Cami says grinning, holding the edges of her skirt and giving a little curtsey.

We're all laughing now, and Mags joins in by twirling round in her yellow dress.

'God, what are people going to think of our outfits?' I ask.

'Who cares?' Cami responds.

'Yeah, who cares?' Mags agrees. 'Although I have to admit to having a bit of a wobble when I got dressed this morning.'

'Yeah, me too,' Cami grimaces. 'Hopefully people will just think we're wearing bright colours to celebrate Mum's life.'

'When really we're celebrating her death?' I say, my expression grim.

'I kind of wish she could see us now,' Mags says.

'What? All wearing her least favourite colours on us?' Cami says. 'Yellow makes you look sallow, Magnooooolia,' she says, imitating Mum's nasty tone.

'You look like a tart, Cameeeeelia,' I spit Mum-style.

'Orange does NOT go with your skin tone, Peeeony,' Mags joins in.

We're still laughing when the hearse pulls in, and quickly compose our faces, nudging each other like silly schoolgirls.

By the time we reach the big black car we are dignified once more. On the outside at least.

As Cami greets the undertaker, my eyes stray to the back of the hearse where a simple wicker coffin lies under an equally simple wreath of white lilies. There are no other flowers. We are the other flowers.

I nudge Mags and whisper in her ear. 'Have we done the

right thing?' We'd talked long and hard about Mum's funeral. She'd left a letter with her solicitor expressing her wishes, and they included a mahogany casket and burial. Here we were about to cremate her in a glorified picnic basket.

Mags nods vigorously. 'Yes, stop worrying.'

I nod, still not feeling entirely reassured. Something just feels off. I shrug off the feeling and turn my attention to Cami who's finished speaking to the undertaker and has turned back towards us.

'Okay?' she asks, smiling at me.

'Mm hm.'

A small group of people has gathered in the car park. I recognise Mum's neighbour Pamela and a couple of other people from her road. The others are all older people, around Mum's age, probably from the village. I smile in their direction. I can't help wondering what they'll make of our dresses and the lack of floral tributes. We'd specified no flowers, with donations to a local children's charity instead, but had finally agreed on traditional white lilies for the coffin as the least that society expected. Cami had baulked briefly at the inclusion of her middle namesake being used, but had come round to it.

The three of us stepped away from the hearse as they began the business of unloading the coffin. I couldn't imagine the body of our mother lying within. I could only imagine her vital and spiteful and spitting in the kitchen of the old house as we tore into each other. It was hard to believe she was dead. Hard to believe death had dared come for her. Had she chosen to die? Made up her mind and just done it? Given up the will to live. Nobody could make her do anything she didn't want to in life, so… I leave the thought hanging and watch as the pallbearers hoist the coffin onto their shoulders and settle it comfortably.

I feel a hand take mine. 'Okay?' Cami's voice breaks through my thoughts.

I nod, unable to speak. I don't know what I'm feeling. I squeeze Cami's hand. We follow the coffin into the chapel and take our seats in the front row. I shiver involuntarily, causing my sisters, seated either side of me, to look at me with concern. 'I'm okay,' I tell them. They each take one of my hands as we watch the pallbearers gently lower the casket onto the stand in front of the curtained area. There are large floral displays either side of the curtains and I can't help examining them.

'None of our flowers, thankfully,' I say quietly.

'What?' Mags asks in a loud whisper.

'No peonies, etc.,' I say, nodding in the direction of the flower arrangements.

'Oh. Good!' Mags says.

I glance round at the rear of the chapel where the other mourners are seating themselves behind us. I'm surprised to see DS Peters coming through the door. He sees me and raises a hand in greeting. I watch as he takes a seat at the back, before nudging Cami and nodding in his direction.

Cami spots the police officer and raises her eyebrows at me, indicating Mags with her eyes.

I just shake my head. The last thing we need is for Mags to know he's here.

Chapter 43
Dearly beloved

Mags

I haven't let go of Rose's hand since we sat down. I'd felt her shudder. I didn't know if it was from the chill in the chapel, or the occasion itself. I haven't let on to her and Cami that I've spotted DS Peters sitting at the back. I'd felt eyes on the back of my head and turned to find him watching me. He'd smiled and nodded. I felt my face colour, smiling shyly and turning quickly away. I really wish I didn't find him so bloody attractive. It feels more inappropriate than ever today. I shake my thoughts back to the present. The view isn't nearly as appealing though.

The former vicar from Mum's local church has kindly come to officiate. He's known us all our lives and must be well into his eighties. He's wearing his dog collar, but with a sweater and jacket, rather than robes; a pair of small, metal-rimmed glasses perch on his large nose and a few wisps of grey hair waft over his head. He looks like a kindly grandfather. He'd always been sweet to us as children when Mum had dragged us to church every so often. I can't help wondering, as I watch him settling himself in front of the lectern, what would have happened if Rose had felt she could confide in him all those years ago. I feel a lump in my throat which has nothing to do with the reason we're here. Will the guilt ever go away? I wonder.

Reverend Carmichael has started to speak now, thanking everyone for being here. Rose squeezes my hand and I return the pressure, drawing strength from her and sending mine in return.

'Flora Jessop was born in the small village of Yaxley in Suffolk in 1942…' he began, 'the only child of Joan and Frederick who owned the village store.'

My mind begins to drift as he speaks of Mum's early life, to the meeting we'd had with him a few short weeks earlier to discuss the funeral. It had all been rather uncomfortable when he'd asked if one or all of us would like to get up and speak or read.

'Um…' Cami'd begun, looking round at Rose and me, silently asking for help.

'No,' Rose had said flatly after an awkward pause.

The reverend had raised his eyebrows slightly and inclined his head. 'Of course, I realise it might be too emotional to get up and speak. I understand completely, and am happy to read your words for you. It may be that other mourners will want to get up and say a few words about your mother.'

I can think of a few words I'd like to say about her. The thought had popped unbidden into my head and I glanced guiltily around at my sisters. I suspect similar thoughts had also occurred to them.

Shortly after we'd arrived, a middle-aged lady (apparently the reverend's housekeeper – I'm pretty sure he never married) had brought a tray of tea things in. I reached for the cup and saucer on the low table in front of me, grateful to have something to do with my hands. We were in an old-fashioned, and masculine, sitting room. The armchairs had antimacassars on the backs and arms, and there were dark wooden bookshelves lining the walls, heaving with leather-bound tomes. The room smelled of beeswax polish and there was a faint whiff of tobacco in the air. The presence of a pipe on the mantelpiece explained it.

'So, as I was saying, if you would like to prepare some notes for me, things you'd like me to say about your mother, or memories you would like to share, then that would be a good place to start,' reverend Carmichael continued.

Christ, I thought, *this was a nightmare. Did we just lie? Make up some non-existent happy memories about her? Wasn't there some generic funeral speak he could use?* I looked helplessly at my sisters who were clearly experiencing the same dilemma.

The reverend stopped speaking and looked at us expectantly.

Rose, perhaps feeling responsible as the eldest, finally responded. 'We'll have a think and get back to you with something,' she said.

I sighed with relief.

'Also, if your mother had any favourite hymns or pieces of music,' the reverend continued.

I was drawing a blank again, but Rose was nodding and saying 'Of course.' I wondered if she actually knew, or was just fobbing him off. I lowered my gaze into my teacup once more, feeling awkward. I just wanted this to be over. It felt so awful to have nothing positive to say about our dead mother. Other than that she was dead.

We'd left soon after, with promises to be in touch with the required readings, etc., and now here we were with our words coming out of the old vicar's mouth.

We'd agonised over what to say. Whether or not we should look at Mum through rose-tinted spectacles and embellish the facts, or just outright lie. Eventually, we'd decided to keep it to a fairly factual account of her life. Anything else felt too hypocritical.

'Flora is survived by her three beloved daughters...'

Those words break through to me and I have to choke back a laugh. I feel Rose stiffen next to me and we squeeze each other's hands hard. Glancing across at Cami, her expression is stony. I know we're all thinking the same thing, that we never felt beloved by her.

I'm not aware I'm crying until I taste the first salty tear in the corner of my mouth. Silent tears are streaming down my face unchecked. I fumble in my pocket for the ever-present tissue and wipe them away, hoping no-one has noticed. I don't want to be cry-baby-Mags, and I don't want DS Peters to see me making a fool of myself.

I know I haven't got away with it when Rose lets go of my hand and her arm snakes over my shoulders, pulling me closer. Cami looks round at me too and mouths 'You okay?' I nod. 'I'm fine, really.'

I compose myself once more and sit up straight, forcing Rose's arm away. I will not be the baby. I just won't.

Returning my attention to the front, the reverend is asking if anyone would like to get up and say a few words about Mum. I half expect to see tumbleweed blow across in front of us, and am totally unprepared for what happens next.

Chapter 44
Our father

Mags

I hear a sharp intake of breath when he passes us in the aisle. I'm honestly not sure if it comes from Rose or Cami. Or both of them. I can feel my eyebrows knit as I try and bring an image to mind. It's been so long since I saw him.

'Is that Dad?' I ask in a whisper.

'It most certainly is,' Rose whispers.

Cami just nods.

'This should be interesting,' Rose, whispering again.

As he passes us, he turns and smiles. It feels like a smile that speaks volumes. It speaks of love and sorrow and regret. The three of us exchange looks, unable to believe our own eyes, and looking for confirmation in two other pairs.

Cami shrugs, shaking her head in disbelief.

'God, what on earth's he going to say?' Rose hisses at us.

'Nothing good,' I mutter from behind my hand.

We wait as Dad swaps places with the vicar, holding our collective breaths. This can't be good. This man, this husband, who left so many years ago, what good can he possibly have to say about the woman he hated?

'I hadn't seen Flora for many years,' he begins. 'She was not

310

an easy woman…'

Oh God, here we go.

'… to live with and our marriage did not last long. So, perhaps you are wondering why I am here today…'

Yep.

'I am here today for the three beautiful daughters she gave me: for Rose, for Cami, and for Mags. The daughters I have failed. The daughters I abandoned. I'm so very sorry,' he says, looking squarely at us, the sadness on his face adding emphasis to his words, desperate to be believed. 'Please believe me when I tell you I thought about you every day, and regretted leaving the way I did. I did not leave you, I left your mother. I know I behaved badly, and there is no excuse I can make, no forgiveness I can expect. You deserved better and I'm sorry I left you with her. I should have fought for you, tried harder to see you. I was weak, a coward, and to exclude her from my life, I excluded you too.'

I'm stunned at this public declaration, my mouth hanging open in disbelief. Is this really happening? I look round at Rose and Cami and see similar expressions. Dad's not done yet though.

'I have had to live with my guilt every single day. I have coped by putting the three of you out of my mind so the guilt didn't destroy me. No excuse. I was spineless. I hope you will give me a chance to make it up to you, but I have no expectation of it. I know I don't deserve it. I know these are just words, but please give me a chance to prove how sorry I am. Let me prove it with my actions. Let me be a father to you, and I will spend the rest of my life, however long that may be, making it up to you,' he finishes, his eyes never leaving us.

A stunned silence fills the room. I'm too shocked to speak, as I'm sure Cami and Rose are. I'm too embarrassed to look around at the rest of the congregation. What must they think?

Reverend Carmichael suddenly comes to his senses and puts his hand on Dad's arm, ushering him away from the lectern, before addressing us once more.

'Well, um, thank you for those... um... heartfelt words. Does anyone else have anything they would like to say about... er... Flora?' I can see him mentally crossing his fingers that nobody sticks their hand up. After a few seconds, he looks over at us. Three heads shake a negative response. I just want the ordeal to be over.

A look of relief washes over the vicar's face. 'Let us bow our heads in a moment of prayer, and quietly remember Flora.'

I bow my head and close my eyes, trying to dredge up a happy memory of Mum. It breaks my heart that I can't come up with one. There must surely have been some happy times? Before Rose got so angry. Before Dad left, and Mum became so bitter. If there are, they are too dim and distant to shine through the murky misery of my childhood. The prayers are only so much background noise, but I hear my voice quietly uttering 'Amen' in the appropriate place as I look up once more.

Reverend Carmichael is announcing the piece of music we chose for the committal, and soon the dulcet tones of Engelbert Humperdinck fill the room. We'd struggled to choose something as none of us remembered Mum listening to music when we were kids, but we'd found a few old records in some of Mum's belongings and 'The Last Waltz' was one of them.

I watch as the curtains begin to close around the coffin, and suddenly it's all too much for me.

Rose

So, that just happened. Our father, who art not in heaven –
although he might as well have been for all the contact we've
had with him – just made a tit of himself in front of everyone.
Mags is in bits. I'm not sure if it's because of Dad or the final
disappearing of Mum's coffin behind the curtains. Maybe a bit
of both. Our bloody parents.

After Dad finished unburdening himself of the guilt he'd felt
at abandoning us as kids, he'd walked past us with his head
down, back to the rear of the room. I think I saw the tracks of
tears down his cheeks, but I couldn't swear to it. Might have
been wishful thinking on my part. I really want his remorse to
be genuine. I turned to watch him and saw DS Peters get to
his feet. The next thing I knew the two of them were heading
out the door at the back. Surely the detective wasn't going to
speak to him about what'd been going on? Not today. Not at
Mum's funeral.

My attention was brought back to the matter at hand –
the cremation of our dearly departed mother. May she rest in
pieces. Certainly Mags had gone to a million of them. Turning
to Cami, I raise my eyebrows and sigh, and we both cuddle
Mags closer, swapping her snotty tissues for clean ones until
the sobbing subsides.

Becoming awkwardly aware that the congregation are waiting for us to get up and go, I link my arm through Mags'.

'C'mon,' I say gently. 'We have to go. Everyone's waiting.
Let's go outside and get some fresh air.'

Mags just nods and sniffs, but gets up and follows me crab-
like out of the pew.

'I'll stay and greet people and thank them for coming,' I tell my sisters. 'Go and find a quiet spot somewhere and I'll come and find you.'

Cami and Mags both start to object, but I shush them. 'It's fine, really, go on.'

'But...' Mags persists.

I know what she's going to say. What will people think?

'It doesn't matter, Mags. It's not about them. Who cares what they think?' I say, squeezing her arm and then pushing her gently away.

Cami's eyes meet mine and she nods gently, before leading Mags away into the gardens.

Taking a deep breath I prepare to smile and shake hands. I can see questions on people's faces, but I ignore them and don't let them engage me in conversation, sending them away curious and unsatisfied. *Oh well. Life's a bitch, eh*, I think as I utter another 'Thank you for coming'.

Thankfully the congregation's small and it's not long before I'm shaking the final hand – the vicar's – and thanking him for everything.

'Mum would've loved it, thank you,' I hear myself saying, on some sort of autopilot. Really I'm thinking nothing of the sort as we'd totally gone against the old bat's wishes. If there is such a place as hell, old Nick was about to meet his match.

As I watch the vicar walking away I spot DS Peters in the car park talking to Dad and a surge of mixed emotions rushes through me. Dad has his head bowed and looks totally dejected at whatever DS Peters is saying. Identifying one of the emotions as panic, I walk briskly over to them.

'DS Peters,' I say, nodding at him. 'Dad.' The word sounds

odd coming from my mouth.

Hearing my voice, Dad looks up at me. His face contorts in an expression that screams guilt and sorrow, pain and regret. Does he know? Has the policeman told him?

'Have you…? You haven't…?' I begin to ask the officer, unable to finish the question.

He just shakes his head, already knowing what I wanted to ask.

I take a deep breath of relief and feel the flutter in my chest begin to subside. I mouth a 'thank you'. This day is more than trial enough without dealing with the fallout of Dad finding out about my abuse.

'Can I have a quick word before I go, Rose?' DS Peters asks.

'Sure.' I look at Dad, who's just staring at me, his lips trembling and his hands shaking. 'Wait there,' I instruct him in my best bossy teacher voice before walking a few feet away to talk in private.

'How are you holding up?' DS Peters asks.

'Oh, you know, putting a brave face on. I've had a fair bit of practice.'

He smiles wryly. 'She wasn't an easy woman, was she? Still, a difficult day. How's Cami? And Mags? Bearing up, I hope.'

Was it my imagination, or did his voice soften when he said Mags' name?

'They're okay, thanks. Just got to get through this. Cami's pretty stoic. Mags has always been the sensitive one. Just wants everyone to get along and be happy. Sadly, we were never one big happy family. It's always been hard for her.'

He nods. 'It's been hard for all of you.'

'Thank you for not telling Dad,' I say, nodding over at the

rather pitiful figure of my father.

'Of course. Not my place to tell him. I was simply talking to him about your mother and anything he remembered of Ken, which wasn't a great deal. I do think you should tell him yourself though, Rose. He does seem genuinely sorry for leaving you. Maybe he deserves a second chance?'

'Is there really any point in telling him now?' I sigh. 'Look at him. What good will it do? He's an old man, already riddled with guilt. What's the point in adding to that?'

'Well, it's up to you, of course, but speak to him, Rose, see what he has to say for himself.'

'Maybe. We'll see.'

'Well, I must get back to the station, but I'm sure we'll talk soon. Take care, Rose, and give my best to your sisters.' With that, he rests his hand briefly on my shoulder before turning and walking away.

A thought strikes me and I call out after him. 'The necklace. Did you find any DNA?'

DS Peters stops and turns back to me. 'We did,' he says, nodding.

'And? Was it?'

He nods again. 'It was Anna-May's.'

I watch him walk away, feeling suddenly very weary. I rub my fingers over my eyes. I could really do with a large gin and for today to be over, but there's the small matter of my father still to deal with. I take a deep breath and walk back over to him.

Chapter 45
The old man

Cami

I felt bad leaving Rose to deal with the mourners alone, but she seemed determined to take charge. The protective big sister still. I took a tearful and trembling Mags into the formal garden behind the main building and we found a bench next to an ornamental pond.

We don't speak for a few minutes. I listen as Mag's breathing regulates and she stops shaking.

'Thanks, Cami. Sorry,' Mags says eventually. 'I didn't want to fall apart today. I'm really sick of being a cry baby.'

'I'll let you off this once, you dopey dartboard,' I say, smiling and nudging her.

Mags laughs, in spite of the occasion. 'It's that bit where the curtains close – gets me every time. Can't seem to help it.'

'It's okay, really. Seeing Dad probably didn't help.'

'Oh God! That's wasn't embarrassing at all, was it?' Mags groans.

'How did you feel, seeing him?' I ask.

'Um... not sure really. I thought I'd be angry, but he looked so old and sad, that I think I just felt sorry for him.'

'Yeah, me too. He didn't look like the Dad who left us all

those years ago, did he?'

Mags shakes her head in agreement. 'Did you believe him? Everything he said about being sorry for leaving?'

'I think so. Not sure I'm ready to forgive him yet, but I'm willing to give him the benefit of the doubt.'

'I just feel sad, really, I think. For all the lost years. All the memories we didn't make.'

'Mm. I can't help wondering if things would've been different if he'd stayed. Or at least maintained some contact with us. You know, for Rose...' I let the sentence hang.

'God, yeah. If anyone has the right to be angry with him, it's Rose, isn't it?'

'We should go and find her, you know, in case Dad...' I say, realisation suddenly dawning that Rose could be alone with him.

'Shit, yes, bloody hell. Why did I have to fall apart?' Mags says, jumping up. 'How do I look?' she asks, wiping her fingers under her eyes and turning to me.

'Full blotchy frog,' I inform her. 'Sorry.'

She groans. 'Christ. Why couldn't we be pretty criers? Don't s'pose you've got any sunglasses in your bag, have you?'

'Want to go all Jackie O, eh? No, sorry, mine are in the car.'

'Bugger,' Mags says.

The penny drops. 'I don't suppose DS Peters is still here. I'm sure he has better things to do than hang around at crematoriums blotchy frog-spotting.'

'Sod off,' Mags says. She's laughing again though, and we link arms and head back in the direction of the car park, arriving just in time to see DS Peters' departing back and Rose walking away from our dad.

I lift my thumbs in a silent question as we approach her, using them to indicate the two men heading off to opposite corners of the car park.

Rose nods grimly. 'I'm okay,' she sighs when we're close enough to hug. 'You two?'

'We're fine,' I say.

'Yes, fine, sorry for deserting you,' Mags says, looking sheepish.

'It's fine, really. You just missed DS Peters,' Rose says.

'Um… good,' Mags says, looking even more sheepish, and indicating the state of her face with an exaggerated smile and show of her hands.

Rose laughs. 'Not that you care what he thinks, of course?'

'Nope. Not a bit,' Mags says, before raising crossed fingers and laughing. 'Old habits, I guess.'

Mags is saved from any more ribbing by the ping of a text message arriving as soon as I turn my mobile back on.

'Lydia,' I say. 'Just checking we're okay.'

'Ah, that's nice,' Rose says. 'Shame she couldn't be here.'

I just nod, not wanting to admit that Lydia had wanted to come, but I put her off, still not ready to share her, even with my sisters. We'd had our first argument over it, Lydia and I, until I made her understand I wanted her to meet Rose and Mags under happier circumstances.

'Did you speak to Dad?' I ask Rose, eager to change the subject, even to one so fraught with complications.

'Briefly. I've invited him to meet us at Mum's in about an hour. Hope that's okay?'

Mags and I grimace, but nod our agreement.

'We could've gone to mine,' I say. 'Would've been warmer at least.'

'Sorry, I wasn't sure how you'd feel about having him in your house. Let's face it, we hardly know the man,' Rose says.

'It's fine. We'll probably need to put the heating on at Mum's though, and I'm not sure there's anything to eat or drink,' I say.

'Well, how about you two go straight to Mum's and get the heating on, and I'll grab a few bits from Tesco's? Meet you back there,' Rose suggests.

'Sounds like a plan,' I say.

'Anything you want?' Rose asks.

'Could you get me a can of Coke please?' Mags asks.

'Sure thing. Cami?'

'Um... milk for tea I s'pose,' I say.

'God, you should have something stronger than tea today,' Mags interjects. 'Get wine. Or gin, or whatever the hell you fancy. You don't have to protect me, I'm fine, really.'

'Gin it is then,' Rose says.

We part company at our cars with promises to 'see you soon' and Mags and I drive to Mum's house.

The chill hits us as we open the front door and I see Mags shiver involuntarily.

'I'm keeping my coat on until the heating kicks in,' she says, heading into the kitchen to click the boiler on.

We sit in the kitchen waiting for Rose to arrive, elbows resting on the flowery tablecloth of our childhoods. I can't help wondering what's going through Mags' head. It's already been one hell of a day, and it's not over yet. I imagine she could really do with a drink. I know I could.

It's not long before we hear the front door open and Rose bustles in with a couple of shopping bags which she dumps unceremoniously on the table.

'Just got the usual essentials,' she says, pulling things out of the bags. 'Gin, tonic, Kettle Chips, chocolate. Oh, and your Coke, Mags.'

'Thank you. Dad'll be here soon. That's not gonna be weird at all. I wonder if he drinks gin?' Mags wonders aloud.

'Dunno. I got milk for tea as well, just in case.'

'We really don't know much about him at all, do we?' I say.

'Nope,' Rose says shaking her head. 'Just that he's spineless.'

'I really don't remember him at all. From our childhoods, I mean,' Mags says.

'You were too little,' Rose says.

'You didn't miss much, from what I can remember,' I add.

'Cami's right,' Rose agrees.

'What are we going to say to him?' Mags asks.

I shrug. 'Just play it by ear, I reckon. Hear him out.'

Rose and Mags nod and silence descends on the kitchen, apart from the rustle of bags and the clink of ice and glass.

When the doorbell goes, we all look at one another, nobody moving as we wonder who should answer the door.

'I'll go,' I say finally, pushing my chair back and heading to the hall.

I hear Mags saying she feels a bit nervous.

'It'll be fine,' I call over my shoulder. I open the front door to find the old man I recognise from the crematorium there. 'Hello, Dad.'

'Hello, Cami,' he says. 'Thank you for agreeing to see me.'

'Of course,' I say, closing the door behind him. I resist the urge to tell him I hadn't really had a say in the matter, and lead him through to the kitchen where two faces look up expectantly.

Chapter 46
One more night

Rose

'Oof,' Cami says.

'Oof indeed.' Dad's just left and I feel exhausted, as I'm sure she and Mags do. He hadn't actually stayed that long in the end, telling us he'd like to see us again soon, under happier circumstances. I'd had to bite my tongue at that point, resisting the urge to tell him circumstances were unlikely to get much happier any time soon with the ongoing shit show of our lives.

I am angry with him. I can feel it simmering just below the surface. I'm just too damned tired to face it right now.

Cami'd made him a cup of tea and refilled our gin glasses.

'Still got the same old tablecloth, I see,' he'd said. 'She always did love her flowers.'

An awkward silence ensued, none of us knowing what to say to this stranger, this man whose seed had thrice impregnated a woman he claimed to despise. Our father. The father we never had. Did he have any right to come back into our lives now? Did we even want him to? I think we all had a lot of questions, but were simply too exhausted to ask them.

What followed was basically him repeating what he'd said at the crematorium. He seemed genuinely remorseful, I will say that for him, but was it too little too late?

After he's gone, with promises to be in touch again soon, we take our drinks into the lounge, collapsing onto the sofa, bone-tired and emotionally drained.

'Quite a day, huh?' Cami says.

'Yep. I feel knackered,' Mags nods, sipping from her glass of Coke.

'Me too. Shall we order some food?' I suggest. 'Get it delivered here? I can't drive now.'

'Good idea, I'm way too tiddly too,' Cami says. 'Curry? I'll find the menu.'

'I could collect,' Mags offers. 'Designated driver, ya know. And other things beginning with double dee.'

'Nah, let's get it delivered. Way too much effort to go out again,' I say.

Thirty minutes later and we're eating curry off trays on our laps.

'Ugh, eaten too much,' Mags says, sinking back into the sofa cushions and holding her stomach.

'Me too,' Cami groans.

'Me three,' I add through my final mouthful of Rogan Josh.

'Here, I'll rinse these,' Mags offers, reaching out for our plates. 'Make myself useful for once. Top up?'

'Um…' I begin.

'Rose, I'm quite capable of pouring you a gin without swigging from the bottle myself. Probably,' she adds with a wink.

'Sorry, thank you, a top up would be lovely.'

'I know it can't be easy for you both – finding out about all my problems and not wanting to lead me back into temptation, but I really just want you to treat me normally. I'm honestly fine.'

'Righty oh then, make mine a double!' I say, laughing.

'Coming right up!' Mags says, smiling as she heads to the kitchen with the dishes.

'God, I am absolutely knackered,' I tell Cami, stifling a yawn.

'Me too. I literally feel too tired to move at the moment.'

'Strange being here again, all three of us,' I say, looking around the room at the old familiar ornaments and pictures. Some bear witness to the angry scenes which took place in years gone by, their glue seams visible to the naked eye.

'Feels different now she's gone though, don't you think?' Cami asks.

'Mm, yeah, I s'pose it does. It's like it's been exorcised or something.'

'What's been exorcised?' Mags asks as she comes back in bearing full glasses.

'The house. Now Mum's gone. Feels calmer somehow.'

'I was just thinking that in the kitchen. And... tell me to shut up if it's a bad idea, but...'

'Shut up!' Cami and I say simultaneously, laughing.

'Dicks. Seriously, I was thinking...'

'Shut up!' we yell again.

We're all laughing now, and clutching our over-full stomachs.

'Sorry, Mags,' Cami says eventually. 'What were you trying to say?'

'I was going to say, would it be too weird if we stayed here tonight? One last time. Lay the ghosts to rest sort of thing. What do you think?'

'Shut up! Sorry, um... I'm not sure...' I say.

'I'm game,' Cami shrugs. 'Up to you, Rose.'

'I s'pose we could, although I'm not sure I fancy sleeping in my old bedroom. Or on my own for that matter.'

'We could put cushions and things downstairs and camp out,' Mags suggests, looking at us with a hopeful expression, an echo of the little girl who just wanted to make everyone happy.

'Oh, why not then,' I give in.

'Yay!' Mags cries. 'It'll be fun.'

'You have a strange idea of fun, Mags. Sleeping on the floor at my age is not my idea of a good time,' I tell her.

'You'll be fine. I'll round up some bedding,' Mags grins and leaves the room once more.

'I have to say, I'm not overjoyed at staying here overnight, but did you see Mags' face, and how happy it made her?' I say to Cami.

'Yeah, bless her. It won't kill us and it'll mean the world to her. The estate agent's coming to show people round tomorrow, so we might as well say our goodbyes to it now.'

'Can you believe Mum left everything to the cat sanctuary?' I say.

Cami chuckles. 'Yep, totally.'

'She didn't even really like cats.'

'I s'pose she liked us even less,' Cami says with a wry smile.

'What a cow,' I sigh.

'Who's a cow?' Mags asks, coming in with arms full of pillows and blankets.

'Mum. Spiteful to the end, you know, her will and leaving everything to the cats,' I say.

'Oh, yeah! She didn't even really like cats that much, did she?'

Cami and I laugh. 'No, she didn't.'

'It really is the end of an era, isn't it?' Mags says with a sigh.

'Yep, closing doors to the past and moving on with our lives,' Cami says.

'I'll drink to that,' I say, lifting my glass. 'To us, and new beginnings. Cheers!'

'Not all the doors to the past are closed, though, are they? With Dad back, for one thing. Maybe that door's just opening,' Mags says.

'Yeah, true, although I may still slam it in his face. And, not forgetting the door next door. Be happy to finally nail that one shut when the police finish their investigation,' I say grimly.

'I'm sure that won't be long now. Unless they find DNA on that necklace, I can't see what else they can do. Even then, Ken's dead, Mum's dead, there's no-one left who might actually know the truth,' Cami says.

'Shit!' I exclaim. 'Sorry, I forgot to tell you – they did find DNA and it was Anna-May's. DS Peters confirmed it earlier. With everything else that was going on, it totally slipped my mind.'

Cami and Mags are silent for a few moments as they process the news.

'He's taken his secrets to the grave, hasn't he? And we'll never know what happened to Anna-May, or what Mum knew or didn't know,' Mags says.

'I think she knew,' I say quietly. 'At some level, she knew.'

'Have you thought about what you're going to do with Ken's house?' Cami asks, in an obvious subject change.

I sigh. 'Give it to a women's charity I think. The will stipulates I can't sell it, but doesn't say I can't give it away. I certainly don't want it or the proceeds of a future sale anyway.'

'I think that sounds like a great idea. Maybe some good can

come from all this,' Cami smiles.

'Or I can still burn it down?' I grin.

'Burn them both down!' Mags says.

'You just want a load of firemen to turn up!' I say.

'So sue me!' Mags says grinning.

'Changing the subject for a moment,' Cami says when we all stop laughing. 'I'm… um… I'm getting married.'

'What the?' I say, nearly choking on my umpteenth gin.

'Oh my God! Cami, that's amazing!' Mags says. 'Oh, I'm gonna cry!'

Cami and I laugh. 'Shut up!'

'That really is wonderful news, Cami, and I'm thrilled for you. You do know we still haven't met Lydia though, don't you?' I say.

'I know, I know, and I'm sorry. It's just with everything that's been going on… you know…'

'We do know, and it's fine,' I smile at her.

'When? Have you got a date?' Mags asks.

'Ooh! Will Dad be giving you away now he's back?' from Rose.

'In June, and no, Dad will definitely NOT be giving me away. There are only two people in the world I want by my side when I walk up the aisle, and that's you two muppets.'

'Oh my God, really? Yay! I'm gonna cry again,' Mags says, beaming.

'Happy tears, eh, Mags?' I say.

'The happiest!' Mags says, dabbing at her eyes with her sleeve.

It's a happy trio who snuggle down for the night under a mound of duvets and blankets, giggling like schoolgirls, making a happy memory together in the house that had given us so few.

Chapter 47
The three sisters

Rose

We talk into the wee small hours, Cami and I gin-soaked and Mags simply on a high being with us. I'm actually glad we decided to stay the night, even though I'm sure I'll ache like mad in the morning. It's a small price to pay to strengthen the bonds we've built in recent months, and end this chapter of our lives on a happy note.

Eventually the other two doze off. Cami's breathing is quiet and slow, and Mags is talking in her sleep as she had when we were little. I lie in the dark listening to them sleep, thinking about everything that's happened and what's still to come now the police have identified the necklace as belonging to Anna-May. I'm wondering if we'll ever find out what happened to her as I finally drift off to sleep.

Mags

I fall asleep with a smile on my face, feeling happier than I can remember in a long time, if ever. I never want this closeness we three have now to go away. I know I'm better now, stronger, and I can do this life thing on my own, without the need of a man's approval. Even if DS Peters asked me out, I'm pretty sure I could turn him down. Probably.

Cami

It feels strange lying so close to my sisters. I don't dislike the feeling, but I miss Lydia. I can't wait to see her tomorrow. Then I'm never going to spend another night without her by my side. Mags is chattering away nineteen to the dozen. She's so happy to be with us. I hope she can find true happiness without needing a man to boost her self-esteem. And Rose; I truly hope Rose can find her way through this and know real contentment. She deserves it. I'm glad she has her girls to focus on, a reason to keep going. I can feel my eyelids growing heavy now. Time to sleep and find Lydia in my dreams.

Mags

'Cami!' I say, gently shaking her shoulder.

Cami mumbles something in her sleep but doesn't wake.

'Cami! Wake up. Rose has gone,' I repeat as I fumble in the dark for my phone. Checking the time I see it's just after four. Dawn is still a couple of hours away.

Cami groans, but starts to come to. 'What? Gone where? She's probably in the loo. Go back to sleep,' she says, rolling away on to her side.

'I don't think she is in the loo. She's been gone too long, and I can't hear anything,' I persist.

'Are you sure? Go and check. It's too early and I'm too hungover for this.'

'Okay, I'll check,' I say, crawling out from under the duvets. The house is chilly and I hunt around for my jumper, pulling it on before checking the downstairs loo and the upstairs bathroom. Returning to the lounge, I turn on a lamp and tell Cami.

'She's not here,' I say in a loud whisper.

'Oh, for God's sake. Where on earth is she?' As she speaks, however, Cami is heaving herself up and reaching for her glasses on a nearby side table. 'Bloody hell, Rose. Ow, my head.'

Together we check every room of the house. No Rose.

'Is her car still outside?' Cami asks.

'Yes, and her handbag's still here.'

'Mobile?'

'Haven't seen it. Shall we try phoning it?'

'Yep. I'll do it.'

I wait while Cami switches her own phone on and tries Rose's number, pulling my sleeves down over my cold hands and trying to ignore the slight feeling of panic that has started in my chest. The feeling grows when we hear a ringing and find Rose's phone on the floor by the pile of cushions.

'Bugger,' Cami says, pressing end call.

'Where the hell is she?'

'Well, she can't have gone far. Her car's still here.'

'She wouldn't have gone next door, would she?'

'I can't imagine why?' Cami says, looking puzzled.

'She wouldn't... you know...'

'Wouldn't what?'

'Um... set fire to the house...'

Cami pauses. 'No. She wouldn't. Would she? Shit.'

'Let's go round and check. Just to be on the safe side. I can't think where else she could possibly be.'

'Okay. Let me find my shoes,' Cami says.

A couple of minutes later and we're at Ken's front door, torches from our phones lighting the way. The door is locked and there's no light showing from inside.

'Round the back?' I suggest.

We head round to the back of the property, but still there's no sign of Rose and the house is in darkness.

We're standing on the patio, shivering and wondering what to do next when a faint noise reaches our ears. It sounds like someone grunting with exertion and then swearing.

Looking up the garden, we can just make out movement in the corner.

'Is that...?' Cami peers into the night.

'Rose? I think so.'

'For God's sake. What the hell is she up to? Come on.'

We pull our coats around us and walk the length of the garden.

We find Rose by the bonfire patch, sweaty and swearing and digging ineffectually with a shovel.

'What the fuck are you doing?' Cami asks.

I just stand there staring in disbelief. Has our big sister finally lost the plot?

Rose doesn't answer, just carries on ramming the shovel into the earth.

'Rose!' Cami says, louder this time. 'What the hell are you doing?'

'What does it look like I'm doing?'

'Well, it looks like you're digging. Maybe a better question would be why?'

'She's here. I know she is,' Rose says, banging the shovel into the ashen ground once more. 'Why's this so bloody hard? You see people digging graves in films all the time. It shouldn't be this bloody hard,' she puffs.

'Well, for starters, you're using a shovel instead of a spade,' Cami informs her. 'But who's here? What are you on about?'

I can feel a look of complete puzzlement on my own face. 'Who's here, Rose? Who do you mean? Your doll?' I ask, thinking of the dolls' house she'd burned on this spot not so long ago.

Rose stops and looks at me as if I'm stupid. 'What? No, Anna-May. She's here. He buried her here. I just know it.'

I look at Cami, not knowing what to say. She's clearly lost for words too.

Rose's impatience with us is palpable.

'Think about it,' she says. 'He always had a bonfire here. There was always a heap of stuff to be burned and nothing was ever planted. Did you ever see it as anything other than the bonfire heap? No, because it never was.'

Cami and I remain silent.

'I just know she's here... I woke up and I just knew... she's here,' Rose repeats.

'Rose...' Cami begins, gently touching her arm.

Rose shrugs her off. 'No, I know you think I'm mad, but I'm right, I know I am. So, are you going to stand there like a pair of lemons, or are you going to help me?'

It's clear the only way we're going to convince Rose she's wrong is to dig up the patch.

'Okay, well, for starters, we need spades. Mags, check the shed. I'll go next door and get Mum's,' Cami instructs.

Before long, we're all digging in a rough circle around the bonfire heap. It's slow, heavy work and we have to stop every few minutes. Thankfully, the years of bonfires and layers of ash mean the soil is not too compacted. If anyone saw us they would think we were completely bonkers.

'How deep do we have to dig?' I ask after we've dug down a couple of feet.

'Until we find her,' Rose says.

Cami looks across at me and raises her eyebrows. I shrug my hands and shake my head, not knowing what to say.

'Six feet,' Rose says to no-one in particular. 'That's how deep they always dig in films.'

I don't like to point out that we're not in a movie and that this is madness.

We keep digging and digging, wondering when it will be enough, and how we get Rose to stop.

We're about four feet down when my spade hits something. 'I've hit a tree root, I think.'

Rose immediately grabs one of the phones and shines it onto the spot. She kneels down to take a closer look. My eyes meet Cami's. It feels like Rose and sanity have finally parted company.

The next thing we know, Rose is digging frantically with her bare hands. I start to cry. I don't know what to do.

'Rose. Rose. Stop,' Cami says gently.

But Rose doesn't stop.

'What do we do?' I ask, rubbing muddy fingers across my face.

Cami just shakes her head, and we watch helplessly as our sister scrabbles in the soil.

I don't know how long we stand there, just watching, wondering what to do.

Finally, Rose sits back on her haunches, shining the light into the earth. 'Look!' she says triumphantly.

Cami and I crouch down and peer at the spot she's pointing to.

There, in the cold, damp earth, two empty eye sockets stare back at us from an unmistakably human skull.

THE END

Acknowledgements

Thank you for reading *The Bonfire Buddleia*. I really hope you enjoyed it. It wasn't always an easy book to write, but I hope I have done justice to some difficult human experiences. I would never wish to make light of such things. This book took a year to write in the end. I started writing it in January 2021, alone at my dining table as has been my writing habit for the past six years. Then, in April, life rather took over as I met my new partner, moved house, and a million other things filled my head besides writing. *Buddleia* has been waiting patiently in the wings since I turned to a life of crime with *The Write Way to Die* series.

I still write alone, but now my desk looks out at the viaduct in Folkestone, the seaside town which is now my home. I feel like I'm always on holiday here, it's a wonderful, creative community to live in. I'd like to say thank you to all the amazing people I've met here, and the new friends I've made.

There are always people I need to thank, people without whom I could not imagine life. My son, Sam, now twenty and still making me so proud. My partner, Dirk, photographer extraordinaire and number one ideas guy. And Kathy, best friend and confidante, and so much cheaper than therapy!

My grateful thanks go to Emma Brown for her invaluable proofreading, and to the brilliant Charlotte Mouncey at Bookstyle for producing a beautiful book as ever. *The Bonfire Buddleia* also has the honour of being the first book to be published by Hut 22 Books.

The book is dedicated to my big sisters, Ros and Carrie. Thankfully our childhoods were much happier than those of my fictional sisters! I love you both.